"H stopp Fran asked, g curious. "You haven't stopped working since I met you."

"It's not always so bad," Edgar murmured.

They were silent for a moment before he went on. "I guess my brothers are probably right—I've been working more and not taking time to slow down and have fun like I used to."

"Too afraid some eligible girl might catch your fancy?" she asked, only half teasing.

He snorted. "Didn't stop you," he said, reaching up to tweak her nose.

"Ha." She swatted at his hand, and he captured her fingers. Slowly, he interlaced their fingers, surrounding her hand with the warmth of his larger one.

She turned to meet his gaze straight on. From only inches away, the intensity of his blue eyes caught her breath.

He moved toward her and gently kissed her forehead, a brush of his beard against her skin. She waited for him to apologize or say the kiss had been a mistake, but none of that was forthcoming. Was he…beginning to soften toward her?

Books by Lacy Williams

Love Inspired Historical

Marrying Miss Marshal
The Homesteader's Sweetheart
Counterfeit Cowboy
*Roping the Wrangler
*Return of the Cowboy Doctor
*The Wrangler's Inconvenient Wife

*Wyoming Legacy

LACY WILLIAMS

is a wife and mom from Oklahoma. Her first novel won an ACFW Genesis Award while it was still unpublished. She has loved romance books and movies from a young age and promises readers happy endings in all her stories. Lacy combines her love of dogs with her passion for literacy by volunteering with her therapy dog, Mr. Bingley, in a local Kids Reading to Dogs program.

Lacy loves to hear from readers. You can email her at lacyjwilliams@gmail.com. She also posts short stories and does giveaways at her website, www.lacywilliams.net, and you can follow her on Facebook (lacywilliamsbooks) or Twitter @lacy_williams.

The Wrangler's Inconvenient Wife

LACY WILLIAMS

HARLEQUIN® LOVE INSPIRED® HISTORICAL

Recycling programs
for this product may
not exist in your area.

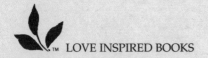 **LOVE INSPIRED BOOKS**

ISBN-13: 978-0-373-28274-6

THE WRANGLER'S INCONVENIENT WIFE

www.Harlequin.com

Printed in U.S.A.

"For I know the plans I have for you," declares the Lord, "plans to prosper you and not to harm you, plans to give you hope and a future."
—*Jeremiah* 29:11

With thanks to Regina Jennings and Mischelle Creager for their help in whipping this manuscript into shape.

Also a thank you to Emily Rodmell, for her editorial input.

For Megan Frances, the sister-in-law I never knew to ask for but God blessed me with anyway. Love you!

Chapter One

Wyoming, late spring, 1900

Being the responsible one was rougher than he expected.

Edgar White had been up half the night with a calving heifer, now a proud mama cow. But instead of burrowing into his bunk and sleeping the morning away, he was working as a trail boss, driving a herd of cattle to meet the morning train.

And wrangling his younger brothers was turning out to be even more difficult than handling a bunch of ornery, smelly beasts.

On his trusted cow pony, he was half dozing, dreaming of getting back to his bedroll with only half an eye on the herd when the far-off whistle brought him fully alert and upright in the saddle. They would have another half hour after the train arrived in Bear Creek to load the animals, but there was no sense in lollygagging around. It would be the work of a quarter hour to push the animals into town to the loading pens near the station.

Since the lion's share of work on the family ranch

had fallen to him these past couple of years, twenty-four-year-old Edgar was always prepared. He followed the most logical course. Was early for his engagements.

His adopted brothers, all six of them, called him boring.

Out of all the guys his pa had taken in before marrying Penny, Edgar was the only one who didn't dream of leaving home on some grand adventure one day. Even Davy, the quiet one, dreamed of traveling back East when he had the cash to do so.

But his adoptive pa, Jonas, must've thought Edgar's steadfastness was a good thing, because he'd left Edgar in charge while he and his wife, Penny, had taken fifteen-year-old Breanna, Edgar's adopted sister, and their smaller children on a trip to Boston for several weeks. Oscar, the eldest brother and now a happy husband with children of his own, had surprised his wife, Sarah, by declaring they were going on the trip, too—sort of as a belated honeymoon. Edgar would never have wanted to travel with that many little ones, but the womenfolk had talked of nothing else for weeks.

Maxwell, his second-eldest brother, was living in Denver while his wife, Hattie, finished her training to become a doctor. They both planned to return to the area within the year. With Oscar and Maxwell gone, it meant Edgar was the eldest still at home.

The eldest, and the one charged with the most responsibility. He needed to get the cattle to Jonas's buyer and take care of the ranch in his pa's absence. He didn't mind. Work was something he knew, and he refused to let his adoptive parents down.

Urging his horse into a canter, Edgar rounded up the last few slow-moving steers, pushing them over the train tracks toward the station on the edge of town.

He had his hat off and was waving the all clear to his brother Seb, who was riding flank near the middle of the herd, when he saw the break in the tracks.

Somehow a section of the track had split. The ground was cracked open beneath the dirt and grass, maybe from the dry winter they'd had, and the connection was broken.

There was no doubt that if the train hit this area at full speed it would derail. Passengers could be hurt or killed. A glance to the east showed the line of smoke puffing nearer, though the train wasn't in sight yet. From here he couldn't tell if it was slowing, but if the engineer didn't know about the damage to the tracks, every passenger on board was at risk.

It wasn't his business, didn't have a thing to do with his cattle or the job, but Edgar couldn't let innocent people get hurt, not if there was a chance he could prevent it.

He whistled shrilly and Seb turned, twisting in his saddle. "What's a matter?" the younger brother shouted.

"Take the cattle on in! I'll follow." Edgar waved him on, because the animals could be injured, too, if the train derailed.

Seb waved his acquiescence and wheeled the horse back to keep the animals in line.

Edgar took off with a cry of "Ha!" to spur his horse on. The large animal responded quickly, breaking into a gallop that nearly blew Edgar's hat off.

The train maintained its speed, chugging quickly toward Edgar as he raced alongside the tracks. Even if he got the attention of the engineer, could it be stopped in time?

Briefly considering a warning shot from his rifle, Edgar dismissed the thought. The engineer might think he was some kind of robber or something. Instead, he loosened the bandanna from around his neck. He clutched the material in his hand as he leaned over the horse's neck, urging the animal with his body for more speed.

As he neared the train, he began waving the dark blue cloth, hoping the engineer could see it. Hoping the man would throw the brakes.

He knew there was a chance the engineer wouldn't stop. He whispered a prayer under his breath for the safety of the passengers he could now see through the windows on the passenger car.

And the train began to slow with a squeal of brakes against the rails.

Would it stop in time?

"What's going on? Are we already there?"

Will anyone take us in?

Fran Morris heard the unasked question from her fifteen-year-old sister, Emma. And she didn't have an answer for any of the three.

Bracing herself against the seat in front of her inside the crowded passenger car, she peered through the window to see only grassy fields. Not a town in sight.

That was the answer to one question.

From the second row at the front—where the group of gray-bedecked orphans were easily seen and ogled by the other passengers—she would be one of the first to know what was going on when the car's doors opened.

But they weren't in Bear Creek yet. With only two more towns scheduled for orphan train stops, they were running out of time to find a new home—and to find safety.

"I don't know what's happening, Emma," she murmured to her younger sister as she craned her neck to better see out the black-smudged window.

Not even a barn in sight.

"Just sit tight." The words had been a mantra of sorts for the two of them since they'd left Memphis three days before. Stay out of sight. Unnoticed. Safe.

Would she ever feel safe again?

In her nineteen years, she'd never imagined leaving Memphis, the city where she'd been born and raised. And now here she was in the plains of Wyoming. Alone, except for her sister to take care of. All because one man had become obsessed with her sister. With no family to protect them, it was up to Fran to keep Emma out of Underhill's reach.

The train's momentum changed, throwing her forward in the seat. The squeal of brakes became a shriek. Voices cried out from all around.

Emma fell off the seat into the aisle.

"Emma!"

But Fran couldn't catch her balance, either. She was knocked back against the seat, shoulder banging against the window, sending pain radiating up her arm. She cried out.

"Fran!"

Emma's voice was lost in the shouts and cacophony as the train seemed to lift beneath them, then listed to one side.

Screams ripped through the compartment.

Fran reached for anything she could use to steady herself. There was nothing. "Emma!"

Passengers screamed. Metal groaned. The car leaned, everything seemed to pause momentarily and then the train crashed onto its side.

Fran was slammed bodily into the window, then the

seat in front of her before everything went still. She found herself collapsed in a small ball between the two seats, her backside now on the window.

Her ears rang. Her head hurt. So did her shoulder.

"Emma?" When she could force her voice to work, it emerged in a whisper, and was lost among the cries of those nearby. She reached around, tried to shuffle to the edge of the seat where Emma had been before the wreck had happened. What had caused them to derail?

"Emma? Emma!"

Worry that her sister hadn't answered had Fran scrambling toward the aisle as best she could in the lopsided car.

Metal screeched and a bright shaft of light hit her face as she crawled into the aisle. The door, now overhead, had opened.

Emma was nowhere in sight.

Luggage was strewn about, blocking her attempt at movement. People all around struggled to right themselves, without much success.

She peered up to see the shadow of a head and shoulders in the doorway above her.

Then a big pair of boots dropped into her line of vision, landing with a reverberating thud.

"You all right, miss?"

She followed the deep drawl up and up and up, taking in the giant bear of a man from those tree-size legs to the broad shoulders to the unkempt blond beard and long hair beneath his cowboy hat.

Inappropriate and ill timed as it was, when she met his sky blue eyes, she felt a shock of attraction, a lightning bolt through her nervous system like nothing she'd ever felt before.

For this mountain of a man?

"I need to find my sister." Was that tentative whisper her voice? Perhaps she was more shaken from the crash than she'd thought.

"Let's get you out of here first."

"No—"

But the man didn't even seem to hear her protest. He clasped her waist and lifted her toward the door where she could see a man in uniform waiting with arms outstretched.

She struggled, but it didn't faze the huge man one bit. He shoved her into the conductor's waiting arms, and she was unceremoniously deposited onto the side of the train car.

"Best slide down the top, missy," the gray-mustached man said. "Less parts for you to get caught on." He motioned toward one side of the derailed train car.

There was no way she was leaving without Emma, not after she'd overheard a man inquiring about them in Lincoln, Nebraska, the day before. Keeping Emma out of Mr. Underhill's reach was imperative.

"I'll wait on my sister. I want to make sure she wasn't injured." And to make sure she was safe. Fran had scoured the passenger car and not seen the man she'd seen briefly on the Lincoln train platform, but it was too much to hope that they'd outrun those who were searching for them.

"Then you'd better move aside. Got a lot of folks to get off this train."

Fran moved a few yards down the side of the train and carefully perched above one of the windows. She wrapped her arms about her knees, worry making her tremble. What if Emma had been hurt?

Edgar had waved until his arm ached, but the conductor hadn't been able to stop in time to avoid the broken tracks.

Watching helplessly wasn't a thing he liked to do, but it had been all he could do to control his horse in the face of the awful accident. The steam engine and this passenger car lay prone on their sides, but had uncoupled from a second passenger car that tilted precariously over the broken tracks. He'd left the people on that car to figure out how to get themselves off and rushed to help the other car, meeting up with the badly shaken conductor. Although the conductor had heard stories of the boiler spilling hot coals in a crash like this, it appeared the machinery was stable for now, not at risk of catching fire.

Edgar worked like a dog to get the passengers off the downed train.

As he worked, Edgar could still hear the little spitfire he'd come across first questioning the uniformed man. Some of the passengers he lifted up to the conductor were injured, some not.

Even the murmur of her voice shook him.

He'd never had such a visceral reaction to a woman before, until this little slip of a thing with her big brown doe eyes.

For someone who made a practice of staying away from the opposite sex, it was gut-wrenching. He definitely needed to get off this train and back to the relative solitude of his pa's ranch.

But he couldn't leave the passengers behind, not when they needed help. Several had been injured by falling luggage or had been thrown around when the train derailed.

He was sweating, and felt more exhausted than he did after a long day of branding.

He boosted a mother and her crying toddler, both

of whom seemed to be blessedly uninjured, to the conductor.

The muscles in his arms shook.

A shadow moved in one of the windows above him. He looked up to see the young woman staring down into the car, peering through the windows.

Their eyes connected, and he felt like someone had taken a cinch to his chest.

Suddenly, the walls were closing in on him.

"I've gotta take a breather," he told the conductor. It had been at least an hour with no break. He was due.

The man nodded and moved back from the opening.

"What? No..." He could hear the girl begin to protest, even through the glass and metal. Her head appeared above the opening, partially blocking his way. "My sister..."

He boosted himself up, forcing her to move back or bump into him.

She didn't go far. Just squatted on her haunches a couple feet away.

Her nearness sent prickles up the back of his neck. His reaction irritated him.

"I won't be any good to anybody if I don't rest a moment," he told her, looking off toward the Laramie Mountains in the distance.

The sun beat down on his shoulders, but at least outside of the enclosed car, the breeze cooled him a bit.

"What about the other men?" the girl insisted.

He looked around, exaggerating the movement. Several men in fancy duds that he'd pulled from the train sat on their cabooses. The conductor was short of stature and wouldn't be any good at boosting people up. Looked like it was Edgar or nobody.

"Everybody still in that passenger car is shook up,"

he explained, trying to hold on to his patience. "And those fellas down there don't look like they're gonna be much help."

"Frances! Miss Morris!" A woman's shout from below turned the gal's head briefly, but she waved the older woman off, concentrating only on her mission to rescue her sister. He could relate a little bit—if one of his brothers was in danger, he would've physically moved the train to get to them.

"Get down here this instant. I need all the orphans to stay together," the woman ordered.

Orphan.

The word stilled everything around them, dampened the noise and commotion.

And suddenly he saw the drab gray dress and plain, scuffed boots peeking out from beneath.

He'd thought she was of age—wouldn't have let himself be attracted to her if she was too young—but apparently he was wrong.

She was an orphan on a westbound train. Just like he had been sixteen years ago.

This time when their eyes met, he didn't fight the connection, although nothing would ever come of it. It swelled between them into something almost tangible.

"I'm not leaving my sister behind. We have to get her out of there," she said, voice low and intense.

"I will. I promise." And he never broke his promises.

"Miss Morris, I insist—"

"I'm of age!" the young woman called down.

The matron's outraged gasp told him something was very wrong.

And in a matter of moments, he—and everyone else in the vicinity—knew what it was.

The orphan girl was a liar.

The pretty young woman had pulled the wool over the orphanage chaperone's eyes and gotten a free ride out west. She was apparently over eighteen, which made him feel a little less like a lecher for his unforeseen attraction to her.

But her age didn't matter. She wasn't trustworthy. It figured.

He knew better than anyone that women couldn't be trusted. His past had taught him that. Save the rare exception, like his adoptive ma, Penny, not a one of them was safe.

Knowing didn't help the sick feeling in the pit of his stomach as he threw himself back into rearranging luggage and unearthing passengers in the upended train car. He was somehow disappointed in the petite young woman.

"You need a hand in there?"

Relief mixed with frustration as his brother Matty's head popped in the opening above Edgar.

"I've got some men from town down here ready to get the rest of the folks off this train," his brother reported.

"I need the doc," he returned, looking down on a child with an obviously broken arm.

He bent to comfort the small boy, at the same time looking around for a mother or father to match with the tyke. Voices called out from farther down in the car, but it would take some doing to get to those folks, blocked off as they were.

Matty turned and shouted down, his words distorted because of the distance, but clearly relaying Edgar's need. Hopefully Doc Powell, Maxwell's father-in-law, had arrived with the other men.

Matty lowered his bottom half through the opening

and dropped inside, his boots clanging against the inside wall of the passenger car. He quickly joined Edgar at the boy's side, shouldering aside a large valise without being asked. That was one thing to like about his brother—he did what was asked without complaining.

"Doc's on his way."

"The cattle?" Ed grunted, dislodging another trunk until they could wiggle the boy free of his former seat. "And where's Ricky?" Matty, Ricky and Seb had all been pushing the cattle to town.

"Don't know about Rick, but Seb and I heard the train crash and tucked the cattle into ol' Mr. Fredrick's south pasture. We might have to round up a few strays tonight, but they should mostly stay put. Doubt the train is going to run this afternoon anyway."

Edgar should've known his brothers wouldn't just turn the cattle loose—they all owed as much to their pa as he did. But Matty's conclusion about the train troubled him. They only had a few days to get the cattle to his pa's buyer. If the train was out, what were they going to do?

He worked to keep a single-minded focus on that thought, on his task. But he couldn't quite ignore the tightening of his gut when thoughts of the pretty young woman crept back in.

Emma was one of the last ones off the train.

But when Emma's feet hit the ground and she ran toward Fran, blinding relief rushed through her.

They embraced, Fran squeezing her sister as tightly as she could. "Are you hurt?"

Emma shook her head. She was trembling, whether from fright or from the adrenaline of the wreck and its aftermath, Fran didn't know.

She watched as the cowboy and two others with him who were dressed similarly—although notably better groomed—jumped off the overturned train. They were the last three off.

The rest of the passengers had disembarked, and now so had the three cowboys who'd come to their aid. She wished she could thank them.

But Fran clutched Emma's hand in hers, not daring to move from beneath the watchful eyes of the orphanage's assigned chaperone and the sheriff.

Her sister was scratched and bruised, same as Fran was, but had no major injuries. It was much to be thankful for.

But being discovered in her deception was a disaster. One she hadn't prepared for.

"I want her arrested." The matron's voice rang out, hushing the rumble of other voices as passengers loaded up in wagons all around.

Fran winced.

She attempted a brave smile at her sister and sent a fervent prayer winging upward. The Lord hadn't helped her any in Memphis and she questioned whether He would now, but she vowed to make herself like the annoying widow in that parable and keep on petitioning until she got the help she needed.

She didn't know if what she'd done was enough to be jailed and punished for—it wasn't as if she'd *stolen* from the orphanage. But as Mr. Underhill had threatened her before she and Emma had snuck out of Memphis, an orphan like her didn't have a lot of credibility. His threats and his crazed obsession with her sister had made it necessary to leave, and without any money, the orphan train had given them their only option.

The sheriff's sudden shrill whistle broke into her

wildly racing thoughts and brought the cowboys into their periphery. The two younger men came first, while the blond man who'd taken her off the train seemed almost reluctant, his steps dragging.

"Doc's going to be tied up with those last two gals, and I've got to help get the rest of these folks to town." The sheriff motioned around.

Several wagons had already departed, following the railroad tracks. Two empty wagons remained, one waiting for the injured girls lying next to the train car.

"Can y'all help me keep track of these two? Deliver them to my office?" The sheriff jerked his thumb toward Fran and Emma.

Fran saw the tension of the moment in the set of the bigger cowboy's jaw. Even unkempt as he was, the rugged lines of his face showed a stark handsomeness.

Not that she needed to be noticing. She should be worrying about the predicament she'd found herself in. At least she and Emma had made it a far piece from Memphis before she'd been found out.

But was it far enough? It had only been a day since she'd overheard the man on the Lincoln platform. He'd been looking for her and Emma by name, but they'd managed to avoid him and get onto the westbound train without being seen. No doubt he was one of Mr. Underhill's henchmen, hired to find them.

"These two gals in trouble?" the youngest of the cowboys asked curiously.

"It's that one," the matron said, pointing a shaking finger in Fran's direction. "She pretended to be an underage orphan. She used the resources set aside for those in need and defrauded us."

Yes. She guessed she had done all that. But it wasn't as if she had had any other choice.

The sheriff looked a bit skeptical. "Circuit judge is in town today. Let's see what he says afore we do anything else. You boys take them on for me, all right?"

Fran patted the special inside pocket she'd sewn into the drab frock the orphanage had given her. The crinkle of paper—her baptismal certificate that was her proof of identity—reassured her. She would face what she had to.

Emma's safety was paramount. Fran squeezed her sister, who looked more than a little worried, and followed the men on foot.

And they still had a chance. If she could locate this Jonas White she'd heard about, perhaps he would help.

"Howdy, miss."

The two younger men came along either side of Fran and Emma, smiling widely as if they hadn't just heard the accusation against her.

The closest one was a few years younger than the mountain man, closer to her own age. With smiling brown eyes and brown curls peeking from beneath his hat, he seemed the complete opposite of the gruff cowboy.

The one she was still intensely aware of as he strode several paces ahead, seeming to ignore them.

"Name's Seb. That's Edgar." He nodded toward the blond cowboy.

Edgar. An ordinary name for such an intense, enigmatic man.

"And I'm Matty." The second younger cowboy tipped his Stetson from Emma's opposite side. He was blond as well, but she could only see a hint of his curls beneath his hat. His brown eyes sparkled.

And still she felt a pull, some unusual sort of draw from deep in her midsection, toward the first man.

"I'm Fran Morris. My sister, Emma."

Both cowboys doffed their hats. "Nice to meet ya, ladies."

She couldn't help but notice that the unkempt cowboy continued to ignore them.

"You'll have to forgive our brother." Matty followed her gaze and nodded to the taller man ahead. "He don't get off the ranch much and forgets how to talk to women."

They were brothers?

Beside her, Seb guffawed. She caught a glimpse of Edgar's profile. Above his beard, his skin had reddened. Was it from the sun? Or could he be embarrassed by his brother's words?

She glanced away, unsure.

There were mountains in the far distance, but only prairie surrounded them. It was almost frightening in its barrenness. Especially if someone was following them—she imagined one could see a far distance on these plains, and she felt bare and conspicuous out in the open.

"How far is it to Bear Creek?" she asked.

"'Bout a quarter mile." Seb's smile was as easy and natural as the rest of him.

Fran sent a reassuring smile to Emma, but her sister remained pale, withdrawn from the conversation. Fearful.

"Do you know how the train derailed? Is that a normal occurrence?" Fran asked, trying to distract herself from worries over her sister.

Emma had remained near silent since they'd left the Girls' Academy in the dead of night. She'd barely spoken to *Fran.* How could she prove to Emma that she could keep them safe when the plan she'd hastily concocted was unraveling around them?

Both near cowboys shrugged, but it was Matty who spoke. "Never seen it happen before. Got a glimpse of the broken tracks, but I don't know for sure what caused it. Could've been some kind of sinkhole."

Ed looked over his shoulder at them. Or perhaps just at his brothers. His gaze seemed to skip right over Fran as if she didn't exist.

She couldn't understand it. They'd seemed to share a moment on top of the displaced train. Then the matron had started harping on Fran and she'd known her slight untruth had been discovered, but why would the man turn cold just because of that?

It shouldn't sting so badly, but it did. Then again, what experience did she have with men? Very little. And that had hardly been positive.

She stared at the back of his head, willing him to turn back around, to acknowledge her.

Which was silly and fanciful.

"Have you lived in Bear Creek long?" she asked Seb, purposefully turning toward him so as to ignore his older brother.

"Our pa's ranch is out of town a bit, toward the west. Been here since before I can remember, so nearly my whole life. Where you two gals headed?"

"Here, I guess," she murmured. She highly doubted the matron would agree to let them travel farther west with the other orphans. The best Fran could hope for was that this circuit judge and the sheriff would be sympathetic to her situation and that she could find work in this area.

If she couldn't, she didn't know what she and Emma

would do. They couldn't go back to Memphis. That wasn't an option.

She looked around at the vast empty sky and grassy land. What job opportunities could there be for her here? She'd hoped to secure a position as a teacher or perhaps as a clerk.

But what would she and Emma do if Fran *couldn't* get work?

Chapter Two

Edgar was tired to the bone.

After the physical efforts required to get all the passengers off the train, he was plumb worn-out.

And a little displeased about having to walk back to town. Seb had told him someone had appropriated his horse for an injured passenger and he could pick it up at the train station back in town.

He didn't mind that so much as he minded having to escort the Morris sisters to the sheriff's office-cum-jail.

Listening to them prattle on with two of his brothers.

He felt old.

A lot older than his twenty-four years.

Stodgy, even.

During his teen years, he'd been the prankster of the family. None of his brothers would've considered him dull. Ever.

And then Oscar and Maxwell, the two eldest, had gotten married. Jonas and Penny had started having more kids. And more and more of the burden of running the ranch had fallen to Edgar. He'd stopped having as much time for practical jokes. He hadn't really *meant* to become more serious natured; it had just *happened* as he'd taken on added responsibility.

He didn't begrudge his older brothers their happiness, even if he did sometimes wonder if it could last. He didn't hold it against his pa that Jonas wanted to spend time with the youngest kids instead of working, working, working on the ranch.

Edgar planned on staying unmarried, so it seemed a natural conclusion that he would pick up the slack on the growing ranch. He wasn't lonely. Didn't think he would be even if all of his younger brothers got themselves hitched. He would have plenty of nieces and nephews around to keep him busy.

He still wanted to strangle his brothers for charming Fran Morris.

Obviously, both had somehow sensed Edgar's muddled feelings about the pretty liar and had immediately gravitated toward her.

Or else either—or both—were attracted to her themselves. She'd claimed to be *of age,* but if she was, she wasn't much more than eighteen. Seb's age. Matty was twenty.

And even liars could be pretty.

Edgar suddenly felt as if he'd swallowed a hot branding iron as fire mushroomed in his esophagus.

He sent a glare over his shoulder. Seb had the audacity to wink. That boy.

Face hot, Edgar turned away, stomping forward. They were getting close to Bear Creek, but to his estimation, they couldn't get there fast enough.

Finally, they reached the outskirts of town. Then the sheriff's office.

Naturally, it was locked up tightly.

"Stay there," he ordered when the older girl shifted impatiently.

She didn't even seem to hear him as she sank down onto the boardwalk step.

Even in its threadbare condition, her simple dress was a reminder of how out of place she would be in one of the cells. He'd only been in the building once, when he and Jonas had had to spring Ricky after a night of carousing. Thankfully his sometimes-errant brother had thus far stuck close to home while Jonas and Penny were on their trip.

He turned away, crossing his arms over his chest. At least she wasn't trying to run off, not like he would be if the law wanted him.

Seb's thoughts seemed to mirror his own as his youngest brother sidled close. "We ain't really gonna let 'em get locked up, are we?"

"Not our business," Edgar said with a grunt.

He glanced at Matty, who was lounging against a post several feet away, just waiting.

But he couldn't keep his eyes from skittering over his shoulder at the pair of girls. Fran had one shoe off, and he could see her bare foot peeking out beneath the hem of her skirt. Her toes were blistered and red.

He steeled himself against the irrational urge to help her. She probably wasn't used to walking. Her shoe, obviously a hand-me-down, was battered. The thing probably didn't fit right and had rubbed her toes raw.

Her toes were not his problem.

Her younger sister knelt at her side, speaking in a low, urgent tone. He couldn't make out the words. The girl hadn't spoken to anyone else that he'd noticed. Was she shy or just shaken up from the train wreck?

Suddenly, one of the girls' stomachs rumbled. Loudly.

He did not feel a twinge of pity.

Emma blushed, her expression turning chagrined.

Matty shook his head. "I'm going to run down to the café."

Edgar reached out an arm, temporarily blocking his brother's progress down the street.

Matty gave him a level stare. Unblinking. "No telling how long the sheriff will be."

After a long, hard afternoon, Edgar's own stomach wouldn't have minded a bit of sustenance. He narrowed his eyes at his brother. "Bring some wet cloths for her foot," he growled.

He didn't acknowledge the soft "Thank you" from behind him.

Where was the sheriff?

He did not look at Fran or her sister and did not feel their curious gazes on him. He didn't.

Edgar exhaled and pushed back the brim of his hat.

"You heard anything about the train schedule?" He directed the question at Seb, but it was another who answered. Ricky.

"Station's closed."

His other twenty-year-old brother strode up to their little group. "I was at the station a minute ago and heard the news, then passed Matty on the street and he told me where you were."

Ricky tipped his hat to the two gals, a charming smile oozing across his face.

Edgar stepped in front of the girls, blocking them from Ricky's sight. "Where have you been?"

Seb had said he'd disappeared before the cattle had made it to Mr. Fredrick's place. Edgar had his suspicions, but would Ricky admit to where he'd been?

His brother squared his shoulders and set his jaw, steel gray eyes flashing. "Around."

Likely spending time with one of his many sweethearts. Where Edgar shied away from women at all costs, Ricky had been caught kissing behind the barn—and the church and the schoolhouse—too many times to count.

"Job's not finished," Edgar told his brother. "I need you with me, not out fooling around."

Ricky rolled his shoulders beneath his faded work shirt, as if he was looking for a wrestling match. His brother's penchant for using his fists to communicate had been a recent development, started when Ricky was caught flirting with another young buck's sweetheart. Normally Edgar would've been happy to oblige him, but not this time.

"Pa left me in charge while he's gone," he reminded his younger brother.

Ricky had no argument for that.

They stared at each other for a long, tense moment. For a few seconds, Edgar thought Ricky would turn and walk away.

"Until those cattle are delivered to Pa's buyer, I need you to quit with the tomfoolery and help me. You owe Pa that much."

The reminder of everything Jonas had done for them was a low blow, but Ricky gave a tight nod.

"Now, what do you mean the station's closed?" Edgar asked.

Ricky shrugged, looking across the street with hooded eyes. "The agent said the tracks are out both east and westbound and that he'd had a wire from Calvin. Their station is closed, too."

"When do they think it'll be repaired? Not in time

for our shipment anyway." Edgar answered his own question, thinking aloud.

"Agent said Tuck's Station has the closest operational rail stop." The small town was about halfway to Cheyenne, a good forty-five miles.

Edgar took off his Stetson and ran one hand through his hair, again noticing how long and messy it had gotten. It was a wonder Penny hadn't taken him to task and cut it for him, but then she'd been busy with preparations for their trip to Boston.

He idly scanned the area, still unable to believe that the railroad they'd relied on for years to ship their livestock could let them down like this. The agreement between his pa and the buyer had been for delivery in Cheyenne by June 1. Edgar had planned for an early delivery, but now they would be pushing it to get the cattle there on time.

It looked like they were going to be forced to do a cattle drive. They hadn't had one in years, not with the railroad making things convenient for local ranchers. With it being spring, others might be affected by the outage, as the White ranch was going to be. Maybe he could rustle up some additional funds by helping out their neighbors, taking their cattle for sale, as well.

Raised voices from down the street brought his gaze around and stalled his thoughts. Here came the sheriff, with the matron, the circuit judge and several other folks trailing behind.

The pretty liar looked up from her seat on the step and their gazes collided.

He quickly shifted his feet, breaking the almost palpable contact and turning away. He needed to get on his way. Had things to attend to.

And yet his feet felt like bricks, heavy and unmovable. And he had to wait on Matty anyway.

"I want her prosecuted to the fullest extent of the law—" The chaperone lady's voice was loud enough to carry down the street.

He'd heard her outside the overturned train car, going on and on about how Fran had cheated the orphanage that had sent the kids West. He figured everyone who'd been on the passenger car, plus those who'd come from town to help, had heard about the girl and the situation, and that the matron wanted her to pay.

And between the two groups of folks, the entire population of Bear Creek was likely to hear the story before sundown. Especially since he'd spotted Matilda Carter, the biggest gossip in town, in the group. She was likely to spread the story like wildfire.

If the girl wasn't a real orphan—at least not an underage one—and if the folks in town were turned against her, she wouldn't be able to find a decent job and would have to move on. He could only hope.

Except he did feel a little twinge behind his breastbone. He knew what it felt like to have all your choices taken from you. He'd been the last orphan at the last stop on the orphan train when he'd been sent West. And no one had wanted him. Not one family had taken a look at his mug and said, "That kid needs a family," or even, "That kid looks like a hard worker."

Until Jonas had arrived. If his pa hadn't come along, Edgar didn't know what he would've done—he'd had no way to survive on his own back then.

He didn't want to feel any sympathy for her. He didn't want to feel anything for her. He wanted her gone.

Matty came up the street from the other direction, towing a cloth-wrapped basket from the local cafe.

The itch on the back of Edgar's neck told him it was time to get out of there.

Fran had a hard time concentrating on all the voices arguing around her. Her nose had picked up on something savory from the basket Matty had brought back and it seemed her hunger pains had taken over her brain.

She forced herself back to the conversation at hand.

Maybe God was finally listening to her prayers. The circuit judge seemed to be fair, although he didn't seem entirely sympathetic to her side of things.

"So this girl is, in fact, an orphan, is that right?" He looked to Fran for confirmation.

Fran nodded. She desperately wished it wasn't true. Her parents' deaths and then her brother Daniel's desertion had started the downward spiral for her and Emma. Now it was on Fran's shoulders to protect the both of them.

"This orphan lied about her age and thus received the benefit from the orphanage and the Children's Help Association of food, clothing…" The man's lip curled in a slight sneer as he looked at her worn dress.

Fran felt the same way about the simple—and cheaply made—gray frock she'd been given when she and Emma had been accepted into the orphan train program. It was plain, with no adornments, and the color did nothing for her complexion. Its only redeeming quality had been that it was clean.

"Did she defraud the program in any other way?"

"No, sir," the matron said.

"Are you able to pay back these costs, small though they may be?" he asked Fran.

"No. I have no money to speak of."

"And why did you lie? Why come West and risk being separated from your sister?"

Tears sprang to Fran's eyes at the thought. She blinked them away. This was no place to break down.

She'd known it was possible they might be forced to separate, but by some blessing, no one had inquired about taking on either of them.

Again, her eyes found the burly cowboy—he really was a bear of a man—but he quickly looked away.

"It is a matter of a rather sensitive nature. I will tell you. But…in a more private setting."

She wasn't oblivious to the curious stares of the other passengers and the people passing by on the streets of the small town called Bear Creek.

The judge considered her, his gaze taking her measure.

She wouldn't lie again. She might've been forced to fudge her age to stay with Emma at the orphanage, but she had been taught since early youth that lying was wrong. If matters hadn't been so desperate, she would never have done it in the first place.

"Suffice it to say, if I had had another choice, I wouldn't have lied."

The judge tapped one long index finger against his chin. "You know, I believe you."

Her heart thumped once. In anticipation or fear, she didn't know.

"I can't jail this young lady. The amount she needs to repay is so minuscule that it would not be worth my time prosecuting or holding her."

The matron protested, voice going even louder. Fran didn't hear what she said over the rushing in her ears.

Emma threw shaking arms around Fran and they embraced, squeezing tight.

"However, I can't just let you go, miss."

Fran's hopes crashed around her feet at the judge's words. She froze, Emma murmuring her dismay beside her.

"Your sister is still a ward of the Children's Help Association until she's placed out. Even though you're of age, they likely can't release her to you because you have no way of supporting yourself."

"I'll get a job," Fran said quickly. "I was planning to work. I'm good with figures, and I'm a quick learner."

The judge sighed. "After all these dramatics…" He sent a stern look at the matron, who was frowning, still clearly upset that her claims had been dismissed. "In a town this small, I can guarantee that everyone now knows your business and that you've lied and been made a spectacle of. Not a lot of folks around here want to risk hiring someone with a reputation like that."

Her stomach swooped low. She tasted bitter disappointment. So, then, what was she supposed to do?

The four cowboys were getting ready to leave—she could tell by their shifting feet. In desperation, she said the first thing she could think of. "What about Jonas White?"

Everyone around her froze.

The sheriff, who'd been standing silently nearby while the judge questioned her, now spoke up. "Do you know Jonas?"

"No—that is to say, someone in the last town said a Mr. Jonas White might take us in."

It wasn't an outright lie. But the comment had come from a man in a fine suit and had been disparaging.

More to the effect of, "That Jonas White will take in any kind of riffraff."

Edgar's head came up slowly, the brim of his hat hiding his eyes until the last possible moment, when they locked on her.

"Boys?" the sheriff asked.

Fran knew her surprise showed on her face. All of them were somehow related to this Jonas?

"None of these boys told you their surname? They all belong to Jonas White. They are his sons."

"My pa's out of town." Edgar looked uncomfortable, like he'd rather be anywhere other than where he was. "So I'm afraid he can't help you. Sorry."

But he didn't look sorry. He looked relieved.

"All she needs is a place to stay," the fourth brother said, the one whose name she hadn't caught. He looked so totally different than the other three that it was a wonder they were related.

"She can't stay on a ranch with a bunch of bachelors," Edgar argued.

"She could if she was married to one of them." Seb's simple sentence changed the tone of the entire conversation. Edgar's gaze landed on hers and something, some connection rose between them, silent but clear.

His face above his beard reddened. She didn't think it was embarrassment turning his skin that shade of pink.

For the briefest moment, Fran considered it. Considered that the burly cowboy would certainly be able to protect her and Emma if Mr. Underhill was able to track them this far. Considered what it might be like to lean on someone like him, someone who could obviously handle the difficulties life threw at him.

Until he spoke.

"No," the cowboy said. There was a very final ring to the word.

"I'll take her in." Another male voice joined the hubbub that had ensued in their little group since Fran Morris had uttered the name Jonas White, this one coming from the shadows of the alley beside the jail.

A man with the look of a gambler, in a fancy black vest and trousers, stepped into their circle of conversation. John Graves.

Edgar had seen him around town, knew he owned one of the saloons, but he wasn't acquainted with the man on a personal level.

"I've got a room she can board in, and I've got work. I'll even take the sister, too."

"She don't wanna be no saloon girl," Matty protested.

Fran recoiled with a little gasp. She took a half step in front of her sister. Maybe protecting her from the man's calculating gaze.

"It wouldn't appear she has any other choice," Graves said coolly.

"That's no life for a lady," Ricky broke in.

His eyes met Edgar's, and Edgar saw the shadows of a life that the other man rarely spoke of—his childhood. Ricky knew from personal experience it wasn't any kind of life for a woman, liar or not. And Edgar believed his brother.

"I'll marry her."

Seb.

Had everyone around him gone crazy?

"You're not marrying her," he told his brother in no uncertain terms.

"Well, someone has to be responsible for them," the circuit judge said.

"I can take care of us both—" Seb argued.

Voices broke out all around then, Seb's and Matty's right in the mix, arguing.

Edgar could just imagine his fun-loving, cheerful brother being shackled to someone who would ruin his life. Pretty she may be, but she was a manipulative liar to boot. His naive brother had no idea what he was getting into.

He couldn't let that happen to Seb.

"You're not marrying her," Edgar repeated. Loud enough to silence everyone around him. "I am."

Chapter Three

This day wasn't turning out as expected.

Inside the jail, with his brothers and her sister looking on wide-eyed, Edgar stood before the circuit judge, new fiancée at his side, ready and willing to get hitched.

Well, not ready.

And not willing, exactly.

He'd planned to stay a bachelor forever.

But he was going to do this.

He took off his hat and put it on the desk. When he looked up, he caught his bride ogling his hair. He reached up.

It was a long, tangled mess. His ma would never forgive him when she found out about this.

He ran a hand through it and shrugged.

Her big brown eyes didn't lose their slightly wild look.

"Can you give us a minute?" he growled at the room in general.

The circuit judge looked like he would protest, but Matty clapped him on the shoulder and the room's occupants edged away into the periphery.

His bride looked like she couldn't catch her breath.

"You gonna swoon?"

Her gaze narrowed on him. "Of course not."

"You look pretty pale."

She frowned, that pretty mouth turning down. "Perhaps I'm just overcome with the anticipation of marrying *you*."

The smile that spread across his lips shocked him. And her, too—he could see it in her face.

She crossed her arms over her middle. He supposed she wanted to appear composed or irritated, but the way she held so tightly to her elbows made it look more like she was holding herself together.

Like she wasn't any happier about this than he was.

He didn't like feeling sorry for her. "Let's just get this over with, all right? I've got things to do this afternoon. I've got a herd of cattle to get on the move. And I know your sister is plumb worn-out."

He had no intention of letting his new wife stay on the ranch permanently, no matter if they were married or not. But he needed some time to figure out what to do with her.

She peered up at him suspiciously. "Will you…seek an annulment?"

He ground his back teeth and shook his head slowly. "But don't get your hopes up."

She crooked her brows at him.

"I'll give you my name and I'll get you settled somewhere, but that's all this is."

Moments after Edgar White's emphatic statement, the others had rejoined them, and Fran stood across from her bridegroom. Close enough to see the muscle ticking in his cheek.

Neither one of them wanted this marriage. But she certainly didn't want to become a saloon girl.

And perhaps the men chasing Emma would be deterred by this cowboy and his brothers. They made a formidable crew indeed. Was it enough to escape Mr. Underhill and his senseless crusade to have Emma?

She didn't know. But she was willing to try anything to save her sister.

"Are you even old enough to get married?" the cowboy before her grumbled.

Her chin hitched before she'd even realized it. "I'm nineteen."

The circuit judge cleared his throat. "Shall I begin?"

The next moments passed so quickly, Fran didn't register all the words that were spoken. She did notice the emotion that darkened Edgar's face when the circuit judge asked if he would *love* her, *honor* her and *comfort* her. She didn't know what it meant, but she remembered his intense statement on top of that overturned train, that he kept his promises. Would he really?

And then it was over. She didn't know what she had expected, but it certainly wasn't for her new husband to clasp her hand loosely in his great, warm paw, or to lean forward and buss her cheek with a kiss—a warm brush of his beard with only a hint of his smooth lips.

They were married.

The afternoon passed in a whirlwind. They obtained a wagon from the livery in town, then visited two ranches on their way to the property her new husband shared with his family.

At each place, when she was introduced as Edgar's wife, there were shocked gasps, quickly hidden behind upraised hands. And cowboys with wiggling eyebrows.

It seemed common knowledge among all the residents that her new husband had never intended to marry at all.

And wasn't that a fine start to a new marriage, real or not?

It wasn't as if he was making the stops to show her off, either. It was more as if he was too afraid to let her out of his sight.

What did he think, that she intended to rob him blind? They hadn't met under the best of circumstances, but she didn't think her one untruth deserved this level of distrust. It stung, but she was determined to smile until her teeth ached if she had to and be as quiet and pliant as she could be. She wouldn't cause trouble for her husband, not when he'd done everything he could to prevent her from being sent to that saloon.

He seemed single-minded in his determination to get his cattle to a place called Tuck's Station. But that didn't stop him from making arrangements with his neighbors, who also had cattle to ship. These partnerships would ultimately net him a larger profit, she learned just by being silent and listening.

Her paper husband seemed to have a head for business.

Finally, they loaded up in the wagon and he informed her they were returning to his home. She was drooping on the bench seat next to him, thankful for his looming presence, even though he retained a respectable distance between them.

"Why did you want to marry me?"

His sudden gruff question caught her off guard and she spoke without thinking. "It isn't as if I was given much choice."

He considered that for a moment.

"You know anything about being a rancher's wife?"

"No."

Her quick answer must have surprised him, as his chin quirked downward.

"What?" she asked.

"Figured you'd say yes. No matter if you knew anything or not."

She bristled. "I don't make a practice of telling untruths."

She could sense that he didn't believe her. Before she could protest or explain, he changed the subject. "You know how to cook?"

"Not much. But I'm willing to learn." Fran knew her new husband didn't believe a word she said.

She didn't guess she blamed him.

She would do everything she could to make up for the trouble she had caused, even if she was only on his ranch for a few days. She would never be able to repay him for the protection that taking his name had offered both her and Emma.

"Know how to gather eggs out of the chicken coop?"

"No."

"Know how to butcher a hog?"

She shook her head.

"How about planting a vegetable garden? Riding a horse? Driving a wagon?"

"None of the above."

"So you're a city girl?"

"Through and through." And she could only hope that Mr. Underhill would never think she would take Emma west to a small town like Bear Creek.

And if her new husband hoped to scare her off with a list of chores, he'd better try harder. She would do anything to protect her sister, even work like a dog.

"Emma and I will pull our own weight. We won't be a burden to you and your family."

He only harrumphed in response.

The setting sun finally slipped over the horizon, and the night air quickly cooled around them.

"Emma, put your shawl on. And mine, too."

She glanced over her shoulder to make sure Emma complied. Her sister's silence was unnatural and another niggle of worry slid through her calm facade.

Had something more happened with Mr. Underhill that Fran hadn't been aware of? Something that had damaged her sister?

The two threadbare garments were the only things the Children's Help Association had seen fit to give them, other than the dresses and shoes. Although, Fran supposed, it was almost summer and perhaps they wouldn't need warmer garments. For now, though, she would hate for her sister to take a chill. Right at this moment, it was the only thing she could do for Emma.

For herself, she simply crossed her arms to ward off the wind that had kicked up.

She refused to ask the man beside her how much longer their ride would be. The question might be seen as a complaint, and she was determined not to cause even that much trouble.

She hoped that if she could hide out for a few days and make a plan for her and Emma, maybe their troubles with Mr. Underhill would be over. His obsession with Emma *had* to end now, didn't it? Even if he found them, they had a place now.

There were still the accusations against her. If Daniel were here, she'd be able to ask her attorney brother how they could be disputed. Of course, if Daniel were here, they wouldn't be in this mess.

Even with her new husband, the fear that had shaken her in Lincoln wasn't letting up yet. Especially because the man beside her didn't really want a wife.

"Here we are."

The wagon topped a crest and she saw the shadows of several buildings. In the dim moonlight, she thought the sprawling, low cabin must be the main house and the larger buildings across the yard must be the barn and bunkhouse.

Edgar seemed to be waiting for her response, almost as if he expected her to demand he return her to town. It was true the home was certainly more rustic than what she was accustomed to in Memphis, at least from the outside.

But there was no going back for her and Emma.

When she remained silent, the taciturn man beside her pulled the horses to a stop halfway between the barn and house.

He left her to get out of the wagon herself. She missed one of the spokes on the wheel and nearly toppled. At least he helped Emma climb down from the back.

He thrust a basket of food into her hands. The last farmer's wife had insisted they take it. "There'll be some bread and eggs in the kitchen for your breakfast. You can bunk down in my sister's bedroom. Should be a quilt on the bed. Don't be messing with any of her personal stuff."

She frowned at him. "Of course not. But what about your sister? Will we displace her?"

"She's in Boston with my folks. She's adopted, like the rest of us older boys."

Adopted. Everything clicked into place. It explained the differences in their appearance. And temperaments. Seb seemed sweet, if a bit ornery. Matty and Ricky had been kind, but a bit distracted. And Edgar... Well, she didn't really know him, did she? But he certainly seemed upset that his plans had been derailed as much as the train had.

"Anyway, my parents have custody over her, but she got a notion to go back to Boston and see where her birth family hails from. It must be a girl thing, I don't know...."

The unspoken meaning to his words was that he had no interest in knowing more about his own birth family.

For a moment, he stared off into the darkness.

Emma shifted beside Fran. She'd remained quiet all throughout the wedding and while the girls had been allowed a short break to eat the supper Matty had provided. Fran knew her sister must be as tired as she was from the long days of travel and fear.

"Where will you stay?" Fran asked softly.

"In the bunkhouse with the rest of the boys. There's five of us brothers plus another hired hand, so if you try to make off with any horseflesh, someone will hear."

He looked pointedly at her.

She bristled. "I already told you, I don't know how to ride a horse."

He shrugged.

"I've got to get the cattle delivered to Tuck's Station— that's forty-five miles west of here. I'll be leaving shortly after first light. Be back in a few days."

He narrowed his eyes at her.

"My brother Davy will be here watching over you until I get back. We'll talk about living arrangements then."

The way he spoke almost seemed like a threat. She could tell him she didn't want more from him than the protection of his name, but she knew he wouldn't believe her. She didn't truly expect him to stand between her and Mr. Underhill if it came to that. Why would he?

"Thank you for today," she said instead.

He appeared flabbergasted.

"And I'm sorry to have inconvenienced you."

His brows crinkled as he looked down on her.

Then he stalked away into the darkness without another word.

I'm sorry to have inconvenienced you.

Edgar mouthed the words, mocking their speaker as he shoved the last of the provisions in the back of the covered wagon and slammed the tailgate. The contraption with its extra nooks and crannies for their food items had been nicknamed a chuck wagon by some long-ago cowboy.

Inconvenienced him?

Was she kidding?

Not only had she put a kink in his plans to get his pa's cattle where they needed to go, but she'd forced him into a situation that would require some doing to take care of.

But she'd seemed genuine in her remorse.

Obviously, marrying him had been a better choice for her than working at the saloon. He couldn't blame her for that, even though he could blame her for everything else. Like getting on that orphan train in the first place. What could have forced a gal like her, orphan or not, into going West and leaving her life behind?

Frustrated that he couldn't seem to get his thoughts off his new problem wife, he stalked into the barn, where he planned to bed down instead of the bunkhouse.

For one, he'd be able to get the chuck wagon hitched

quickly in the morning and get off the ranch before he even had a chance to see Fran or her sister.

And he'd be able to watch over the house better from here.

It sat wrong with him, settling the two girls in his ma's house, in Breanna's bedroom. It was true there weren't a lot of valuables to be had around the place, but if they messed up his family's home, he'd never forgive himself.

He didn't expect to get a lot of sleep that night.

And another benefit of sleeping in the barn? He didn't have to face his brothers again.

He'd spoken to them briefly about his new plan to get the cattle delivered to the buyer. Teaming up with two of their nearest neighbors, who also had cattle to sell, would make things easier on them and provide more eyes to watch over the cattle.

He'd barely gotten his plan laid out before the brothers had started razzing him. Even Davy, who was quiet natured, had apparently been filled in and was teasing him about his new wife.

And that was when he'd commanded Davy to watch over the homestead in his absence and rushed out of the bunkhouse to pack up the chuck wagon. His feelings about Fran were so muddled. Mostly he just wanted her gone.

She was pretty enough, he guessed. But he couldn't trust her.

The soft light that had been shining from Breanna's bedroom went dark. Finally.

He folded himself into the bedroll, just inside the barn door that he'd cracked open. The night before, he'd been up all night helping that mama cow, and now he wanted nothing more than to slip away into sleep, but he forced himself to keep his gritty eyes open. The hint of moonlight didn't offer much, but he could distinguish the darker line of the house from the night sky.

For some strange reason, he really hoped that his new wife *wouldn't* be found sneaking out of the house.

Fran curled up beneath the quilt next to her sleeping sister, mind racing.

It was a snug house, well built. Different from what she was used to. A small white dog had greeted them at the back step until Edgar had shooed it away.

Edgar and his brothers were leaving in the morning, along with another couple of cowhands. He had said he would leave her under the care of his brother Davy, but what if…

What if the man she'd overheard on the Lincoln platform was still hunting them on Mr. Underhill's behalf? What if he tracked her here?

She'd married Edgar for the protection he could afford her—she'd seen how he had rushed to rescue a bunch of people he didn't know from the train wreck—but how could she rely on his protection if he wasn't there? How could one cowboy who didn't even know her go up against Mr. Underhill and his associates?

Edgar had said he would be gone for a few days, but what if she didn't have that long?

Emma stirred beneath the thin quilt, and Fran's drooping eyes flew open as an idea hit her.

What if she and Emma went on the cattle drive with the men? Surely they could help in some way. This solution would keep her and Emma from staying in one place. They would be on the move.

And near Edgar.

It would be hard for Mr. Underhill to track them if they just disappeared.

The more she thought about it, the more sense it made.

She only hoped her new husband wouldn't be too mad about it.

It was still dark outside when Fran was roused by the blow of a horse nearby. The confining wall next to her bed was unfamiliar, and why was Emma pressed against her back so closely? She could barely breathe.

She came awake at the murmur of a man's voice.

She was in the wagon. She'd been unable to sleep most of the night, praying they wouldn't be discovered, but she must've finally drifted off.

And the man nearby was Edgar White. Her paper husband.

Memories of the day before, the anxious train ride and then the terrifying wreck—and her new husband—tightened Fran's chest until she wanted to gasp for air. But she didn't. She didn't want to be discovered, not here in this uncomfortable wagon bed and not yet, after they'd taken so much trouble to sneak across the yard and into the conveyance in the first place, in the dark of night.

Emma moved beside her, softly rustling the old blanket Fran had draped over them to hide them if anyone should look in the back of the covered wagon before the journey had begun. Fran placed a gentle hand on the crown of her sister's head, a sign of comfort they'd used at a small age in their parents' home, and Emma stilled.

Metal jangled—possibly the horses' harnesses?—and Fran braved a whisper, hoping the man was far enough away from the wagon that he wouldn't hear. "Just go back to sleep."

The entire wagon shifted and creaked under a heavy weight. He must be climbing onto the bench seat now. Fran was reminded how very large her husband was. What if he was angry when he discovered them? She didn't really know him. Would he become violent?

The realization she might be putting Emma in danger again frightened her.

The thought that there would be other cowboys around was small comfort. She would simply have to find a way to prove her worth and hope he wouldn't be extremely angry.

He clucked softly to the horses, and then it was too late to change her mind as the wagon jostled forward.

Emma's breathing evened out as the wagon continuously bumped along. Fran's mind raced ahead, leaving her unable to return to sleep. Was she doing the right thing?

She couldn't have imagined Underhill's man on the train platform in Lincoln. And even though he hadn't been on the train to Bear Creek, if he'd tracked them that far, he could track them the rest of the way. Which meant she and Emma might be only a day or two in front of Mr. Underhill. If this didn't work, if they couldn't get to Tuck's Station with the driving cattle and find a way to hide, she would never forgive herself. She was tired of running, but if it came down to it, she would keep moving for Emma's sake.

Soft light filtered through the canvas above them when the creaking wagon slowed and stopped.

Unusual noises of many feet and jostling people confounded Fran. It was barely light outside. Surely the entire town didn't wake and gather this early, rustic as the place was. But what was going on? Then she realized it wasn't people she was hearing at all. It must be the cattle. A loud lowing from nearby confirmed it.

The wagon shifted and then released like a spring. Edgar must've disembarked.

"You're driving the wagon," he said, not attempting to be quiet any longer. "The other boys ready to go?"

"Aw, why do I hafta drive first?" Fran thought she recognized the second speaker as Seb, though she hadn't seen him since yesterday afternoon, after the rushed wedding.

"You wanna take a guess why?" There was the sound of flesh meeting flesh—a friendly punch on the arm, perhaps?—and an "oomph" of expelled air, as if the two grown men were wrestling. Surely that couldn't be right. But then, her brother Daniel had been much older than she and Emma were, and they had never been close enough to tease.

"C'mon, we gotta get moving," Edgar said. "Let me get my horse untied."

With only her nose poking out of the thin blanket, Fran was still able to see his shadow as it loomed over the side of the wagon. She held her breath, praying he wasn't going to open the back flap and discover them. Sounds of leather against wood echoed right near her ear.

Then came another male voice, one she didn't recognize. "Excuse me."

"Morning." Whoever it was didn't get the same effusive greeting Edgar had given his brother. Someone he didn't know well?

The wagon shifted again, much less this time, as Seb must've gotten into the wagon seat.

"I'm looking for two young ladies that arrived on a train yesterday."

Fran's breath lodged uncomfortably in her throat. Could this be the same man from the Lincoln station two days before? Or someone else Mr. Underhill had hired to find them?

"Both small of stature, dark haired."

"No young ladies here," said Edgar, his voice stiff.

Fran strained to hear over the pounding of her heart in her ears. Would he direct the man to his family's ranch and give them up?

"They're only a couple of runaways, see, and I've got to get word back home."

This time the stranger got no response.

Leather creaked and a horse blew again. Edgar mounting up? Hooves thumped in the packed dirt and from behind her, Seb clucked to the horses and set the wagon in motion.

It seemed they were safe for now. But how long could it last?

Chapter Four

"**I**'m so bored," Emma burst out, sending the blanket flying. "I can't breathe under this thing, and I can't lie still another moment!"

Fran was joyful for a moment that Emma had spoken, even in an outburst, but then she sent a panicked look to the front of the wagon, where indeed Seb was revealed to be sitting. Now looking over his shoulder right at her, he winked. And whistled shrilly.

"Whoa," he shouted to the horses, and began slowing the wagon.

By the time they had rolled to a stop, she could see through the front opening of the canvas as Edgar rode a beautiful big black horse toward them.

"What's going on?" he called out.

Seb jabbed his finger over his shoulder, and Edgar's eyes flicked back into the wagon, widening in surprise when they clashed with Fran's gaze.

"What are you doing? How did you get in there?"

He didn't sound happy to see her. At all.

Seb cleared his throat.

Edgar shot a look at his brother as he swung one muscled leg over the horse and dismounted. He rounded

the wagon, briefly stepping out of sight and then opened
the back flap and took the tailgate down.

"Hop down."

Fran slid her legs over the side and dropped to the
ground, but after a morning spent nearly motionless
trying not to be noticed, her legs were like jelly.

Edgar's strong, wide hand settled at her waist, both
steadying and unsettling her.

He frowned down at her, quickly releasing his hold
on her as she straightened her spine. "Watch your step,"
he ordered.

Bossy man.

He stared down at her for a long moment, looking
half confused and half angry. Beneath his cowboy hat,
his eyes were stormy.

At their feet, a barking white dog interrupted the
moment.

"What's that critter doing here?" Edgar threw the
words at Seb.

Behind her, Seb chuckled as he rounded the wagon
and helped Emma down. "He's been following the
wagon all morning. Thought he'd turn back, but he
hasn't."

He caught his brother's eye, and the chuckle turned
into a cough that he quickly tried to hide behind his
own hat.

"May I...have a moment to stretch my legs?" Emma's soft question seemed to affect the man in charge,
softening him the slightest bit.

"I guess."

Fran watched Emma swirl through the golden
grasses at their feet. She bent and said something soft
to the dog, reaching out to pat its head.

Her sister's small animation was such a relief after

several days of near silence that Fran would've braved Edgar's wrath all over again, just for this moment.

Edgar clamped a hand on his brother's shoulder. "Ride ahead and tell Ricky the wagon had a delay but we'll be on the way shortly."

Seb didn't question his brother's order, but he looked back over his shoulder as he walked away.

"What am I supposed to do with you?" her paper husband asked, still with that torn look on his face.

Fran swallowed hard. The unending prairie surrounded them, not a house in sight. Edgar wouldn't just leave them here in the middle of nowhere, would he?

His frown gave her no answer.

"What exactly did you think you were doing? Did you think you were going to ride along in the wagon without being caught?"

"I hoped by the time we were found, it would be too far away from civilization for you to turn us back."

Edgar had to look away from the woman's saucy, endearing grin. He waited for his rolling stomach to settle. The two biscuits he'd downed for breakfast that morning must've been bad.

It was the only thing he could think of that would have caused that hitch in his breathing when he'd touched her and that swoop in his stomach when she smiled.

What he couldn't explain was the dizzying relief he felt when he'd realized both sisters had hidden in the wagon.

The man that had approached him at the holding yard had asked after two small dark-haired young women. Which could easily have been Fran and Emma. But for some reason Edgar couldn't explain, he had held back from answering the man.

Or maybe he could explain it. The man had had the look of a crook or a confidence man, with beady eyes and a half-chewed cigar hanging from one corner of his mouth. He'd been much too sly...too oily. Edgar had had a bad feeling about him, but had trusted that Davy would be able to keep the two women safe on Jonas's ranch. Mostly.

It was the relief at their presence that made him edgy, and he crossed his arms over his chest. "What are you doing here? Why'd you sneak onto that wagon?"

"I thought I could help with your cattle drive. You'll be tired after a long day in the saddle, and I can cook supper—I can at least take on that one task so you don't have to do it."

She had a lot to learn about the life of a rancher. She'd just described about every day of his life. Long hours in the saddle and then chores at home. "You said you couldn't cook."

"I said I couldn't cook *much*. But I've been reading these and I think I've got the idea...."

She turned back to the wagon and then held up a small wooden box that had been tucked inside. A box he recognized from his ma's kitchen. "You stole my ma's recipe box?"

"I didn't *steal* it. I borrowed it."

She clutched it protectively to her chest, as if offended that he would suggest she would take something of his ma's.

The corner of his mouth wanted to tick upward, so he narrowed his eyes instead. "Why'd you really hide in that wagon all morning?"

She huffed and looked past his shoulder. So did he.

Nearby, her sister walked through some tall meadow grasses, hands gently touching the tops of some tall buffalo grass. Emma's eyes were on the horizon—she wasn't paying any attention to them—and she looked almost peaceful.

The younger girl's previous soft question had twisted something in his gut. She was afraid of something. Something that had been enough to send them West?

He looked back to her sister, watching Fran until she spoke again, eyes still on Emma.

"I thought it might be better if we kept moving, rather than stay in one place. Even with your brother for protection."

"You gonna tell me what you're runnin' from?"

She considered him with her big brown eyes. "Not today."

He shifted his boots, nodding toward the double tracks the wagon had left in the soft grass as it had traveled along. "I oughta leave you out here to find your way back to Bear Creek."

Her eyes widened, a flicker of fear or uncertainty flashing through them.

For some reason, his chest started aching. It made his voice gruff when he spoke.

"It'd take too long to drive you back. You'll have to ride along. But when we get to Tuck's Station, you and I will have a serious talk about what the future holds."

He started off toward where he'd left his big black grazing and tossed his last words over his shoulder. "I'll send Ricky back to teach you how to drive the wagon. Might as well make yourself useful."

He'd been thinking on it all morning. His ma frequented a seamstress in Calvin, a good thirty miles from Bear Creek, who was in high demand. If she could use a helper, he might be able to use his ma's connection to talk her into taking on the two girls.

Then all he would have to do would be find a place for them to board, and he could wash his hands of the whole situation.

Calvin was close enough that he could help if she needed it, but he wouldn't have a woman messing up his orderly life.

It was a workable solution. He could only hope.

Fran had never been so glad to see the sun dipping toward the horizon.

Surely now the man beside her would have mercy and stop this torture.

The wagon topped a rise, and she saw the cattle spread out in a loose knot before them, dust flying. She'd never thought one could choke on dust, but she'd been proved wrong. She felt as if she'd swallowed several mouthfuls of it over the course of the day.

Edgar rode point, all the way out front, tall in the saddle of his big black horse. The other cowboys kept strategic places around the herd. Ricky, beside her on the wagon seat, had explained the placement when her curiosity had prompted her to ask.

Swing riders were about a third of the way back, flank riders two-thirds back and tail riders were at the very rear of the herd. Ricky hadn't explained what the young Seb had done to deserve eating trail dust all day long, but it was obvious that riding behind the herd wasn't a coveted position.

Driving the chuck wagon wasn't much better.

"Shouldn't we be stopping soon?"

She'd vowed not to ask, but the screaming pain from

her shoulders and arms wouldn't let her keep silent any longer.

Ricky chuckled and took the reins from her.

A half gasp, half sigh escaped as the tension from driving the two massive animals harnessed in front of her was suddenly gone.

"Ooh…" she moaned, reaching up to rub her left shoulder, which felt a little worse than the other.

"I was waiting on you to say something," the man beside her said. "You lasted a lot longer than I thought you would."

Because she hadn't wanted to give Edgar the satisfaction of knowing he'd assigned her a task she couldn't do.

She glanced behind them to check on Emma, who'd walked beside the wagon for a long time that afternoon, watching after the little white dog. Ricky had told them it belonged to his sister, Breanna.

Several times during the day, Emma had listened in on Fran and Ricky's conversations, although she hadn't spoken again after her question to Edgar. She had dropped off to sleep inside the conveyance not long ago. Now she slept on, something she hadn't been able to do on the train out of Memphis. What was it about being out on this open plain that calmed Emma?

Fran hoped she'd done the right thing by not telling Emma her suspicions that they were being followed. Her sister's peace was so fragile. Fran would do anything to keep away the plaguing fear and desperation.

"Ed's calling a halt." Ricky pointed to where Edgar appeared to be talking with one of the other cowboys, then the taller, broader man rode back to speak to each of them in turn.

"Let's drive a little farther and see if we can't find a place near that stream to camp for the night."

"What stream?" She strained her eyes but didn't see anything resembling the sparkle of water, only an endless prairie and a snaking line of trees.

"It's beneath the trees—it's what's sustaining them."

"Ah."

By the time they'd found a campsite Ricky deemed good enough—somewhat close to the stream she still couldn't see and somewhat flat—Fran was drooping with exhaustion. Even though she'd ridden on the bench seat most of the day, the strain of guiding the two horses in their traces had taken a toll.

It was a relief to stand on firm ground and stretch her back. She hadn't realized her legs would be sore from bracing against the front of the wagon. She twisted from side to side, loosening muscles that had stiffened with the same activity all day.

"Ed will leave a couple of fellas with the cattle, but the rest of them will be along soon for supper. You want some help?" Ricky asked.

Edgar hadn't specifically told her to cook the evening meal. He hadn't specifically told her not to, either.

During her only break from driving the team, she'd catalogued everything in the wagon, from the cast iron frying pan to the large ham hanging from the cross poles to the covered jugs of flour and salt.

She had an idea of what she thought she could cook without botching it too badly. But she was at a loss for how to begin.

"How do I... We'll need a fire, won't we?"

The charming cowboy grinned at her. "Seems like you're starting to think like a rancher's wife after all."

Fran preened a little with the praise and leaned as far as she could into the wagon to wake her sister.

"Emma. I'll need you to start peeling potatoes. We've got a lot to do."

She was determined to prove to her taciturn husband that she could pull her own weight and not be a burden until they got to Tuck's Station.

Hours later, Fran was dozing over her food when an empty plate and tin mug clattered to the ground in front of her.

She startled awake, heart pounding, to see her husband stalking off away from the fire and into the night.

"Mighty good fixin's, ma'am."

Fran looked up as Matty knelt next to her and added his empty dishes to the pile.

She shouldn't have been miffed. She'd expected very little from her paper husband, but the man could have at least praised her effort. Awful though it had been.

"Don't lie. The ham was only half cooked and the potatoes were burned."

"I was trying to be nice. The food wasn't inedible. And the bread was all right."

She gave him a look. "The bread was baked before we left home."

"And I did a fine job of it, too." He smiled, but she couldn't help looking out after the retreating back of her husband.

"He's not very friendly, is he?" she asked. But there had been a moment when she'd been discovered in the wagon... He wasn't always standoffish, but perhaps that was how he wanted her to see him. She just didn't know why.

"He'll come around. He's mostly mad at me and Seb right now. And a little worried about getting the cattle where they need to go. I think he doesn't quite know what to do with you."

She shrugged, too tired to think anymore about what she might do to make this trip a little more bearable for Edgar.

Her gaze fell on the dirty cast iron skillet and the pile of plates that was growing as another cowboy added his.

"I have to wash all of these, don't I?"

Matty's eyes had a definite twinkle. Or maybe the fire was playing tricks on her. "Somebody's got to."

She sighed. "Where?"

He nodded, and she followed the bob of his head to the line of dark trees against the night sky.

"The creek?"

His nod was anything but reassuring.

"There's not anything…dangerous out there, is there?"

"Shouldn't be. Your sister gonna help?"

"I've already sent her to bed. She's exhausted."

"Oh, *she* is?"

Fran shooed off the pesky cowboy, who only chuckled as he went. She gathered the rest of the cowboys' plates and utensils and piled them all in the large skillet. Then she flung a towel over her shoulder and tossed a small chunk of soap on top of the whole heap and began lugging it toward the dark silhouette of the trees.

By the time her eyes had adjusted to the darkness that made the firelight seem overly bright, she'd stumbled on a large tree root, knocked her elbow into a thick tree trunk and submerged one booted foot completely in the icy-cold creek.

But at least she'd held on to the pan and all the dishes.

With the bottom of her skirt already drenched, she

figured she couldn't do much worse by kneeling on the creek bank to wash the dishes.

The farther she'd gone from the campsite, the quieter it had gotten. Now all she could hear was the rustle of leaves in the night breeze and her own heartbeat. She realized she was holding her breath, and tried to force her shoulders down. Surely the men wouldn't have let her come out here if it was dangerous.

But she couldn't quite believe it, and so she rushed to scrub the dishes clean as quickly as she could.

She was elbow deep in the freezing water when a twig snapped behind her. She whirled, and the tin cup she'd been scrubbing flew from her fingers and landed in the water with a *plunk*.

"Oh!" she cried in dismay, quickly leaning out to reach for the cup. The bank beneath her knees shifted.

"Watch it!"

Edgar.

His voice registered just as he grabbed the back of her dress and kept her from tumbling headfirst into the water.

Her relief melded with irritation that he'd snuck up on her, and she slapped at his hand. "Let go!"

He did, but caught her as she went off-balance a second time and this time drew her away from the water's edge.

"You made me drop a cup—it's there." She was breathless from fear, not from his nearness. Mostly.

"Leave it. I'll come fetch it in the morning."

Well.

In the near complete darkness beneath the canopy of the trees, his presence seemed larger as he held her loosely by the waist. He smelled of horse and man, and with him this close, with her hands resting on his broad chest, she didn't feel any fear at all.

He seemed to realize exactly how close they'd become at the same moment she did.

He released her and took a giant step back. "What's taking so long?"

"I thought you were a bear!" she said at the same moment.

There was a beat of silence.

"A bear?"

"Or a mountain lion."

She sensed more than saw his smile in the darkness. She remembered the one time he'd smiled, at the sheriff's office. Did she, in particular, bring out his frown?

"I scouted this area before it got dark," he said. "No tracks or sign from any bears or mountain lions. Maybe a turtle, or a rabbit or two."

"Ha."

"You about done with those dishes?"

"Almost there. Are you done checking up on me?" She knelt at the bank again, expecting him to return to the campsite, but to her surprise, he joined her, his big shoulder bumping hers as he reached for a plate.

"Are you surprised by what I accomplished today?"

He seemed stumped by the question, staying silent for a long moment as he scrubbed his plate with his hand.

"A little," he finally said.

Their hands tangled as they both reached for the last cup. He tugged it away from her grasp quickly, exhaling loudly in the silence.

Why was he so prickly? Her single experience with the opposite sex made her unsure. Was it her or the fact that she'd ruined his bachelor status? She couldn't help that she'd forced him into a situation he wanted out of. She didn't know if they would have enough time together to make peace.

She gathered the dishes and put them into the now clean cast iron skillet, wondering if she dared to ask him.

She didn't.

She stood and stretched her back as she waited for him to finish the cup.

"You're sore from driving the wagon?"

"Mmm-hmm."

"Regretting riding along this morning?"

She thought about it for a moment. "No." She'd worked hard that day, but it was a good feeling knowing she'd also protected her sister.

He stood, picking up the skillet when she would've reached for it.

But he didn't move. He stood in the darkness, and she could feel his gaze on her.

"Why'd you marry me anyway?" he asked.

She hesitated. It was almost the same question he'd asked the night before. He deserved more of an answer than he'd gotten out of her then, if only because he'd allowed them to tag along without much complaint.

Finally she said, "I did it for Emma."

Chapter Five

I did it for Emma.

Edgar lay in his bedroll, wide-awake when he should've been sleeping. Dawn was going to come early.

And he kept hearing Fran's soft-spoken words.

Did the woman never think about herself?

She'd babied her sister all day—he'd witnessed some of it himself, and Ricky had told him about what he'd missed.

His brother had also sung her praises. How she'd driven the wagon until just before they'd made camp for the night. How she was smart, and proper.

Then he'd watched her cooking supper, and though it hadn't been the best meal he'd ever had—it reminded him a bit of his ma before she'd really learned how to cook—he was reluctantly impressed that she'd made the effort.

And then she'd done the dishes.

He'd needed distance when they'd returned from washing the dishes, so he'd sent her to bed in the wagon with her sister. He wanted to like her—too much.

Fran reminded him of both his ma and his sister, Breanna. Willing to work hard. Protective of her family.

But she was holding something back, too. He needed to remember that.

There was a reason he didn't trust women. Between his birth mother and the other woman who had lied to him, his whole life had changed at a young age. Penny had earned his trust with her steadfastness to Jonas and their mismatched family. And while he'd known Breanna since she was a tot, he'd seen her twist the truth to her own ends a time or two.

Women didn't play fair. And couldn't be trusted.

He'd done his best to stay away from Fran all day, riding as far away from the chuck wagon as he could manage.

And even so, he'd found himself constantly looking over his shoulder, finding her on the wagon seat next to Ricky. He'd stuck her with his brother all day, hoping she would succumb to Ricky's charm and give Edgar a reason to dislike her. At supper, she'd given his brother the same treatment she'd given everyone else: basic kindness.

Edgar didn't want to like her, but he did.

Movement in the grass between the bedroll where he'd bedded down and the snoring figure of Seb had Edgar turning his head slowly to one side.

What he saw froze him in place.

The dancing firelight glistened off the patterned back of a snake as it slithered between the brothers. In the cool evening air, the reptile probably sought the heat from the fire.

A very faint rattling noise told Edgar that the situation was dangerous. It was a rattlesnake.

If Seb rolled over in his sleep, the snake might decide to strike. And that could be deadly for his brother.

If Edgar tried to wake his brother, there was a chance Seb might move around and get bit.

And, less important but still a concern, where was that pup of Breanna's? He didn't need his sister's pet getting itself killed.

He couldn't trust that the reptile would keep moving.

But he could save his brother.

Edgar swung out his arm with a yell, sending the snake flying away into the darkness, but a sharp sting in his hand told him the move hadn't been entirely successful.

"Wha—" Seb woke with a confused yawn.

"Rattlesnake," Edgar bit out. He scooted closer to the fire, trying to see the puncture wounds in the meaty part of his palm, just below his thumb.

Seb came instantly awake, as did Chester, the hired cowpoke on his other side.

"Where?" Seb asked.

"What's going on?" Fran poked her head out of the back of the wagon.

"I tossed him back thataway." Edgar jerked his good thumb over his shoulder.

"I'll get him." Chester unsheathed a long, deadly looking knife from its leather scabbard.

"Didn't know he was sleeping with that beneath his pillow," Seb muttered. He untangled himself from his bedroll and joined Edgar near the fire.

"Tossed who?" asked Fran. She sounded genuinely concerned.

"A rattlesnake." Seb leaned in close to Edgar's hand. "It don't look too bad."

"Well, it hurts something awful." Edgar thought his hand was swelling, and pain radiated up his arm.

"How bad is it?"

Edgar looked up. Blinked. The bite must be worse than he thought, because he was hallucinating that his pretty wife—the little liar—was kneeling at his side in her rumpled, ugly dress, her dark hair down around her shoulders.

With bare feet.

"Woman, didn't you hear him say rattlesnake? Put some boots on."

She furrowed her brows at him, managing to communicate displeasure, but it struck him as funny.

"We should put a tourniquet on," she murmured to Seb.

"I'll get some rope." Seb was off and running.

"Where's Ricky?" she asked, holding on to his wrist. Her hands were soft and cool against his skin.

"Out with the cattle. Him and Jack and Matty. Why?" Pain was traveling all the way up his arm now. He gritted his teeth against it, a metallic tang filling his mouth.

A loose lock of hair fell across her cheek. He was mesmerized by how it danced there in the slight breeze.

"Here's the rope." Seb skidded to a halt beside him, dirt and grass dusting up beneath his feet. He held out a coil.

"If ya ain't gonna put manure on it, ya need ta suck out the poison," Chester said.

She looked up to the other two men standing nearby. "Shouldn't someone be saddling up? Will you take him to the doctor?"

"Not if they value their horse, they won't. You see any gas lamps to light the way?"

She looked up at him, perturbed, then around them, taking in the darkness surrounding their little beacon of light, the campfire.

"You need a doctor," she said.

"Well, I ain't gonna have one. In case you forgot, town's a half-day ride for a fast horse."

She took the coil of rope from Seb and made a loop under his armpit and to the top of his shoulder. Her hands were shaking, her movements jerky and angry, but she didn't tighten it too much.

"In the morning—" she started.

"In the morning, we're moving out," he interrupted her. "We've got a buyer waiting."

He could see from the set of her chin that she wasn't happy with that answer.

Someone threw a log on the fire, sending sparks flying with a whoosh, and he jumped, heart pounding. Through the haze of his pain, the sparks seemed to dance against the backdrop of the night sky.

He felt hot all of a sudden and might've swooned a bit, losing focus for a moment. He heard her voice, maybe talking to the two others, but he couldn't make out the words.

Someone settled him back in his bedroll. He thought to protest that it was too hot near the fire, but then the soft, cool brush of his wife's fingers against his brow brought his focus back in close, to her face. He realized he'd ended up with his head in Fran's lap.

She was mad. Fightin' mad. Her eyes sparked down on him. He let his gaze travel over her features, something he hadn't allowed up until now.

"You've got freckles across your nose," he said in a whisper.

She scrunched said feature at him.

She said something to someone standing off to the side, but he was dizzy and couldn't make out the words. All he knew was that she kept that cool, small hand pressed against his forehead.

And it made him feel better.

And that made him mad, too.

She could be widowed by morning.

The realization didn't sit well as Fran dipped a cloth into a pail of water she'd made Seb fetch from the stream.

She wasn't going anywhere in the dark by herself. A rattlesnake!

"I thought you said there wasn't anything dangerous in the woods," she said.

But she forced her hands to be gentle as she wiped the sweat beading on his brow.

"Did not," he mumbled. "I said there weren't any bears or cougars."

She wanted to thump the man, she really did, but she refrained. Barely.

Why was he so stubborn? He could've sent one of the others for the doctor. Surely, it couldn't be that dangerous to ride at night...

But looking at the moonless, star-filled sky, she knew he was likely putting the protection of his hands above his own welfare. Stubborn man.

"How bad is the pain?" she asked.

"Pretty bad. But it seems to be localized."

Was that a good thing? She didn't know.

When she and Seb had bent over and examined the wound, there had been no visible puncture marks, only a furrow where the snake's fang might've scratched through Edgar's skin. Perhaps it would be worse if the fangs had punctured directly?

"Where's my brother? I don't need to be babied."

"I believe he's gone back to his bedroll," she snapped. Seb had first ridden out to the other brothers, relaying

Edgar's wishes. Then he'd only gone back to sleep after her insistence that she would care for Edgar in the night. After seeing how long a day the cowboys had had in the saddle, if her stubborn husband insisted they move on in the morning, all the men needed as much rest as they could get.

Edgar struggled to his elbows, but the effort cost him. His face went pale above his beard.

"Why don't *you* go back to bed," he ordered her weakly. But then he lay his head back down in her lap.

And began to shiver.

She pulled the bedroll up around his shoulders, being careful of his injured hand.

She stopped bathing his face as the chills racked his body, then started back up again a few minutes later as he began to sweat again.

Thankfully, Emma had never woken. Fran didn't want to give her sister something else to fear out here.

The fire began to die down again. Gradually she could see less and less detail in the wagon and bedrolls, their little camp.

And still the prone man struggled. Should she call for Seb? But what could the younger man do? There was no doctor nearby, no help.

"What will they do if you die?" she asked quietly. Because she didn't dare ask, "What will *I* do if you die?"

"Not gonna die," came his slightly slurred response. "Seen someone bit by a rattlesnake before. If I was gonna die, it would've already happened."

Well, that was a relief.

"Might get infected, could lose the arm, but…" he trailed off as if he'd forgotten what he was talking about.

His pain was obviously affecting his responses. He'd

hardly spoken to her before this, except at their abbreviated wedding. She should have compassion for him.

But she couldn't waste this opportunity to find out a bit more about the man she'd married.

"Why is it so important for you to get the cattle where they're going?"

"Promised my pa," he mumbled.

"Surely he would understand if you had to delay in order to save your arm."

He smiled, eyes closed. "Pa would." Then his lips turned down in a frown. "My own pride wouldn't. I owe it to him."

"Why?"

His eyes still closed, he didn't respond for a long time. Then, quietly, "He took me in when no one else wanted me."

She'd known he was an orphan, of course. The latent pain still in his voice, emotion that she somehow knew this man rarely shared...

"Bear Creek was the last stop on a long orphan train. I was ten."

Her breath caught. She hadn't known they'd shared a similar experience. Was that why he'd been so offended that she'd lied about her age and taken advantage?

"How long ago?"

"Almost fifteen years now." So he was almost twenty-five. Six years her senior.

"What kind of man is your father? And your mother?" She couldn't picture the people who would take in so many orphans.

"Jonas took us in before Penny ever came along. Seven of us boys and Breanna."

How extraordinary.

His tremors began to ease and so did the tension etched in the lines of his face.

She ran her fingers through his long hair. The water from her ministrations had loosened some of the trail dust, and in the dying firelight, the clean locks shone gold.

Her touch seemed to comfort him.

"That's nice," he mumbled.

She did it again.

"Do you remember your mama rocking you? When you were little?" His soft question sent her heart up into her throat.

"No," she whispered, somehow knowing this connection between them was fragile. Not wanting to break it.

Emma had been a baby in most of Fran's earliest memories, her mother busy tending to chores required to care for an infant.

"I do," he said. There was a long pause. "This feels like that."

He drifted off, the final lines above his brow smoothing.

Leaving her with more questions than ever about this enigmatic cowboy.

Edgar woke completely disoriented, with a throbbing pain in his favored hand.

He was...outdoors. The sky was dark, but the eastern horizon was turning gray.

It only took a moment for memories to rush in.

The snake.

The bite.

Passing the night with his pretty little wife. The liar.

His head felt stuffed with cotton, pillowed on the same. He was unbearably warm, which was unusual for this time of year when the nights still got cool. Then he realized she was sorta…wrapped around him. His head rested on her folded knees, she was stretched beside him, her head resting on his shoulder.

She'd stayed with him all night?

The warmth that expanded his chest was uncomfortably new. How long had it been since someone had cared for him like that?

Maybe never.

The question was: Why had she done it? Out of some sense of duty since he'd married her?

He couldn't imagine another reason.

And he didn't like it anyway.

And then he started to remember her soft questions in the middle of the night. What was she trying to accomplish, pushing him for information? He didn't like her questions about his family. Was she trying to find a soft spot? To what purpose?

"Lemme up," he grumbled, shifting her and jostling her head.

She bolted up, the movement sliding her knees out from beneath his head. Without the support, his head clunked against the ground. He growled.

"Oh, I'm sorry." She knelt at his shoulder and slid those slim, cool hands into his hair and around the back of his head. What was her angle?

"Help me get up," he gruffed. He pushed to his elbow, and his head only spun a little. He took it as a good sign.

"How is he?" asked another voice. Ricky. With Matty rushing right on his tail, looking concerned. Seb and Chester must've relieved them in the night, just like they were supposed to do.

"About as cranky as a bear," came her quick answer.

But she didn't let go of his elbow until he was all the way upright.

"So back to normal, then?" Matty said.

And Edgar's wife beamed a smile at the other man.

It rubbed him the wrong way. "I'm right here," he growled.

And that set the three of them laughing.

He started to stomp off—more like limp off—but Matty stopped him. "Let's have a look at the hand, you old grizzly."

Edgar reluctantly held up his mitt for inspection. It was colorful and grotesque, swollen yellow and purple. The skin around the bite was pink and puffy, but there were no red streaks going up his arm that might indicate poison.

"Looks like I ain't gonna make you a widow yet," Edgar said.

She frowned at him, and he remembered her worrying over him in the darkest part of the night.

"You wanna ride back to town and see the doc?" Ricky asked grudgingly.

"I want to go visit the woods and then get saddled up." He limped off because he couldn't stomp the way he wanted.

And by the time he'd done his private business in the woods, he knew he wasn't riding anywhere that day. Except in the front of the wagon.

His legs were trembling, his equilibrium was off and he only had the use of one hand. He was sweaty and weak, a feeling he hated.

It made him cranky when he walked back to camp and saw one of the cowhands bent close and saying something to Fran.

"Make sure the cook fire's out," he barked. "Don't need a prairie fire chasing our flank."

She glared at him but went back to the smoking ashes.

Ricky waited near his saddled horse. It was obvious Edgar's brother had something to say. He tried to beat him to it. "You look exhausted."

"Bet I look better'n you do. Guess you're in the wagon today, huh?" But the lines around his brother's mouth didn't lift in a smile.

"Trouble sleeping in your bedroll after the snake incident?"

"Somethin' like that." But the shadows in Ricky's eyes remained.

Edgar needed to get these cattle to sale. He knew there was something eatin' his brother, but if the other man wasn't offering it up, what was he to do? They weren't women, who could share gossip and hurt feelings. If Ricky wanted help, he'd ask for it.

"Go easy on her," Ricky said. "Seems she and the sister have had a rough time of it."

Edgar's temper flared. But before he could get into it with Ricky, the other man swung up into his saddle and spurred his horse.

Finally, Edgar approached the chuck wagon. Wary, like a man should be when facing an unknown predator.

She met him with a cup of coffee. He took it.

"Thanks." His ma would skin him if he didn't practice basic politeness.

"You're welcome," she said a little too sweetly. She brushed a hank of hair out of her face. The sleeves and skirt of her dress were soaked as though she'd carried several pails of water up to douse the fire.

"This the cup from the bottom of the creek?" After

the hullabaloo with the snake, their moment of close-
ness the night before seemed a long way off.

"Mmm-hmm." She loaded up a last crate in the back
of the wagon.

He choked on the first sip of the sludge. "Tastes like
you didn't wash the sediment out of it."

She looked at him with wide, innocent eyes. "Might
serve you right after the way you've been barking at
me all morning."

Then she laughed, a tinkling, full sound with her
head thrown back and the pale skin of her throat exposed.

And if it didn't beat all, he found a smile wanting to
curl up the edges of his mouth.

He turned away and climbed into the wagon instead.

He knew she hadn't put anything in the coffee—it
was just awful on its own, probably the last of the pot.
But that was just the kind of prank his old self would
have pulled. Right now he was too worried about getting the cattle sold and untangling the mess she'd made
for him to do something like that.

And why did she have him thinking about pranks
anyway? They had a job to do.

He gritted his teeth as she climbed onto the bench
beside him.

Fran had a brother. And though Daniel was much
older, she knew that when men were injured or sick,
they tended to be a mite grumpy.

But her husband took the cake.

He'd allowed her to drive the wagon. Probably because his right hand was pretty worthless.

Riding on the bench seat beside him, she barely had
room to move.

And he hadn't spoken all morning, except to grunt one-syllable responses.

She was getting tired of it.

Emma had elected to walk, and was trailing the wagon, but not by much. Fran knew, because she couldn't quell the urge to keep looking back and checking on her sister.

After only a couple hours behind the reins, her shoulders protested all the driving she'd done the day before. She tried to shift her shoulders unobtrusively, but she caught her husband's sideways glance.

He still didn't talk.

"Are you ever going to say anything?" she blurted.

Now he gave her a long look with those blue eyes. "You want to talk?" he asked. And his wolfish smile had her shifting uncomfortably on the hard bench seat. "Seems you do owe me some answers after interrogating me last night."

Heat scorched her cheeks. So he had remembered her impertinent questions. But if he thought she would be embarrassed, he was wrong. "I suppose it's only fair," she offered.

Their eyes held, his challenging, hers steady.

"What happened to your parents? How did you end up—"

"At the orphanage?" she finished for him.

He had the grace to look slightly abashed at the probing question. She answered anyway.

"My parents were affluent." She said it simply. "There were several farms passed down through the generations—cotton and corn, mostly. Tennessee is very fertile. But we lived in the city. I was sent to a finishing school when I was fourteen, just like my mother before me. I got to see my family on holidays. I remember our last Christmas together. We had a roast goose, and my brother gave me the most beautiful calligraphy set...."

She shook herself out of the happy memory. "But that isn't what you asked."

He pointed to a depression in the prairie, and she did her best to guide the horses around it.

"Emma joined me at the school when she was fourteen. Shortly after her arrival, we were pulled into the headmistress's parlor, where we received the news in a letter from our brother, Daniel. Our parents had died. A fever of some kind."

She took a moment to steady her breathing, blink back the tears. It had happened two years before, but it still hit her hard.

"Daniel is ten years my senior. He was an attorney in Nashville. He wanted Emma and I to continue our schooling until he could settle things with our parents' probate. Things were all right for a month or so, but our tuition came due. I had my eighteenth birthday, but couldn't reach Dan, though both the headmistress and myself sent several letters. The headmistress allowed me to stay on and work in exchange for board, but Emma's tuition remained unpaid. Finally, the headmistress was notified that no one by the name of Daniel Morris resided at the boardinghouse where he had previously stayed. He was gone. Disappeared."

She stared out over the gently flowing grasses to the cattle well ahead of them, small black-and-red specks in the distance. Ah, there was a rider, kicking up a plume of dust.

"He just left you there?" Edgar prompted. "Abandoned you?"

Her eyes stung and she sniffed, squinting in the sunlight. She shrugged. "I don't know what happened to him. I can't countenance that he would've just left us without any correspondence. We weren't close, but... he wouldn't have just forgotten his responsibility to us."

"So you think something happened to him?"

"I don't know. Our grandparents were already gone, and there was no other family to contact. I tried contacting my papa's business associates, tried writing our old neighbors. Someone told me there had been loans taken against our family home—that they defaulted with my papa's death. The house and its contents were sold at auction by the bank."

Tears burned behind her eyes at the remembrance. Not only had Daniel disappeared, but the house she'd grown up in had been lost to her. There had been no money, no support, nothing.

She'd lost everything.

She looked over her shoulder again, through the back flap of the wagon, ostensibly to check on Emma again, but really to try to escape the painful conversation. Emma dawdled behind the wagon with the white dog. With the wide prairie behind her, Fran should be able to see any approaching threat. But the relative security of the prairie didn't remove her unease, her sense that something—someone—was still coming for them.

"Emma!" she called. "Come into the wagon for a while. You'll burn under the sun."

Emma waved. Whether that meant she was coming, Fran couldn't tell.

"You coddle her," Edgar said.

"Don't you spoil your younger sister?" she asked.

She felt his gaze on her as she focused on navigating what must've once been a dry creek bed.

"Breanna has chores like the rest of us." He paused

a moment, as if considering. "She does have an independent spirit."

"And seven older brothers."

That won a smile. It was a small smile, but she counted it as a victory.

"All young women should be spoiled and pampered by those who love them," she said. She turned once more to see Emma approaching the wagon.

"And you?" he asked.

She purposely misunderstood him. With Daniel gone, she was not likely to be spoiled or pampered. And she had Emma's safety to think of.

"I'm all she has left," she murmured.

Chapter Six

Moments after her emotional disclosure, Edgar waited as Fran pulled up the horses. The wagon rolled to a stop, and she allowed time for her sister to hop into the back.

How'd he get here anyway? Stuck in a wagon with two females while his brothers drove the cattle. Doing his job for him.

They'd barely gotten moving again when the dark head so like his wife's popped behind them in the back.

"Will we stop for lunch?" Emma asked softly.

She was as quiet as a mouse. Her knees were tucked up against her chest, making herself as small as possible. Fran's comment about Breanna had hit him particularly hard. He couldn't help comparing the two. Breanna was brash and independent, free-spirited. Emma was quiet, withdrawn. What had happened to her?

"We didn't yesterday," Fran reminded her sister gently. "There were a couple of biscuits left over from breakfast. I wrapped them in a cloth—there on top of the crate—"

Twisting next to him, his wife's dark hair brushed his jaw and sent sparks flying through him, just like the campfire the night before.

"You mind?" he asked as mildly as he could.

"Sorry." She straightened, shoulders up around her ears now.

His sorry stomach rumbled.

Emma's hand appeared between him and Fran, a biscuit proffered on the small palm.

He nodded his thanks and chomped into it. "Good, huh?" he said through a mouthful.

Fran looked at him with mild horror written on her features, but his wink earned a soft "mmm-hmm" of agreement from Emma—also through a mouthful.

"Emma!" Fran gasped, obviously embarrassed. "Manners!"

He laughed. "Who's out here to see?" he asked through the next bite, crumbs flying.

Emma giggled very softly, but it definitely was a sound of happiness.

Fran looked at him askance. One corner of her mouth lifted and she didn't correct him.

A few minutes later, Emma asked another soft-spoken question. "We don't have time to stop.... We'll drive until it gets dark. What's the big rush to get to where we're going?"

"Tuck's Station."

"Yes, there. Why the hurry?"

"Because my pa made a deal with the buyer for delivery, and the train's not running. We've got to get the cattle there on time."

"So you always fulfill your obligations perfectly?" Fran broke in.

She made him sound just like his brothers did. Boring.

"I have fun." And that didn't sound petulant at all.

"What kind of things do you like to do?" the pixie behind him asked.

"I…" He couldn't think of one thing offhand. "Well, I…"

Now he sensed Fran's eyes on him, too, but he kept his narrowed eyes on the horizon. "I like riding," he said finally. "Breaking horses."

"Doesn't count," Fran said. "It's part of the work you do, isn't it?"

"I enjoy the work." Most of the time.

"Hmm." Fran's little noise indicated she didn't really believe him.

Emma was silent. Until, after a delayed moment, she asked, "What are your other brothers like?"

Relieved to have the attention off himself, he went with the topic he could talk about.

"My two older brothers are married. Oscar's wife is Sarah. They've got three adopted girls and a son of their own. And another on the way.

"Maxwell's a doctor in Denver. His wife, Hattie, is finishing her medical degree and then they intend to move back to Bear Creek."

"His wife is a doctor, too? How incredible." Fran seemed genuinely impressed, not shocked like some of the other people who knew Hattie's intentions.

"And…what do you think of their wives?"

He tipped his Stetson back on his forehead, thrown by her question. "They're fine, why?"

"I just wondered if you disliked their wives, or if it was only me that you dislike."

Emma had gone silent, wide-eyed in the back of the wagon.

The tips of his ears got hot. But he wasn't going to

apologize for not trusting her, not after what he'd been through as a child and how she came into his life.

He couldn't imagine any other woman of his acquaintance making such an outrageous statement.

"I didn't meet their wives under false pretenses."

She went silent, and he had a moment of regret for his harsh words. Before he could decide whether or not he should apologize, a shadow in the tall prairie grasses next to them caught his attention.

"Pull left," he commanded her, his uninjured hand covering hers and attempting to direct the horses away from the danger.

But it was too late. The right-side wagon wheels dipped into a wash hidden by the tall grasses. With both wheels on that side losing traction, it tipped the wagon at a dangerous angle.

"Whoa!" he shouted to the horses.

Fran fell into him. He heard Emma scrambling, a soft shriek and a rip of fabric—probably the canvas wagon cover. Had Emma fallen through the canvas beneath the wagon? If so, and if they tipped any farther, she could be crushed.

He used his legs to brace, but with Fran leaning into him, he had to throw his bad hand out to the side of the wagon seat to stop their momentum and keep them tumbling down the wash.

He cried out, the pain fierce and fiery up his arm.

But they'd stopped.

The dog barked wildly, still on solid ground and somewhat above them.

"Quiet," he growled, afraid it might spook the horses.

The horses were old hands and hadn't panicked when everything behind them had gone off-kilter. They stood placidly while the wagon listed to one side, in danger of falling completely into the depression.

His wife hadn't panicked, either.

But it sounded like her sister was crying.

"Be still," he told the girl in the back. "You in the wagon?"

A soft sound of assent came.

Fran scrambled to get over the side of the seat—now angled down. When she had her feet on solid ground again, she reached back for him.

"Emma? You hurt?" she called, even as she hooked both arms around his upper arm on the bad side, leaving his good hand for leverage. She might be a tiny thing, but she helped him maintain his balance as he struggled over the wagon seat.

Shuffling and soft sobbing came from behind the canvas. No answer.

"Be still," he commanded again, loudly this time.

Fran wrinkled her entire face up and he saw her protest coming in her slightly opened lips, so he countered it before she could speak. "If things shift again and she moves wrong, the wagon could still topple."

She glanced at the horses. They couldn't see Emma, but they seemed to wordlessly understand the disaster that would be.

He glanced over her head in the direction they'd been going. The herd and the boys had kept moving; they were too far out of yelling distance. One of his brothers would notice their absence, but it might be a while. And Emma might not have that long.

She followed his gaze. "Will they hear us if we yell?"

"Probably not. We need to get her outta there."

The crease above her eyes deepened, showing her

worry, but she followed him around to the back of the wagon.

"Shouldn't we unhitch the horses?"

He shook his head, attempting to loosen the ties holding the canvas closed, forgetting about his swollen hand momentarily. He pulled back with a hiss.

She shifted him out of the way with a gentle shoulder and began unknotting the ties.

"The horses are holding it steady—for now. If we unharness them, the whole thing could go."

"Fran?" Emma's voice sounded frantic with a hint of a sob. There was more shuffling. The wagon shifted an inch and Edgar grabbed the tailgate with one hand, not that he could really stop it if it was going over.

"Be still," he said, words sharp this time. He wasn't used to being questioned—his brothers knew who was in charge and followed his directions without question.

Fran glanced at him, and he saw the worry on her face again.

"Everything's going to be okay," she cooed. "We're trying to get you out, but you have to be patient."

He snorted.

She finally got the ties undone and the flap tucked back enough for him to duck his head and see inside.

The girl was half-buried beneath two crates, her back to the canvas on the low side of the wagon. Another two crates balanced precariously above her head—and if they had any weight in them at all, she could get hurt if they fell on top of her.

She was in a full panic, struggling against the weight pinning one of her legs.

"Emma. Emma."

The girl's eyes finally looked up at Fran's calm, soothing tone just behind his shoulder.

"I'm coming in there with you." Fran glanced up at him, silently asking his permission at the same time as she comforted her sister.

"Coddling," he mumbled.

She tapped his chin with one forefinger. "You seemed to like my coddling last night. You said it reminded you of your ma."

He had? He didn't remember that and didn't want to talk about his ma, so he steadied her as she stepped over the tailgate and into the mess in the back.

"Be careful," he warned her. Not because he was worried about her getting hurt.

She glanced once back over her shoulder at him. He did his best to brace his feet and steady the whole shebang. He felt a little like David against a Goliath of a wagon.

"I'm stuck," Emma said, still struggling. "It's like before…he's got me pinned—"

"Shh." Fran could barely reach, but she put her palm on Emma's cheek. Soothing her.

Her next words made his blood run cold. "We're not in Tennessee anymore, remember? There's no one here but you and me and this cowboy, right?"

She looked back at him, chagrined. Probably hadn't wanted him to hear.

Her sister began to calm, and Edgar's sudden insight as to why they'd fled their orphanage made him hot and angry all at once. Someone had attacked Emma? No wonder she seemed so fragile.

He worked to steady himself. His anger wasn't going to help anybody.

"Can you reach that top crate, there? It's teetering— don't want it to fall on her." He spoke softly and gently, like he might to a horse if it'd spooked.

He directed Fran on moving the crates. She passed them to him out of the wagon so they wouldn't throw anything else off balance.

When she finally got her sister loose, the other girl threw her arms around Fran and clung.

"C'mon outta there," he said. But more tenderly this time.

The girls picked their way through the overturned detritus, and he helped first Emma, then Fran out with his good left hand.

"Seems like you been derailing everything since I met you."

She cocked her head at him, but her eyes were soft and shadowed. "I'm sorry," she apologized. "I didn't see the drop-off."

And for some strange reason, he wanted to comfort her. "Neither did I."

He realized he was still holding on to her elbow, even though they were both on solid ground, and he dropped it quickly.

Emma huddled on the ground nearby. She seemed okay, if shaken. The white dog nuzzled her hand, licked what it could reach of her chin.

"Will you help me unharness the horses?" he asked.

"Let me see your hand first. I heard you—you landed on it, right?"

His ears went hot that she'd heard him squeal like a girl. It *had* hurt. He held out the appendage for her inspection. It was probably quicker than arguing with her.

"Does it hurt any worse than before?"

Looking down on her dark head bent over his hand, that same uncomfortable warmth from the morning lit his chest again. "Not really."

She turned his hand, and her gentle, cool fingers

traced the lines on his palm. "It looks a little better than it did last night, I guess."

She tilted her face up to his, and her eyes were still shadowed. Had they always been that way and he hadn't noticed before?

He looked back at her sister. They needed to talk, but now wasn't the time.

Walking up to the front of the wagon, he could see the herd was farther off. His brothers apparently hadn't noticed they'd fallen behind. It could be a while, and if the wagon went over now, the horses could be injured. Better to unharness them and put them back in the traces when his brothers had gotten the wagon back up.

"What will we do if they don't come for us?" she asked.

"They will." He knew his brothers.

She took a good long look ahead, all around them.

Her sister was sitting on the grass behind the wagon, still shaken up.

"Don't you ever get scared…being out here? Without any help close by? What if that bite on your hand would've been worse? And…no neighbors? It seems sorta lonely."

He followed her gaze across the rolling plain, far out to the horizon. "I guess I've been here long enough to see it different."

He gestured back the way they'd come. "There're neighbors. Old man Miller and his family live over that way, less than an hour on horseback. Longer in the wagon. With Oscar's family nearby and all the rest of us at the homestead, it's never quiet there. And when Maxwell gets back, we'll have our own doc, won't we?"

She gazed up at him, still not fully understanding.

He pointed her to the first buckle on the harness, knowing he wouldn't be able to undo it with his injured hand.

He watched her for a moment, making sure she'd gotten what he wanted. She had.

"I guess there's a…freedom to it," he tried to explain.

She went to the next buckle.

"It's like…when we were teasing back in the wagon, about manners. Out here, they don't matter as much."

She looked up at him sideways as she went to the next and last buckle.

He didn't know if he was botching this explanation or if she was purposely misunderstanding. "I can do what I want to do," he went on. "If I want to raise cattle, I can. Or sheep, or horses. If I keep to myself, no one's going to bother me."

She wrinkled her nose as she trailed him around the front of the horses to the other side. "Don't you mean no one will have any expectations of you?"

He froze, the depth of her question surprising him. "What do you mean?"

She looked at him from the side. "You take care of your papa's ranch, but being so isolated… It keeps people away. Keeps you from having to interact, I guess."

He didn't have an answer, not that she was really asking for one.

"Problems?" a familiar voice asked.

He whipped around to see Ricky already dismounted and another hand not far behind. Had they ridden up and he hadn't noticed? He'd been wrapped up in Fran's discussion.

His brother looked like a thundercloud, but as of late that seemed to be a common expression for him.

Fran moved off to see to Emma.

"Needs a good shove from the lower side," Edgar suggested.

"I can see that." Ricky rounded the wagon, eyes on the ground.

"Not there," Edgar said as his brother knelt to examine one of the wheels that were still above the wash.

His brother sent him a scathing look over his shoulder. "I can see what needs doing. I don't always need you bossing me like I'm a young pup."

Edgar's footsteps faltered, but then he joined up with the other hand at the back of the wagon while Ricky went into the wash.

He could at least help steady the thing, even if he didn't have use of both hands.

Was that what Ricky really thought? That he bossed like a mother hen? Jonas had left him in charge. It was Edgar's responsibility to get those cattle where they needed to be. It was on him if they didn't make it.

They got the wagon back on solid ground, and he moved to his brother as Ricky used the toe of one boot to inspect the spokes in each wheel.

"Pa left me in charge—" he started.

"How could I forget? You keep reminding us at every turn." Ricky wouldn't look directly at him. What was eating him? Could he be jealous?

Then Ricky turned to him. "You know, she might be right about you hiding out on Pa's spread."

Edgar's ears went hot again. So Ricky had heard Fran's conclusion. Did he really think the same, or was he just trying to get under Edgar's skin?

"You really happy there? Because not all the rest of us are."

And with that, he stalked off. Not giving Edgar a chance to really talk to him, not really solving anything.

And making Edgar more worried than ever about getting the cattle to Tuck's Station on time. If Ricky didn't do his share, there was a real chance of some of the cattle getting hurt or falling away from the herd.

Frustrated, he ducked behind the wagon, kicking through the tall grasses.

He hated feeling so distant from his brother. Not being able to solve the problem with Ricky. Hated feeling helpless.

A disgruntled frog hopped away, displaced from some nearby stream.

And the idea that popped into Edgar's mind made him forget about his troubles with his brother. For the moment.

Her husband had been acting strange all afternoon.

But Fran was so happy to be out of the wagon that she dismissed it.

For someone who'd been as irritable as a bear the previous two days and had then spent a good hour that afternoon upset with his brother, and was snakebit to boot, he was smiling to himself quite a bit.

Ever since they'd reorganized all of the items in the back of the wagon.

When she went to get the large pot to make the stew Chester had told her he wanted, she found out why.

She took off the lid, and a large green amphibian leaped toward her.

She was proud that only a small shriek escaped and that no one had been on her side of the wagon to witness her clang the lid down, trapping the frog inside the pot.

She supposed she should be angry at the man, but after his gentle care of Emma earlier, she couldn't muster it.

Or maybe this was just the way Western men courted their womenfolk?

She shook her head, remembering his words about being on his own. There was something deeper underneath them, but she didn't think he wanted to share it with her—if he even knew himself.

"Food on?" asked Chester, bringing the firewood that Edgar had told him to bring.

Seeing the older, grizzled cowboy gave her an idea. "Do you know how to cook a frog?"

She followed his directions, swallowing her squeal when she had to dismember the poor animal. This had better be worth it.

And it was, when she presented her husband with the fried frog legs, arranged neatly on top of his biscuit and stew.

His eyes widened, and the cowboys all around guffawed. Even Emma smiled from her retreat in the wagon.

His eyes sparked. She thought for a moment he might be angry, but then he ripped into one of the legs with his teeth like a mountain man with no manners—harking back to their earlier conversation, no doubt.

He raised the bone to salute her.

And she retreated behind the wagon as the cowboys laughed again—this time her husband included.

Supper was long gone, and Fran was attempting to muster the energy to take the dishes to the stream. They'd made camp about the same distance away from the one they'd found the day before.

She leaned on the corner of the wagon as she attempted to cajole Emma into helping her. The other girl remained holed up inside the canvas-covered box.

"Please come down," Fran said. Suggested. Gently.

Emma shook her head slightly, eyes flickering past the firelight to the shadows beyond. Still afraid.

"Is it Edgar? His brothers?"

"No. They're fine. I don't know…some of the others."

Fran's curiosity piqued. "Has someone said something inappropriate to you?"

"No, just…"

Emma was sensitive. Had always been so. Fran thought her mother probably wouldn't have sent Emma to the finishing school but she'd once overheard her father saying that Emma needed *something* to bring her out of her shell.

And she had become more social around her friends at the Girls' Academy. Until the awful Mr. Underhill had changed everything.

With the visible fear on Emma's face, Fran couldn't push her into getting out of the wagon.

Even if it meant she had to do all the dishes on her own.

She was so tired that it made her answering "fine" sharp.

Emma looked apologetic, but apology didn't really help get the chore done.

Fran wished—for both their sakes—that things were different.

No doubt Emma did, too.

She couldn't let guilt cripple either of them.

She gathered the last of the tin spoons and added the pieces to her stew pot, already filled with the rest of the soiled dishes.

With one last glimpse of Emma making her bed in the wagon, she turned the corner.

Hidden behind the wagon, she heard the voices near

the bedrolls but couldn't be sure if they knew she was there.

"There're at least two of them, judging by the tracks."

She became instantly aware at the serious tone in one of the cowhands' voice. Two of whom?

"Looks like they circled back, kinda like they're following us."

"How long have they been following? Could you tell?" That was Edgar's voice.

Her heart began to pound. Someone was following them?

"Maybe since yesterday. Maybe today. Hard to tell. I tried to catch a glimpse but either they were long gone or holed up for the night."

"Hmm."

"You thinking it's rustlers?"

She was thinking something entirely different. What if Underhill's men had tracked her and Emma this far?

Heart thrumming like a bird's wings, she rose from her crouch by the stew pot.

Should they try to run?

A glance back at the wagon and the slight shadow of Emma's profile within calmed her very slightly.

Emma was safe—for now. The two of them alone on the prairie? It would be much more dangerous for them, wouldn't it?

Knowing Emma was safe for the moment released some of the tension in her shoulders. Only a bit.

If Underhill's men were still chasing them, what could she do?

She grabbed the pot and rushed out into the darkness, tears and fear blinding her. She dropped to her knees at the creek bank, thoughts racing.

They were as good as in the middle of nowhere. In

between two small towns in the wilds of Wyoming. Even if she were able to spirit Emma away, where could they go for help?

She scrubbed the first plate violently. She washed the second the same way, acting out her anger and the fear twisting her gut.

It didn't help.

She wanted to shout at God. They'd made a deal, hadn't they? She would do anything if He would keep Emma safe.

And now this.

Tears rushed in again. With Emma around all day, she had no release for the fear and frustration that constantly hounded her. But now, in the darkness, there was no one to see her.

She bowed her head and let them come silently.

She knew God didn't owe her anything. That she couldn't really strike a deal with Him. She vaguely remembered a Bible verse about His sun shining on the good and evil both.

But she'd begged for God's protection for Emma. Where was His answer?

A branch cracked behind her, and she whirled, one hand brushing at the tears on her cheeks, the other scrambling through her dishes for anything that might be used as a weapon. A knife, perhaps?

She came up with a spoon.

A man crashed through some brush several yards away and she shrieked, knowing she was probably too far away for the men back at the campfire to hear her.

How could she have been so foolish as to come out here alone?

Chapter Seven

"Kinda foolish to come out here by yourself."

Edgar had seen cornered animals before. Knew to be ready for her to run or to turn and take a swipe at him.

But she'd been surprising him from the beginning.

Edgar saw his wife drop her shoulders and a silver utensil she'd been holding. She took a swipe at her face. Was she crying?

"Aw, snakeskin."

Like his pa and most of his brothers, he had no idea what to do with a crying woman.

He tiptoed closer. Warily.

She dabbed at her face again, then grabbed up one of the dishes and splashed it into the stream, scrubbing it harder than the thing probably warranted.

"You scared me," she said to her plate.

He had a guess as to why, especially if she'd overheard his conversation with one of the hands, John Michaels.

He'd watched her light out from camp and guessed she had. Would she admit to it?

He squatted beside her. "Sorry. Did you overhear John and me talking?"

She frowned.

And he thought about her promise that she wouldn't lie to him. Her expression made it clear she didn't really want to answer.

Finally there came a reluctant "Yes."

"I don't want you coming out in the dark alone, not without us knowing who's following behind."

She nodded, not looking at him. She switched out one plate for another.

"Anything you want to tell me?"

"No."

He fought the smile that twitched one corner of his mouth up. "Let me rephrase. I'd like to hear about the reason you left Tennessee now."

She sighed and her shoulders drooped. She switched out the plate for the big pot, probably the last thing she had to wash. "I already told you that our parents passed away and then Daniel's tuition payments stopped coming. Emma and I were on the headmistress's last bit of mercy when he came calling. Underhill." She spit the name like it was poison.

"He must've seen Emma out with the other young girls. Picnicking or shopping or some such. I don't know exactly how he became enamored with her."

She scrubbed the pot harder, water splashing up her arm and onto his boots. Like if she scrubbed hard enough, she could rub away the past.

"I think Emma was flattered at first. He was older—probably thirty, much too old for her. She tends toward shyness anyway, always has. But we didn't have any options and I don't know what she was thinking. Maybe that a handsome man was interested in her. She's only fifteen. She didn't know better."

Sounded like an excuse to Edgar. But then, both girls

were away from any family who could've—should've—protected them.

She threw the rag into the pot and wiped her forehead with the back of her hand.

She still didn't look at him. "I always sat in when he called for her. *Always.* Except one day I came in from laundering some of the bedclothes. They were in an embrace, but Emma was struggling against him."

Her hands made fists in her lap, the pot seemingly forgotten on the bank.

"Her dress… The sleeve of her dress was ripped." Fran's voice shook as she spoke the words.

Hot anger swirled in his belly. If anyone dared do something like that to Breanna, they'd have the whole passel of White boys on them so fast…but who had been there to protect Emma? Only her sister.

"I called out, but when one of the teachers came to help, Underhill claimed the embrace was mutual. Emma denied it. Anybody with eyes to see would've known that he'd tried to force himself on her. But the damage was done. The school couldn't have any hint of impropriety, and it was Emma's word against his.

"The headmistress asked us to leave. She was afraid, too—she wouldn't use any of her connections to help us, other than offering to deliver Emma to an orphanage. I don't know where I would've gone…. We were packing our few things when Underhill showed up again. He told Emma he would have her—whether she wanted his attentions or not. It frightened us both. The headmistress escorted us to the orphanage, but Underhill threatened to return. One of the orphanage administrators believed us, though, and put us on the westbound train."

"Did she know your real age?" He couldn't contain the question.

She paused again, looking up at him. Moonlight filtered through the canopy of brushy trees above them. She frowned again. "No. I've always looked younger—"

He could believe it. Her petite stature and pixie features made it a natural assumption.

"By that point I was so afraid that I couldn't see any other way."

"It doesn't make it right," he pointed out.

She sighed. Looked down. "No, it doesn't."

She picked up the pot again and gave it one more swish with the water and rag, then dumped the remaining water in the creek.

"What's his interest in Emma? Do you think he's really followed you all this way?"

"I can only guess his motives," she said quietly. "It's as if he became obsessed with her. I overheard a man asking about us on the platform at the Lincoln stop."

Edgar would've questioned her further, but remembered his ma's issues with just such a man. Why were some men bent on evil? He didn't know, but he did know that the surge of emotion in his chest meant he wouldn't let any harm come to Emma.

"We can't be sure that whoever is following us is after you two. It could've been a farmer curious as to who was passing by. It could be someone interested in our cattle—which isn't good, either. Until we figure out who it is, I want you and Emma to stick close to the wagon or camp. Don't head off by yourselves. Understand?"

Oh, she understood.

Fran was thankful that Edgar wanted to protect Emma. He'd believed her on the most important thing, and that was all that mattered.

But…

Part of her thought maybe she should tell him the rest.

She hadn't lied to him.

But she hadn't told him about Underhill's accusations against her, either. They were entirely untrue, but given that she'd arrived under false pretenses and Edgar still questioned her trustworthiness, she didn't want him to have any reason to doubt her.

She piled the clean dishes back into the pot and rose to stretch her back before she reached for it.

"I'll haul it for you," her husband said.

"Your hand—" she protested, but he'd already picked up the lot of it and was heading back toward camp.

"It doesn't hurt that bad. You coming?"

Walking along next to him the darkness, nothing had been solved, but somehow she felt reassured.

Was it possible God *had* put her on that westbound train here, to Wyoming? Had God set her on a path to meet this man?

Looking up at the shadow of his profile against the starry sky, she was strangely comforted.

Maybe, after days of restless, worry-filled sleep, she would finally rest tonight.

Hours later, Edgar urged his horse across the grassy field, as careful as he could be in the darkness. Morning was coming, and he needed to get back to the cattle camp before it was time to ride out.

His hunt hadn't turned up what he was looking for. They must've hit a patch of unclaimed land, because there seemed to be no farmhouse close. The fact that there were no farmhouses nearby meant that whoever followed them hadn't just been checking on who was passing by.

Which amounted to one of two things.

Rustlers.

Or men coming after their two female stowaways.

Neither option was pleasant.

He was a decent tracker and hadn't been able to find hide nor hair of anybody. John had seen two sets of tracks the day before, but they'd been covered over when Edgar had returned to where John had told him they were. And there weren't that many places to hide out here in the open prairie. Not like there would be closer to the mountain range.

Someone was being extracareful not to be seen.

And that didn't sit well with Edgar.

His hand was still swollen and near to useless, but he had his equilibrium back, and riding in the early morning had been a relief.

He whistled a welcome to Seb, who'd been assigned sentry duty, and was gratified when a return whistle came quickly. The boy must not have been sleeping on the job.

He dismounted as the first rays of light started sliding over the eastern horizon. He tied off his mount and knocked softly on the side of the chuck wagon, where Fran and Emma slept.

There was a frantic rustling, a whisper, then dead silence.

He knocked again. "Fran, it's me."

The canvas flap kicked open and she hissed, "You about scared the life out of me!"

Her pert nose peeked out of the darkness inside. He imagined she was on her knees in the wagon bed, and so they were pretty much face-to-face. Her dark hair tumbled around her shoulders, teased him with the desire to touch it.

His mouth kicked up in a smile at her petulant adorableness before he even realized it.

"C'mon. Rise and shine. We've got work to do."

He heard her soft groan. Knew being out here must be hard on her, if she'd been used to city living and had grown soft from days of train travel. But she hadn't complained yet.

"All right, I'm— Emma!"

Her soft exclamation came only a second before she tumbled out of the wagon.

He caught her against his chest.

And for the first time, didn't want to let her go.

Fran landed hard against her cowboy husband. At least that was the excuse she would give if anyone asked her why she was breathless.

The frantic beat of her heart had changed from the stark fear she'd known at his soft knock against the wagon to something entirely different.

She was attracted to her bear of a husband.

It wasn't light out yet, and standing together in the darkness like this, with his hands at her waist… At least the semidarkness would hide the heat in her cheeks.

Emma was likely watching from inside the wagon. The little goose had shoved her, and only Edgar catching her had stopped Fran from falling facefirst to the ground.

But she forgot about her sister and all their troubles in the safety of his arms.

"Does no one tell you you should cut your hair?" she asked, daring to reach up and touch one of the long locks trailing out beneath his hat. It was surprisingly soft.

"My ma," he gruffed. "But not in a while."

"Hmm."

Was it her imagination, or was he leaning closer…
as if he might kiss her….

"Arf!"

The sharp bark from within the wagon startled them
both and Fran stepped away as his arms fell from her
waist.

"Emma!" she called, coming back to her senses.

Her sister poked her head out, the white dog in her
arms.

"What's that thing doing in there with all the food?"
Edgar demanded.

"I made sure everything was covered," Fran protested, defending her sister. As if there wasn't trail dust
and grass coming in the wagon at all times anyway.

He took off his hat and ran one hand through his
hair, turning away. Agitated.

Because of the dog, or because of their near kiss?

She quickly swept her hair up behind her head,
reaching into the pocket of her dress for the pins she
would use to secure it.

He glanced back at her, eyes intense as he watched
her contain the full tresses. So it had been the almost
kiss that discombobulated him.

"It's good you're both awake. I came after both of
you anyway."

She sniffed the air. Seemed like Chester had already
started the coffee. What more could her husband ask
her to do so early in the morning?

"There're two things a gal needs to know out here
in the West. Seems like I'm going to be the one teaching you and Emma."

There was motion from Emma behind the canvas
cover. Fran had been trying to figure a way to get her
sister out of that wagon and interacting—somehow. If

Emma was curious enough to emerge from the cocoon of the wagon, Fran would be grateful. No matter what the idea was.

"What are the two things?" she asked.

"Shooting and riding."

The corner of his mouth tipped up at the incredulous look that must have been on her face.

"Not milking a cow? Or gathering eggs?" She recited two of the items she could remember from his list of chores that first night.

"Nope. Shooting and riding. You gonna swoon?"

She wrinkled her nose at his reference to the moments just before their wedding.

"No." She sighed. "Lead the way."

She could suffer through, if it would get Emma out of the wagon.

"We've only got time for one this morning. Y'all can take a few private moments, then meet me back here and we'll head off for some practice."

The sun was a half of a burning orange ball on the horizon when she and Emma followed Edgar down to the creek, crossed it in a narrow part and wound back behind to a bluff rising out of the prairie.

"We want to be far enough away from the cattle that they won't startle when we start shooting," he explained. "I've scouted and there's not a house or anything back behind here that might indicate someone's out there. You never want to shoot where there's a chance you might hit someone."

She shivered, imagining what a bullet could do to a human body if they weren't being careful. Beside her, Emma clung to her elbow a little tighter.

On the other hand, being able to protect herself, and her sister, could be something she really needed.

Edgar showed them both a rifle and a pistol, showed them how to tell if either was loaded or unloaded, let them feel the weight of each in their hands.

Then he showed Emma how to load and fire the pistol. The recoil threw Emma back a step, but he was there at her shoulder, showing her the correct way to reload and fire again.

He was so good with Emma. Like the older brother Daniel had never really been. By the time Fran had been old enough to understand, Daniel had been immersed in his studies and preparing for a career in law.

But it was clear to see that Edgar must dote on his younger sister.

He made Emma comfortable. Fran hadn't been sure how her sister would react. But Edgar's gentle teaching had somehow eased her. And after everything she'd been through, that was of utmost importance to Fran.

Then it was Fran's turn behind the weapon. Her hands shook as she leveled the gun on the white scrap of linen Edgar had hung over a bush up against the bluff.

"Steady now," he said.

She couldn't stop thinking about what could happen if she ever had to shoot the thing at a person.

She started to lower the weapon, but he moved up right behind her, so close her bent elbow brushed the fabric of his shirt.

And then she was trembling for an entirely different reason.

Edgar felt the tremor go through Fran.

Having the shakes could get someone shot, so he put his arms around her from behind—she was so petite, the top of her head didn't even reach his chin—and covered her hands with his, steadying her, guiding her to where he knew she'd be able to sight the target.

"Your hand," she whispered.

"Hmm?" he asked.

"Is it…better?"

He imagined she could see it was still yellow and purple, still a little swollen. "The worst of the pain has passed. Go ahead."

She shot once, the sound ringing in his head. She bumped back into him from the recoil.

She was still shaking.

He wanted her to relax a little. So he teased. "You might be worse than my ma when Pa taught her how to shoot."

She tilted her chin and looked back at him. "I'd like to meet her."

Looking down into her warm brown eyes, fringed with those sooty lashes and with that spray of freckles across her nose, he realized he was in trouble.

He knew she'd felt the attraction sparking between them when she'd fallen out of the wagon and into his arms. They both had.

Attraction or not, it didn't change things between them. His past had taught him that he couldn't trust a woman, not when his own birth ma had abandoned him.

"I've been thinking about what happens after I get the cattle to Tuck's Station."

She kept her eyes on the target but spoke softly. "Oh?"

"I know a woman in Calvin—" Wait, that didn't sound right.

She fired a shot. Miss.

He started over. "My ma frequents a seamstress in

Calvin who is always busy. If she's willing to take you and Emma on, it'll be a start for you.

"How are your sewing skills?" he finished lamely.

She broke from his light hold and turned to face him, lowering the gun. "Passable. But I thought—"

He didn't want her thinking anything other than that they were going their separate ways. "I promised to provide for you, and this seems like the most workable solution."

She was silent, looking up at him with an assessing gaze.

"I told you when we got into this marriage that you could have my name. That's all I can give."

That had sounded better in his head.

Her face scrunched and for a moment he thought she might tear up, but she only turned her back to him and raised the gun again. This time, her hands didn't shake at all.

She shot out the rest of the chambered bullets, kicking up dust near the target and once flapping its corner.

When she turned back to him, gun lowered at her side, her lips were set in a firm white line.

He didn't like the silence, the distance between them. It made his gut ache. But it was for the best, right?

"Good job," he praised. "If any of those goons come after you two again, you'll at least have some level of protection against them."

"What 'goons?'" Emma asked, coming near.

He hadn't noticed she'd gotten up from her place among the prairie grasses. The daisy chain she'd been weaving fell to the ground at her feet.

"Fran?" Emma asked.

He and Emma came shoulder to shoulder as they both turned on Fran.

"You didn't tell her?" he asked. He held his hand out for the gun. "Your coddling could put her in danger. She needs to know what's going on."

"Tell me what?" Emma came even closer, hands going to her hips.

Fran smacked the gun into his hand, butt first.

"There was a man asking about us on the Lincoln train platform. He may have followed us. I'm not sure."

"And someone was looking for you back in Bear Creek. And there's a couple of horses following our herd, not close enough for us to get a good look at them," he added.

"So Underhill has...found us?" Emma's chin trembled, and she looked about twelve at that moment, young and scared, looking to her sister for answers.

Fran glared at him before going to her sister and putting an arm around her. "We don't know that for sure. It may be a couple of rustlers."

Emma let out a teary laugh. "Is that any better?"

"Not really," he said honestly. "But the boys and I are all crack shots. If anyone comes close with an unsavory purpose, we'll let 'em know what's what."

He meant the statement to be reassuring, but Emma was still pale and teary, close to how she'd been that first night.

"Look, Emma, we aren't going to let anyone hurt ya."

She just shook her head, eyes wide. Not even arguing.

Fran guided her sister, arm still around her, back toward the wagons. He guessed that meant their shooting lesson was over. It was coming on full daylight now, and the boys had likely already started the cattle moving, leaving him to get the girls going in the wagon. At least he could ride his horse today.

Fran sent him a glare over her shoulder, but he met her stare levelly. He stood by his statement that Emma needed to know they might have been followed. Being prepared was important, especially if unsavory characters showed up.

"What if he catches us, Fran?" Emma's worried whisper carried back to him.

"Don't worry," Fran said. "I won't let anything happen to you."

He couldn't help feeling a bit miffed. It was like they'd completely forgotten that he'd said anything about him and the boys protecting them. Maybe they weren't used to having a man around, but he wasn't going to let some unsavory character get a hold of Emma.

Or someone mess up his pa's deal with the cattle, either.

Chapter Eight

"Isn't there somewhere else we can go?"

Emma's frightened plea tugged at Fran's heart. The girl had been huddled in the wagon all morning, clutching the white dog. Fran knew Edgar didn't want the animal inside with their food staples, but she didn't have the heart to deny her sister the small comfort.

Emma wouldn't even get out of the wagon and walk, like she had the day before.

Fran shot a glare at the cowboy who'd put that fear in Emma's voice.

As if he sensed her ire, Edgar turned around, muscled legs flexing as he stood in the saddle.

He tipped his hat. She turned her face slightly, looking away from him.

He'd ridden his horse all morning, but had stayed close, riding beside the wagon when the cattle had moved out front, then drawing closer to the herd when it was nearer the wagon. The morning was cooler than the day before had been, the sun partially obscured by gray clouds.

She could swat the man for making her tell Emma about the men possibly following them. Her sister didn't need to spend her time worrying about a threat that might not even exist.

Things were under control. Weren't they?

Emma sighed. "Fran?"

She realized she'd been lost in thoughts of the cowboy. "Sorry." She took one hand from the reins and motioned to the landscape around them. Empty except for cows and cowboys.

"Edgar promised to get us to Tuck's Station and then set us up in Calvin. He says it is another small town between Tuck's Station and Bear Creek."

She told Emma of her husband's plans. "By the time we're settled, we'll be free of Underhill." She hoped.

Emma's brows crinkled. "But what about your marriage?"

Fran strove to keep her face from showing any emotion other than smooth serenity. "Edgar thinks we should live separately."

Her sister gave a disbelieving huff. "What's his reasoning? It's obvious there are sparks between you two."

Fran didn't want to talk about it. But she also didn't want her sister's focus to return to their desperate circumstances.

How did she explain to her sister, when she couldn't fully understand it herself? She knew he was attracted to her. But…somehow he found her lacking. Just like Tim, the man who'd come calling when she was still at the Girls' Academy. "Neither of us intended to be married back in Bear Creek. It happened quickly. It was a solution that fit. But he doesn't want a wife," she reminded her sister.

"Then he shouldn't have said vows!"

Emma's perturbed scowl pinched Fran's heart.

"What of your happiness?" Emma asked.

"I'll be happy knowing you're safe."

Her emphatic statement brought the shadows back to her sister's eyes.

"I wish…" Emma sighed, letting the words fade away. "I'd started to like it out here—it's so open."

Pounding hoofbeats brought her gaze up. Emma curled back into a ball.

Edgar rode up to them. "Looks like there might be a storm brewing. We're going to stop for a while."

Relief at being allowed an extra stop was tempered by immediate concern. They were going to pass a storm…in the wagon?

The stream they'd camped near for the past two nights had disappeared. Now the only thing breaking up the smooth, slightly hilled landscape was a nearby copse of scrub trees.

Edgar pointed to it. "Pull the wagon over there. The hands and I are going to settle the cattle as best we can. Then I'll come to help you unhitch. Stay put with the wagon."

She followed his directions, snugging the wagon up as close to the trees as she could before setting the brake. Emma shuffled around in the back as Fran got down, using the front wheel as a step.

It was nice to have a break from the constant jostling of the wagon. Yesterday she'd been on her best behavior with Edgar beside her. She'd done her best to sit still and not fidget, and her muscles were sore today.

In the relative privacy between the wagon and the woods, she stretched her back, then bent at the waist, reaching down to touch her toes. It was unladylike, but it felt good to release muscles unused to the effort of driving a team.

The sky darkened. How had Edgar known they were in for a storm? Years working outdoors, likely.

She decided it was a good idea to ensure the wagon was as watertight as they could make it.

She turned to the front of the wagon. "Emma? Emma, can you come out and help me batten down the canvas? Make sure the dog stays inside." Edgar had mentioned that it was his sister's special pet, and Fran didn't want it running away out of fright if the storm spooked it.

Emma didn't answer verbally, but canvas rustled as if she'd climbed down out of the back.

Stepping on the wheel spokes, Fran could barely reach the ties connecting the canvas to the wooden wagon, but checked to make sure each was secured tightly.

A distant rumble of thunder had her rushing through the next knot and then climbing back into the wagon seat to tie off the front flap that they'd made a practice of leaving open while Emma rode in the wagon and Fran out front.

She'd never weathered a storm out-of-doors. The closest she'd ever been was in one of her father's barns as a small girl. More recently she'd always been in-doors when the weather was frightful. And the slate-gray clouds now swirling above threatened to make this a memorable time.

"Emma, you about done back there?"

There was no answer other than a bark.

"Emma?"

A little unnerved by the escalating weather and her sister's silence, Fran hopped down on the wagon's opposite side. The cattle were more distant than she expected. She could barely make out the cowboys circling the herd.

She turned back to check on Emma's progress, but couldn't see her sister. Had Emma gone around the back of the wagon, and they'd just missed each other?

Fran rushed to the rear, but Emma wasn't there, either. She circled the wagon entirely, heart beginning to pound loud in her ears. She threw open the back flap. No Emma, only the white dog, frantically wiggling toward her, no doubt scared by the worry in her voice.

Skirting the wagon a second time, she kept her eyes on the ground. Edgar and his cowhands had talked about tracking the men following them by their prints in the ground, but she couldn't make out anything in the thick grasses. Not even her own footprints.

Her heart thundered, pulse racing.

Had Underhill's men caught up with them?

The wind kicked up, blowing strands of hair into her eyes. Thunder rolled, much closer this time.

"Emma!" she shouted. "Come out now!" Could her sister be playing a trick? But Emma had never been particularly cruel.

And then she broke.

"Emma!" she screamed.

She went to the horses, but her fear and panic made it impossible to remember how Edgar had instructed her to unhook their harness yesterday. Even if she managed to get one of them untangled from the wagon, she didn't know how to ride it.

It would be quicker to run.

She lifted her skirt and sprinted out into the open, praying she wasn't too late.

* * *

Edgar didn't like the look of the sky. The storm had come up too quickly and threatened to be a real gully washer.

Bursts of lightning preceded thunder, but not by much. It was closing in fast.

The cattle milled disconsolately, bawling and shifting with unease. He'd sent the girls near the patch of woods. He knew from riding through this area before that the land behind the trees shifted into two levels: a taller bluff and the continuing prairie.

He wanted the girls as far away from the animals as they could be—just in case.

He was as nervous as the cattle, but he projected a calm he didn't really feel for both the animal under him and the other cowboys who were looking to him for direction.

If the cattle got spooked by either the lights or the loud, rolling thunder, they could stampede, and that was something that no one out there wanted.

He thought he'd better check on Fran and her sister before the storm really got rolling. He'd shouted his intention to the nearest man and turned his horse to head that way when he spotted one of them running toward the cattle, waving her arms and shouting, though he couldn't make out her words.

From this distance, it would be impossible to tell them apart in the same drab dresses they wore. He suspected it was Fran, and spurred his mount into a gallop. Had something happened? Unease tightened his throat.

Her hair flew out behind her like a banner. She clutched her dress above her knees so she could run at full speed. They met in the middle of the open prairie. He reined in, not wanting to run her over with her horse.

She stopped at his knee, clawing at him, panic evident. "Emma's gone," she gasped. "We stopped and I tried to secure the wagon and she's just gone."

"Wait a minute—she ran off?" He shifted in the saddle, looking to the wagon but seeing nothing out of place. No girl waiting there, either.

"I don't know. What if Underhill's men took her?"

Unless whoever had been following them had circled around in front and specifically hidden in that stand of trees, they wouldn't have had time to grab Emma. More likely she'd wandered away from the wagon. It was still a dangerous proposition, with this storm coming on.

"Did she say anything? Did you see her walk off?"

Fran shook her head in the negative. She couldn't catch her breath to answer and he didn't want to waste any more time. He reached down and swept Fran up into the saddle behind him, ignoring the blast of pain from his injured hand.

"Hold on," he commanded.

Her arms came around him, clasping in front of his midsection. He could feel her breaths heaving, from panic or exertion or both.

He kicked his mount and the horse took off. He made a beeline for the wagon, and when they got there, he urged the horse around the wagon quickly. He couldn't find any evidence that another horseman had come through there.

"She didn't say anything?" he demanded. "Anything about running away?"

"No!" Fran replied, voice urgent. "Why would she? There's nowhere to go."

A bright bolt of lightning split the sky and immediately a loud clap of thunder shook the ground.

If the rain came fast, like it looked like it would, a flash flood was a real possibility.

His horse reared unexpectedly, and it was all he could do to hold on with his thighs and grip the saddle horn with his good hand.

Fran slid away behind him, but with his injury he couldn't reach for her. He barely kept his saddle.

Her arms squeezed his midsection tightly, but he still felt her slipping.

"Whoa, boy, whoa," he managed.

The horse settled, all four feet back on the ground. Fran adjusted herself behind him, breathing hard.

"You okay?" he asked.

She said something, but he couldn't tell if it was in the affirmative.

His own thudding heart made him mistake the first sounds of rain against the hard-packed earth, but the wetness quickly pounded his shoulders, disabusing him of the notion he was getting out of this dry.

He hadn't even had time to put on his slicker.

The immediate pounding rain brought with it the frightening reality of the situation. If Emma was caught out in this in the wrong lay of land, she could be in real danger. And both she and Fran were city girls. Would she even know to find higher ground?

He kicked his horse again, pushing into the brushy trees, squinting in the low light to make out if she hid in any of the shadows. It was slightly darker here, the noise of the raindrops dampened by the foliage around them.

"Emma!" he shouted.

Fran quickly echoed his call, not needing him to instruct her.

Twigs snapped and branches slapped at him as they navigated the small woods. He hoped Fran wasn't getting the same. She burrowed into his back. Maybe that shielded her from some of it.

Finally clearing the wooded area, there was still no sign of Emma.

The rain was pouring even harder now, if that was possible.

Another bolt of lightning rent the sky, and Fran jumped, hands clenching on his sides.

At another time, he might've welcomed the protective feeling that came over him, but now his worry for her sister took front and center.

He urged his horse up the incline to the top of the bluff. It grew steeper the farther they went.

He really hoped Emma had chosen to go upward, but he had a sinking suspicion that if she were trying to hide, she had chosen the lower, more dangerous route.

And all the rainwater running off the taller swath of land to the lower could create a flash flood. Another hundred years and it might wash all the way out into a gully, but for now it just spelled danger. Rushing water and a slip of a girl weren't a good combination.

He wished he'd had time to call for one of his brothers or the other cowboys before he'd rushed off here alone, with only Fran behind him.

But he wouldn't let her down. In their wedding vows, he'd promised to protect her, and that extended to her sister, as well.

Lightning lit the sky again, and that was when he spotted Emma's gray dress against the drenched green grass. She was huddled against the ground.

At least, he hoped it was her and not a wounded animal—it was hard to tell through the sheeting rain.

"Emma!" He shouted, and she moved a little. Was she hurt?

He drew up his horse on the edge of the bluff. The animal shied and a look over the side revealed why. It was a straight drop-off of maybe ten feet. If the horse stepped off it would mean a broken leg for sure—maybe for all of them.

"Is that her?" Fran cried, leaning out so she was more beside him than behind him. She kept a tight grip on his waist. "How can we get down there?"

"I don't know. It's a straight drop-off—"

"You could lower me—"

She was cut off by a loud rush. A wall of water rushed along the bottom of the bluff, separating them from Emma even more. She was feet away from the bluff, but the water still tugged at her dress or feet, he couldn't tell which.

"Why doesn't she get up?" Fran worried aloud.

"I don't know, but we've got to figure a way to get her. If we take the time to go back and find a place to cross, the water may rise even more."

"Lower me down," she said again.

He shook his head, accidentally sending a stream of water from his hat brim into her face. She gasped.

"You're too petite. That water'll sweep your feet right out from under you."

"But Emma—"

"I'm going." He made his voice firm, so there wasn't any question, and swung his leg over the horse's back in preparation to dismount, his opposite foot in the stirrup holding him in place temporarily.

"Guess you're going to get that riding lesson quicker than I planned." Before he could think better of it, he slid his good hand behind her head and pulled her in for a quick kiss, a flash fire of mouths pressed together.

Then he slid off the horse to rescue her sister.

* * *

Head spinning from that impromptu kiss, Fran registered Edgar's slide off the horse.

The shock of his hand on her knee, through the layers of her skirt and petticoat, roused her back to the present disaster.

"You'll have to sit astride."

Her worry for Emma renewed, Fran didn't protest the unladylike move. And Edgar was too busy unstrapping a rope from the side of his saddle to look at her calves anyway.

"The horse knows if you're calm or panicked."

He must've sensed her skepticism, because he looked right up at her, rainwater sliding off the back of his hat. "It's true. Your body might tense up when you get nervous, and your legs will tell the tale."

His palm slid across her knee and he squeezed.

"All right. Project calm," she said.

Lightning flashed, illuminating his face and the serious look he wore. He waited until the thunder had shaken them before he spoke. "We're going to get her. Together."

And she believed him.

"You communicate to the horse with your legs and hands," he said. He pressed her knee into the horse's side. "To move forward." The horse obligingly stepped forward. Edgar followed, still gripping her leg.

Then he pressed her foot into the stirrup. At the same time, his other hand clasped both of hers on the reins and pulled back. The horse stopped.

"And if he...jumps from the lightning again?" she asked. She'd nearly fallen before and had only stayed on the animal's back because she'd been clinging to Edgar.

"Then try to fall where he won't step on you."

How reassuring.

Edgar unfurled the rope and passed part around his back, then knotted it in front of his chest, leaving it only a little loose beneath his arms. He looped a small amount around the knob on top of the saddle. "First, I'm going to climb down the side of the bluff. Just keep the horse standing, all right?"

He slowly turned the horse to face away from the bluff.

She swallowed hard. The horse bobbed its head. She realized she was gripping the reins too tightly and the animal could feel it. She forced her hands to relax.

Edgar squeezed her forearm. "Once I get Emma, I probably won't be able to climb the hill on my own. Wait for me to shout or wave, and then slowly move the horse forward. Don't go too fast, or you'll drag us."

"Okay."

"Sure?"

She smiled a shaky smile. "What choice do I have? We have to get Emma."

He nodded, and she had the sense that he was proud of her. She would be proud if they got Emma back to safety.

"Steady, old boy," he said to the horse with a pat on its neck. He nodded once more to Fran and disappeared.

She turned as far around in the saddle as she dared, in time to see him lever his lower body over the side of the bluff. Quickly, his head and torso disappeared, then reappeared as he moved away from the drop-off.

She prayed silently and fervently as she saw his boots splash into the muddy brown water. He sank to his knees, wobbling a bit before finding his balance.

A glance at Emma revealed the girl still prone on the ground, and Fran's heart thumped wildly, just like it had at the first glimpse she'd gotten of her sister. Had Emma been hurt? Surely this was all Fran's fault. Maybe Edgar was right, and keeping Emma in the dark about their possible pursuers had somehow made the girl feel she should run away.

The rope hanging from the saddle became taut as Edgar knelt over her sister.

She held her breath.

And then the rope slackened as he stood, with Emma's slight body in his arms. Was she alive? Was she hurt?

He disappeared again beneath the lip of the bluff. She worried, as he must be struggling through the dangerous water. Then she saw Edgar's hat waving just above the side of the bluff.

He was ready for her to move.

She turned forward in the saddle and carefully squeezed the horse's flank with her knees the way he'd briefly shown her. The animal plodded forward.

She held the reins as loosely as she dared, using her other hand to wipe a hank of bedraggled hair from her face. She felt like a drowned cat, soaked to the bone, but that wasn't important. Getting Emma back was.

The rope pulled tight, and she craned her neck to look back. At first it was only the rope, tight with tension, then a glimpse of Edgar's hat, then one arm thrown over the jutting bluff.

And then they were both aboveground.

She wanted to jump down from the horse but was afraid what it might do without a rider. Would it drag Edgar and Emma with no direction?

Waiting on the back of the horse was excruciating as Edgar pushed to his knees, and then stood. Emma was limp against his chest, and Fran's heart thundered in her ears. This was all her fault. All of it.

If Emma was all right, she would do anything, *anything* to make things right for her sister.

Chapter Nine

Edgar knew what he would want most if he'd been the one forced to wait.

Reassurance.

So the first thing he said to Fran as he neared the horse was, "She's okay. Twisted her ankle a bit and is shook up."

And when Emma raised her head from his shoulder with a trembling smile, he was rewarded as Fran's eyes welled with tears.

He felt like a hero—in contrast to the heel he'd felt like after their shooting lesson. Had it only been that morning? It seemed so long ago now.

He held the reins while Fran dismounted and embraced her sister. After they were done with their hysterics, he boosted Emma into the saddle.

Shock held him immobile when he turned back and Fran threw herself at him, her arms coming around his shoulders tightly.

His chin brushed the top of her head, the wet, loose strands sticking to his beard.

And he held on.

He didn't mean to encourage her if she was developing affection for him, but he was still reeling a little himself. There had been a moment, when his boots had hit the muddy bottom of that wash with the water roaring against him, that he'd thought he might be swept away himself. Maybe he needed a little reassurance of his own. A firm grip on the fact that he'd done it; he'd made it out of that predicament alive.

That remaining frisson of fear still zinged through him, and that was the reason he let her cling to him now.

And after she had moved back with a quick swipe of her eyes, he kept her hand as they trudged back to the wagon with Emma in the saddle.

By standing up on the wagon seat, he was able to see the herd through the pouring rain when lightning lit up the sky. The boys were circling, trying to keep the animals from stampeding.

He should get back out there, pull his weight.

He looked down on Fran and Emma, huddled together next to his horse. He had a responsibility here, too.

All this responsibility could wear on a man, especially when he had a job to get done.

He started to climb down. Before he got both boots on the ground, Fran said, "You must need to return to the other cowboys. Emma and I will get in the wagon and do our best to dry off. We'll wait for you to come and tell us when to move out."

He turned a raised eyebrow on her. So far she hadn't complained at the man's share of work he'd given her, hadn't argued when he'd told her he would set her up in Calvin. And now this. It seemed she was doing her best to be a compliant little wife, but… "Woman, it's a little late to try to not cause me trouble. From the moment you stepped off that derailed train…"

We'd like to send you two free books from the series you are enjoying now. Your two books have a combined cover price of over $10, but are yours to keep absolutely FREE! We'll even send you two wonderful surprise gifts. You can't lose!

Each of your FREE books is filled with joy, faith and traditional values as men and women open their hearts to each other and join together on a spiritual journey.

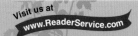

GET 2 FREE BOOKS!

HURRY!
Return this card today to get 2 FREE Books and 2 FREE Bonus Gifts!

▼ DETACH AND MAIL CARD TODAY!

YES! Please send me the **2 FREE books** and **2 FREE gifts** for which I qualify. I understand that I am under no obligation to purchase anything further, as explained on the back of this card.

PLACE FREE GIFTS SEAL HERE

102/302 IDL GEKP

FIRST NAME

LAST NAME

ADDRESS

APT.#

CITY

STATE/PROV.

ZIP/POSTAL CODE

She looked so bedraggled, with her dark hair plastered against her skull and neck in ringlets, those doe-brown eyes looking up at him, that he couldn't hold back a smile.

"You're soaked to the bone," he said.

Her teeth chattered, and Emma wasn't any better, maybe worse with her weight all balanced on one foot.

"And from what I can tell," he went on, "neither one of you has a change of clothes."

Now she blushed, pink rising in her pale cheeks.

"If you get in that wagon, you'll be wet and miserable and it's not like there's all that much room to move around."

She bit her lip, considering his words.

"Besides, you're likely to just get in trouble again if I leave you to your own devices."

She bumped his elbow and this time he grinned, because teasing her felt right.

It was the work of a few minutes to string the canvas he reserved for wrapping up his bedroll at night off the side of the wagon to two of the nearer trees, creating a temporary canopy. The rain pelted into it, but nothing got through.

Then he found the dry tinder and kindling they kept in the bottom of one of the covered cooking pots so they could start a fire in rainy conditions like these.

He'd been wet before, but once he'd stepped foot in that creek, he'd gotten soaked. He couldn't get any wetter, so he set out among the brushy trees and found some twigs and branches that had been sheltered at the base of a fallen log and were mostly dry. Soon he had a nice fire going, and both girls huddled next to it beneath his bedroll blanket, which was mostly dry due to being wrapped tightly.

— Color was coming back into both of their cheeks, and he felt a responding warmth in his gut. He liked taking care of Fran and her sister.

Then he noticed Emma had that little rat dog cradled in her arms, too. Thing was totally dry—must've been hiding in the wagon the whole time.

"Let's have a look at that foot," he said, settling down between the two of them.

Emma looked to Fran for reassurance and Fran nodded.

Emma hiked her skirt up a couple of inches, and he worked at getting her shoe off, but the laces were knotted too tightly and were wet to boot.

"Here. Your hand." Fran knelt before her sister, careful to skirt the fire, and pushed his hands away. She struggled with the laces, too, but stubbornly kept at it until they loosened. "There," she said, sitting back, her satisfaction evident in her raised chin.

He started to take off Emma's old, worn shoe. "You want to tell me what you were thinking, running off like that?"

Fran inhaled sharply. He hadn't said the words unkindly, maybe a little sternly. But look at the danger the girl had put herself in, not to mention him and Fran!

Emma remained silent as he took off the shoe.

"Emma? What made you run off?" he pushed.

"She doesn't have to say. You don't have to answer," Fran told her sister, laying a hand on the girl's shoulder.

"Yes, she does. Your babying her isn't going to solve what's going on here—"

"I'm not babying her!" Fran protested. The color in her face was growing, changing from a healthy pink to a red that he recognized from some of Breanna's tantrums in the past. "She's not a boy, not one of your brothers you can order around." She was really getting fired up now.

He pretended not to hear her, stripping off Emma's sock, careful not to jar her foot.

"She's *my* responsibility, not yours—"

"*You're* my responsibility, so that makes Emma my charge, too. Our wedding might have been short, but I do remember promising to protect you. And that extends to your family," he countered calmly.

"Underhill's men are after *me*," Emma burst out. "Fran's done all this for me, ran away from Memphis, married *you*—" She choked on the emotion she was spewing and put her hands over her eyes as she began to sob.

He let go of her foot and sat back, crossing his arms over his chest.

Fran put her arm around her sister, glaring at him as if to say, *Now look what you've done.*

But then Emma pushed away from Fran, as well. "Maybe if I just let them capture me…maybe if you didn't always have to take care of me, you would be happy. And not have had to marry a cowboy!"

"Is that what you think?" He saw the emotion fill Fran's eyes but she blinked and her words emerged even, with only a small wobble.

"You should've married Tim back in Memphis."

He'd been ready to jump in to their female prattle, but Emma's words surprised him into silence. He rubbed his chest with one hand, uncomfortable with the sudden burning there. Who was Tim? Fran hadn't mentioned a beau before.

"Tim didn't want to marry me," Fran told Emma. She kept her eyes on her sister, not wanting to see anything that might cross her husband's face. He was suspicious enough of her already. Bringing Tim into the mix might make that worse.

And more than that, she didn't want to see his pity.

Tim hadn't wanted to marry her; neither had Edgar. Maybe there was something the matter with her.

"He wanted the benefits of being married, but he never intended to marry me. He didn't love me," she told Emma, something she'd never voiced before. Maybe Edgar was right and she did have a tendency to coddle her sister. Before this, they hadn't talked about Tim and the reason he and Fran had parted ways.

Edgar coughed.

She still didn't look at him. Emma needed her. That was what she had to focus on.

"What exactly do you think I had left in Tennessee? No home. Mother and father gone. No Daniel. You and I are all that's left of our family. Do you remember being back home? You were little. You toddled after me everywhere on the farm."

Tears sprang to her eyes at the poignant memory. It was poignant for more than one reason. Her parents had been alive back then.

Emma's eyes were wet, as well.

"I love you, Emma. We're family. No matter what difficulties we have to go through, we'll get through them together. I won't let that maniac have you."

Fran's fervent words seemed to get through to her sister. Emma began sobbing again into her hands, and this time she let Fran embrace her.

Fran met Edgar's eyes over Emma's head. He looked slightly panicked, like he didn't know what to do with two emotional women. With all those brothers, maybe he didn't.

But she never would have had this moment with Emma if he hadn't pushed. And maybe Emma would have still bottled up those same feelings and done something else rash without things being cleared up.

Her husband had been right.

Not that she was going to tell him so. She didn't want the occurrence to go to his head.

Their gazes caught and held, something crackling between them. Maybe the awareness of that kiss.

Suddenly, his forehead wrinkled and he looked down, breaking the connection.

"You mind if I look at that foot now?" he asked gruffly.

Emma broke away with a small sniffle.

"I'm sorry you had to come after me," she said. "But thank you."

His head was already bent over Emma's foot, but Fran thought his upper cheek and ear—all she could see of his face—had turned pink.

"I would've done the same for my younger sister, Breanna. You two would probably get along," he muttered.

He prodded and twisted Emma's foot, and she gave one wince of pain but nothing more.

"You probably stepped in a hole out there and twisted it. I don't think it's sprained."

"It already feels better," she said softly.

He nodded, handing her sock and shoe back to Emma.

"Storm's still going, and the boys'll be wet and cranky. We didn't make it as far as I would have liked today, but I think we're gonna stop here."

"I'll look at your mama's recipes and see if I can get something started," she offered.

He still didn't look at her. He shoved his arms back into his coat and mashed his hat on his head.

"I should go check on the boys. Don't burn the wagon down," he cautioned.

She couldn't tell if he was being serious or not.

And he was leaving quickly.

"Wait!" she called out.

He ducked beneath the canopy and she followed.

Her hair had almost dried. She hadn't noticed until she stepped back out into the rain and it began clinging to her cheeks and neck again.

"Edgar!"

He turned back, but the mulish frown on his face didn't bode well.

"Don't you think we should talk about what happened back there?" she asked, keeping her voice low. Emma was still right behind her beneath the makeshift tent.

"We just did—with Emma."

"Not that. About the k—" She looked behind her, stepped forward into the rain so Emma wouldn't hear. "About the kiss," she hissed.

The stubborn set of his jaw didn't change. "Nothin' to talk about. It was the heat of the moment. We were in a sticky situation, and it just happened. Don't worry. I won't do it again."

And he turned and ducked behind the wagon.

She had the fleeting thought that he was running away just like Emma had, but what exactly was he scared of? He'd told her they were going to stay married, but he was setting her up in Calvin. His kiss might've hinted that he wanted something more, even though he'd told her differently earlier in the morning.

Was he having second thoughts?

Or was she being foolish, hoping for something she shouldn't?

Did he really think their kiss was a mistake?

Well, she certainly wasn't going to beg him to repeat it, in any case. She had some pride.

Edgar had delayed as long as his rumbling stomach would allow. He planned to take first watch, but he hadn't had any grub since his breakfast biscuit and he was half-starved.

Maybe he could sneak into camp and grab a bowl of whatever Fran had made without her noticing.

He'd waited so long that maybe she and Emma were tucked into the wagon and asleep already.

Praying for small favors, he reined in his horse and ground tied the animal outside the ring of firelight.

After several hours of hard rain, the weather had finally cleared just before sunset. It had given them a beautiful rainbow-colored sky. He'd found himself wondering what Fran thought of it, then shook the errant thought of her away.

He might've lost his focus earlier that afternoon, but he couldn't let it happen again.

Kissed her. He'd *kissed* her.

In all the dramatics following his rescue of Emma, he'd forgotten about it until Fran had confronted him.

He might like her, but it didn't mean things were going to change.

He had a job to do, and losing focus could mean someone would get hurt or the cattle didn't get to the buyer on time.

He couldn't fail his pa.

And he didn't dare risk trusting his heart to a woman.

So he'd been hiding with the cattle all night.

The cook pot was kitty-corner to the wagon and looked like it might have a bit left for him. All he had to do was go get it and slink back into the shadows before Fran saw him.

Except when he was ladling the savory-smelling stew into his bowl, he heard a sniffle from around the side of the wagon.

Was Emma upset again?

He'd known women, especially young women, needed reassuring, but this was getting to be a bit much....

He peered around the corner of the wagon. It wasn't Emma crying softly into her apron. It was Fran.

Fran, who'd suffered in silence while he'd asked her to do things she'd never done before in her life, like driving the wagon and cooking for twelve men.

Was crying.

He must've made some noise, because she looked up. The firelight behind him reflected off the tears on her cheeks.

Another woman might've turned to him, wanted him to see her pain or even fix it, but Fran turned away, ducking behind the other end of the wagon.

Aw, snakeskin.

He couldn't just leave her.

He closed his eyes briefly, then made his way around the wagon, leaving his supper behind.

Fran wasn't curled up in a little ball, like he might've expected.

She was standing tall—still didn't reach his chin, she was so tiny—and wiping her face with the edge of her shawl. Pretending, with a smile, that she was fine.

"You all right?" she asked. "You've had a long day in the saddle. How's your hand?"

He waved it at the silly woman. All his fingers moved like they were supposed to, even if his hand was still sore and swollen.

"What's going on?" he asked. He leveled a look on her, trying to send her a silent message that he wasn't going to take any nonsense answer.

"Oh." She laughed a little, but it sounded too much like a sob to be real. "Just having…a moment. I didn't want Emma to hear."

Her eyes flickered briefly to his face. "Coddling her again," she amended.

If she was trying to throw him off the track, it hadn't worked.

He let his hand close over her elbow, even though he knew he shouldn't touch her. "Fran," he warned.

That was when her chin tilted down, and she squeezed her eyes shut.

"I'm just second-guessing myself," she said.

"What do you mean?" he prompted, when she didn't continue.

She took a tiny breath. Another. Then answered, "Things I might've done differently. What if I'd been more proactive finding work in Memphis? Emma and I could've been long gone from the finishing school when Underhill came calling."

"Or you'd have been completely on your own," he felt compelled to point out.

She wiped her face again.

"Why couldn't that monster have been attracted to me instead?"

He laughed at the absurdity of her words. "You can't be serious. You'd rather have a lunatic like that coming after you?"

"Better me than Emma," she returned stubbornly.

She stepped away, leaving his hand to fall away from her elbow. "Look at me," she demanded.

"I am looking," he said over the lump that rose in his throat, half choking him. Her fierceness drew him. He should leave, but he couldn't make his feet work right.

"What's wrong with me?"

Nothing, far as he could tell.

"Tim didn't want to marry me. *You* don't want to be married to me."

She'd worked herself up into a fine fit now, eyes sparking and hands gesticulating in front of her.

"There must be something wrong with me," she concluded.

If there was, he couldn't see it. That was his problem—he liked her, was attracted to her. And he shouldn't have been. Hadn't his past taught him anything?

But her words stirred up the unwelcome reminder of something he hadn't had time to talk to her about earlier.

"You said you wouldn't lie to me," he reminded her, closing in on her and taking her upper arms in his hands. Her eyes widened as she recognized the gravity of his tone and expression.

"Y-yes."

"Did that Tim fella ever kiss you?"

He saw the answer in her eyes, but waited for the minute shake of her head—barely—before he lowered his head to hers.

He crashed into the kiss like she'd crashed into his life, upending everything in his ordered world.

She met him sweetly, passionately. Her arms clung to his shoulders. One hand even snuck up to the back of his neck and buried itself in his tangled hair. She knocked into the back of his hat brim, and that small shift brought him back to his senses.

He set her away from him, untangling her arms from around him.

Her eyes were big, luminous in the moonlight.

"Don't say that was a mistake," she whispered, lips trembling.

He mashed his hat down on his head. Clenched his hands into fists to keep from reaching for her again.

"It has to be," he said.

And turned and walked out into the darkness.

Chapter Ten

Fran was awake long before the cowboys began rolling out of their bedrolls, their murmurs soft in the semi-darkness.

She let Emma sleep for a bit longer and crept out of the wagon.

She had no desire to see her husband, so she snuck through the dew-wet grasses to find a bit of privacy. Even though he'd told her not to go off alone. She needed a moment to herself.

The sun was a slip of orange light on the horizon, and she watched it grow. The fields all around her remained cloaked in gray as the sky's blue lightened. A line of low-lying clouds at the horizon turned gold.

Bright white light slid into the growing blue in the sky and then began to slide in golden rays across the prairie, turning the green grass golden at its dewy tips. Spreading. Spreading.

Illuminating everything.

Illuminating her.

She glanced behind her to make sure no one was around.

She was utterly humiliated.

Edgar had come to her the night before. Had kissed her breathless.

And apparently found her wanting.

She didn't want to go back to the cowboy camp. Didn't want to drive that wagon all day, her shame visible to everyone.

How could she have kissed him back?

She was falling for him, that was how.

He'd given her the protection of his name, offering her only that.

But in reality, giving so much more. He'd taken her and Emma in, given her a chance to prove herself on the cattle drive.

Helped her in getting away from what was chasing her.

Rescued Emma.

He was so much more than the aloof cowboy he pretended to be.

And she couldn't help admiring him, couldn't help wishing things could have been different. That they'd met under different circumstances.

That he was really attracted to her.

He'd certainly seemed to be, in the throes of that passionate kiss, but…

She froze, her swirling thoughts coalescing into one.

On the afternoon they were married, he'd said and she'd overheard several comments that indicated he never planned to marry. She knew he didn't trust women, but she did not know the reason why.

What if he *was* attracted to her? Even liked her?

But was still wary.

She'd been reacting to the circumstances in her life for what seemed so long. Her parents' deaths, Daniel's desertion. Then spiriting Emma away from Underhill's reach.

What if she were proactive in…well, courting her husband?

What if she could make him fall in love with her? Or at the very least, realize that she could offer him a comfortable home, companionship. Friendship. Reasons they should stay together.

Time was not on her side. She'd overheard some of the cowboys the night before say they should reach Tuck's Station later that day. That only left a day or so for him to finish the sale of the cattle before he tried to settle her and Emma in Calvin.

Could she change his mind in such a short time?

She didn't know, but she had to try. Didn't she?

"Ricky ain't happy."

Matty spoke in a low, concerned tone. Most of the other cowboys had left after they consumed their breakfasts, but some remained close, saddling up for the start of another long day.

Add him to the list of people who were unhappy with Edgar. Fran couldn't be thrilled with him either, not after how he'd treated her the day before. Confusing her. Confusing the both of them.

Tuck's Station couldn't arrive fast enough.

"He tell you why?" Edgar asked finally, curiosity getting the better of him.

"No. He's keeping to himself, real suspicious."

Edgar nodded. "You think he'll finish the job?"

Matty squinted beneath the brim of his Stetson. He chewed on a piece of grass, the thin green line bobbling between his lips when he spoke. "He knows someone's following us. He ain't gonna leave you in danger. Possible danger."

Edgar wasn't so sure his brother's loyalty was to him, not after the last aborted conversation they'd had. "He owes it to Pa to do right by the cattle. We all do."

Matty's eyes shifted over to him. His brow was furrowed. "Pa didn't take us in to count some kind of debt."

"I know."

"You sure?"

Matty's pointed question made Edgar look away, watching the last of the cowboys swing up into the saddle.

Jonas had never asked Edgar to work on the homestead, now the growing ranch. He hadn't had to. Edgar had wanted to pay back his adoptive pa for taking him in and giving him a home when no one else would. Jonas had given him a place to lay his head, love, support, everything.

It mattered. And that was why Edgar had to do this job right.

What would he do if Ricky left the herd and the job behind? They had just enough cowboys to wrangle the animals where they needed to go. Would his brother be selfish enough to leave the job unfinished?

Should Edgar try to talk to him again, smooth things over?

"Someone's glad to see you."

Edgar followed Matty's nod to Fran as she picked her way across the couple of bedrolls that hadn't been secured on their owners' horses. She moved toward where he and his brother sat, downing the remains of their pan-fried biscuits.

She was smiling, beaming at him.

He looked down, examining himself. Had he

smeared some dirt or grease across his body, or otherwise forgotten to button something up?

Nope. Everything seemed in order, from his boots to his chin. He leaned back into the saddle he was propped against and pushed back his Stetson to see her better as she approached.

"Good morning," she greeted.

He narrowed his eyes at her, trying to understand what had happened between last night when he'd left her near tears and this morning.

"Mornin'," he mumbled around a bite of biscuit.

She didn't reprimand him for his poor manners, but leaned down and bussed his cheek.

He choked on his biscuit.

"Let me refill your coffee before I start cleaning up." She took the mug from his suddenly nerveless fingers and turned away.

He registered his brother practically rolling on the ground at the stunned expression he must have been wearing.

"Knock it off," he growled, thumping Matty's leg with his boot.

"You just—hee, hee, hee—you look so thunderstruck!"

He felt thunderstruck.

He was a cad, and she should be angry with him.

Not kissing his cheek like she was happy to see him.

"Quiet," he warned his brother.

"You charmer, you!" Matty was still belly laughing, swiping at tears rolling down his cheeks with one sleeve while he fanned his face with his Stetson.

"What's going on?" Seb asked, plopping down a few feet away. He'd been on the last watch of the night and looked exhausted.

Thank goodness they were only a half day from Tuck's Station.

"Hee, hee, hee—Ed's gone and found the one woman who likes his crotchety nature."

"Shut. Up!" he hissed, looking over his shoulder to make sure she hadn't heard.

Seb brightened, his exhaustion disappearing as he straightened, knocking back his hat with wide eyes.

"There's nothing between us," Edgar insisted. "We're parting ways. I've got an idea to put her up in Calvin."

"Then maybe you shouldn't be kissing her behind the wagon," Matty said, suddenly serious. "Might give her the wrong idea."

Edgar's face and ears went hot.

"Well, I think it's grand that Edgar's finally found someone to love," Seb interjected, clearly trying to play the peacemaker.

"I have *not*." Edgar looked over his shoulder again, but thankfully Fran still hadn't reappeared with his coffee.

He kept his voice low when he turned back to his brothers. "She's a pill, all right? Yeah, I like her, a little, but you both know I wasn't looking for a wife."

Seb shrugged. "You got one, though. Shouldn't waste your chance."

Matty kicked his head back and Edgar shot a look over his shoulder to see Fran approaching. She didn't have his coffee mug—instead she had a pair of kitchen shears. He got a bad feeling in the pit of his stomach.

"I started thinking… If you're going to represent your papa for this deal with the cattle, you should look a little more… A little less…"

He raised one eyebrow at her. "What's wrong with

the way I look?" Not that he didn't know. But he wanted to see what she would say.

She had the grace to blush. "I know spring must be a busy time on a ranch. Maybe you haven't realized it's past time for a haircut."

"And a shave," Seb offered helpfully.

Edgar glared at his brother.

"Well, I don't have a razor," Fran said.

That was good, because he wouldn't trust her that close to him with a blade.

"But I found these shears in the bottom of the wagon and I thought I could at least attempt to..." She waved one limp hand toward him, toward his head specifically.

He waited for her to finish.

She frowned at him.

"To make you more presentable," she finished firmly.

Matty slapped him on the back. "Sounds like a fine idea. You're overdue for a trim."

The mark of a smart man was knowing when he was beat. And Edgar knew, between his two brothers and Fran, he wasn't getting out of this without a haircut. Like it or not.

So he gave in with what grace he could muster.

"Fine," he muttered.

He'd ridden through this area before and knew of a little stream farther past the wooded area. It was a little bit more of a hike than they'd had the first two nights out on the prairie, but by the time he'd built that fire the day before it seemed silly to move the wagon for a little less of a walk to do dishes and water the horses.

He followed her there and stood on the still-swollen bank, waiting for her to tell him what she had planned. He took off his Stetson and tossed it up the bank a few feet for its own protection.

"Why don't you…" She looked him up and down, and he felt the full difference in their heights.

She set down the wooden bucket and a towel he hadn't realized she was carrying and plunked her hand on her hip, biting her lip and assessing him with her eyes.

He wasn't going to make this any easier on her. It had been her idea after all.

Even though he knew his ma would appreciate the thought.

"I suppose you should sit here."

He followed her directions to kneel on the bank of the creek—a little too close for his comfort, but he supposed he'd been dunked the night before and this clean stream wouldn't hurt none. It wasn't deep, even with the extra inch or two from the recent rain.

Then, with a little pressure from her hand on his shoulder, she had him bent over the water, and he heard the soft swoosh as she dipped the bucket.

He yelped at the icy sensation of the entire bucket being poured on his head and splashing onto his shoulders.

Water sluiced down his face and cooled him all the way down the neck of his shirt.

Then she pressed on his shoulders and he sat back on his heels. Her palm rested against his forehead, hot on his now-chilled skin, and she flipped back the hair that had been dripping in his face.

He squinted up at her.

She grinned. "Sorry."

"Sure you are," he growled. But he wasn't angry.

It was a little like when she'd served him the frogs' legs. He could appreciate a good prank, couldn't he?

She combed his hair back from his face with her fingers, and her touch sent the same jolt through him that he'd felt when he'd kissed her the night before.

He needed to distract himself from that. Dwelling on that connection could only bring trouble.

"You're not going to scalp me as punishment for kissing you last night, are you?" he blurted.

Then winced. Way to bring their kiss back to the forefront by throwing it out there in conversation.

"No." She smiled again, a little ornery this time. Both a niggle of worry and a tingle of attraction shivered through him. Or maybe it was the cold bead of water that slid down the back of his collar.

She reached and pulled a bar of soap from the towel. She worked up a lather and then slid her fingers into his hair, massaging the lather into his scalp.

It felt amazing.

He normally didn't give so much attention to his hair during his twice-weekly baths, and even if he did, he doubted his own hands could make his head feel this good. Why was she doing this to him?

"You done this before?" he asked grumpily. He closed his eyes so at least he couldn't see her.

"No. Well, a few times bathing Emma when she was a tot."

He grunted.

"You haven't told me much about yourself," she said as she moved closer and reached around to scrub the back of his scalp.

He squinted one eye at her. At that moment, a few soapsuds slid down over his brow and he squeezed his eye shut, but not before it stung with the soap.

"What do you mean?"

"Well…I know you came to be with your family

after being on an orphan train. But how did you come to meet Jonas?"

Her massaging fingers must've scraped away some of his inhibitions, because he found himself telling her, "Bear Creek was the last stop. And there I was, standing on the platform at the front of the schoolhouse with no one to take me in. By that time, Jonas had taken in Oscar and Seb, and then Matty after the homestead had been settled. Someone said my pa might take on another orphan and they fetched him to town."

He didn't like remembering the pain—kind of the same sting as that soap that had gotten into his eye— of standing there alone.

Of not being chosen.

He'd been humiliated and desperate, but Jonas had simply clapped a hand on his shoulder and said, "Let's go home." And they'd gone.

"Jonas came and got me." That was all he could tell her. The rest was too painful to share.

She pushed him forward until he was worried he might fall into the creek, and then she poured another icy bucketful over his head.

She rinsed him twice more, running her fingers through his hair as she did so, removing all the soap.

Then she pushed him back on his haunches again, combing his hair away from his face.

She smiled at him again. Gently.

She took a comb from her pocket and began sliding it through his heavy, wet locks. Unknotting. Untangling.

Settling him, like he'd seen his brother Oscar do with a horse and brush before.

She walked around behind him and used both hands to set him facing straight forward. He felt her pick up a hank of hair.

She snipped and the hank fell onto his shirt.

Snip. Snip.

Thankfully, it didn't look like she was giving him a lopsided cut.

"And what about before that?"

She'd lulled him into such a relaxed state with her hands and her manner that it took him a moment to track back to their conversation.

"Hmm?"

"What about before you got on the orphan train?"

His head jerked to one side, and she gasped as the shears snipped again.

"Don't!" She dropped the shears to the ground and came to his side, gripping his chin with one firm hand and the back of his head with the other. She brushed his hair away and touched his ear.

His ear. It was a part of him that he barely ever thought about—except to remember to wash behind— but somehow it was entirely too intimate.

"I thought I'd cut you," she murmured.

He couldn't remember anyone else ever touching him there. And it seemed so close that he jerked away. Stood all the way up. Realized he was shaking.

"Is that why you brought me out here?" he demanded. "Did you think you could trade a haircut for my past?"

Fran looked up at Edgar. All the way up.

He'd risen to his full height, and she knew she'd hit on something tender.

Not his ear, because blessedly, she'd somehow managed not to cut him when he'd jerked his head to the side.

Something inside him.

"Sit down." Somehow she managed to keep her voice

even, when she was slightly frightened, trembling at his intensity.

"I don't talk about my childhood," he said. His firmness offered no option.

But she wasn't one to give up easily.

"Sit down," she repeated.

He did. Stiffly this time. Before, his shoulders had lost their tension.

It was all back now.

She massaged the top of his scalp for a moment before she went back to trimming his hair. It didn't help.

"You can trust me," she said, because she couldn't give up, not when she'd seen the potential they might have together.

He didn't respond. A glance at his face showed that stubborn jaw locked in place and his lips thinned with displeasure.

"I told you something very painful for me—about my parents, about why Emma and I had to run."

She didn't know what she thought, perhaps that he would understand that she'd trusted him with her past, but all he said was "I said I don't want to talk about it."

She finished his haircut with jerky movements. Part of her wanted to ruin it, give him a lopsided cut that would make him look ridiculous.

But she refrained.

When she stepped back, brushing a few stray hanks of hair from his shoulders, she froze as she got her first good look at him.

Before, even with his unkempt appearance, he'd been striking.

Now he was handsome. With his hair trimmed short and curling about his collar and ears, and with his beard washed clean and shining blond, she could clearly see the strong cheekbones and defined brow. His blue eyes were clear and steady.

Her husband was one of the handsomest men she'd had the pleasure of seeing.

Of course he ruined all her hard work when he smashed his hat on top of his head.

And he didn't acknowledge her when he stomped back toward the wagon.

But she still wasn't going to give up.

She had a day left to figure this man out, to find a way to make him realize they could have something together.

She was going to take that day.

Edgar spent the morning agitated and as far away from his nosy little wife as he could.

Matty and Seb had both admired his haircut and tried to tease him. But they seemed to have sensed his foul mood, so they circled around the herd in the other direction. Ricky had stayed away in the first place.

The worst part was, he sort of felt she was right.

She *had* opened up to him. Told him everything he'd asked, about her past and her parents.

And he hadn't reciprocated.

It bothered him, probably more than it should've, that there was an unequal trade between them.

But he didn't want to talk about his early childhood. Didn't even like thinking about it. Made a practice of just living his life. He didn't need to dwell on it.

It was over and done.

But the fact that he couldn't quit thinking about Fran and her pushiness and the chasm between them made him wonder if maybe it wasn't over and done with.

He took his hat off and fanned his face with it, the

early-morning sun getting to him. Running a hand through his shorn hair made him think of Fran again, too.

He didn't really think she'd offered to cut his hair to pump him for information. And he appreciated that she wanted to help him look nice for when he met with his pa's buyer.

He was almost relieved when a steer in his vicinity decided to take a meandering side trip. It gave him something to focus on as he galloped his cow pony out and ushered it back to the herd.

Their trip was almost up. And then he and Fran would go their separate ways. She would be in Calvin, and he would be in Bear Creek.

She didn't need to know about his childhood, his insides argued.

John, the cowpoke who'd noticed the riders on their tail before, rode up to him just before noon.

"See any sign of them?" Edgar asked the other man.

John shook his head. "It's strange. Their tracks say they followed us all the way up until last night. I found a small fire where they must've camped. Then nothing."

"No tracks today?"

The man shook his head again. "It's like they decided to give up. You think?"

Edgar pushed back his Stetson, idly scanning the horizon. "Don't know. If you spent two and a half days tracking someone, would *you* just give up?"

John shrugged. "Probably depend on why I was tracking them in the first place. Or if I got myself a better plan."

"Exactly."

Edgar didn't like it.

If the men were after the cattle, their chances were

getting smaller and smaller to make a move, as the cowboys pushed them closer and closer to Tuck's Station.

If they were after Emma, they could beat the crew to the town. The cattle moved slowly. Two men alone on horseback could easily circle around to town and make it there first.

With Fran's tendency to overprotect the girl, he sort of felt like Emma was his own little sister, too. She was Breanna's age. Emotional, like Breanna could be at times.

And she didn't deserve to have someone after her.

He remembered how jumpy Penny had been for months after the man who'd become obsessed with her had tried to abduct her. Edgar had startled her once by rushing into the kitchen and she'd burst into tears, then quickly apologized.

Emma didn't need to be haunted by that kind of fear. She was—sort of—his sister, and he wouldn't let anything happen to her.

"What do you want to do?" John asked, his horse shifting to one side.

"I don't know yet. I'll check in with my brothers and we'll get a plan together for moving into town."

John nodded and rode off.

Edgar stood in his stirrups and surveyed the herd and cowboys.

They'd purposely gone light on manpower when they'd left Bear Creek. Most of the ranches didn't hire cowboys the way they used to, not since fences and the railroad had changed the landscape.

With the extra cattle they'd taken on, they'd make a nice profit.

Rustlers were less of a concern—or had been less of a concern in the past.

Did he have enough cowboys to put up a good fight? He didn't know.

His brothers, especially Ricky, were handy with their rifles. But if this was about Emma, would they be willing to stand and fight? It was his fight, not theirs.

So he would ask.

He spotted Seb dismounting near the wagon. Looked as if Fran had stopped for a stretch. He'd go intercept his brother.

Chapter Eleven

They were back where they'd started.

Emma wouldn't leave the wagon. She'd gotten out once, walked next to the conveyance for only a few minutes, then returned. Now she was huddled inside, that little dog with her.

"If we do find work with a seamstress, at least we won't be stuck in these horrible rags for much longer," Fran said over her shoulder, trying to engage Emma in conversation.

Her sister only hummed in response. Was that a negative or a positive hum?

"Edgar said there's a nice boardinghouse in town, not far from the church and the town square—"

"What if Underhill finds us there?"

Emma's question was spoken so softly that Fran barely heard her over the horses' plodding steps and the creaking of the wagon.

"Edgar won't just leave us unprotected," Fran said. And hoped it was true. He hadn't actually said, but his ire on Emma's behalf seemed to indicate that.

"What if we get settled and Underhill comes back?"

Obviously, Emma's thoughts centered on one thing

only. And Fran couldn't blame her. Emma had been attacked. Although Fran had intervened before her sister had been irreparably hurt, the emotional scars remained, especially for one as sensitive as Emma. It would take time, and lots of reassurances, to heal.

And if Fran's plans to stay close to Edgar panned out, the worry would be unnecessary. But she didn't want to get Emma's hopes up if the stubborn man refused to see reason.

"Once we're established in the community, we'll have friends who will help protect us. And I'm sure there's a lawman, and maybe a town marshal or a sheriff, to watch over the citizens."

"A lot of good that did us in Memphis."

Emma was right. Underhill had been a man of such good standing that no one had dared speak up against him for two orphans—at least that was what the head-mistress thought as she bundled them away.

But if *they* were the ones established in the community, surely it would make a difference.

"What about his accusations against you?" Emma queried.

Fran had nearly forgotten his threats. That was all they were. She'd never even been to the man's home, but he'd claimed she'd stolen from him. It was impossible. If she'd never stepped foot in the place, he couldn't have a witness against her.

And there was nothing he could do to her here, was there?

It didn't bear worrying over.

She needed to figure out a way to win over her husband. And she became more concerned as Edgar spent the morning avoiding her.

How could she figure out a way to get close to him if she couldn't speak to him?

When Seb rode close at about lunchtime, she waved him over.

She pulled the wagon to a stop and secured the brake, then climbed down. Emma remained inside.

"What do you need?" her youngest brother-in-law asked, hopping off his horse.

"Information."

He looked perplexed, so she rushed on. "I botched things with Edgar earlier, asking about his childhood before he came to be with your family."

Seb's face closed. He didn't actually take a step back, but he looked like he wanted to. Uncomfortable.

"He doesn't like to talk about it," Seb hedged.

She knew. "I gathered that. I don't want to use it against him. I *am* his wife...."

She could see Seb softening. She'd grown to like Edgar's brothers, even though she'd really only inter-acted with them in the evenings around the campfire.

"I want to make a go of it," she said softly, for the first time voicing her intentions. "I won't hurt him."

Her words seemed to loosen him. Just enough.

"What do you want to know?" he asked reluctantly.

"How did he come to be on the orphan train? At what age—"

Movement from behind her arrested her words and she turned in time to see Edgar sidestep his horse around the wagon.

His face was dark, a thundercloud of deeply drawn brows, and she knew he'd overheard her pressing his brother for information. "What's going on?"

"Just talkin'," Seb said before she could make her frozen vocal cords work.

"About me." Edgar's voice was low and dangerous—even more so than when they'd been at the creek earlier.

"I asked," she inserted.

His eyes flicked over her and back to Seb, almost as if she hadn't spoken. As if she was being dismissed.

Edgar opened his mouth, but she couldn't let Seb take the blame for something that was her fault.

"I want to know you," she burst out. "You wouldn't tell me, so I asked your brother. That's all."

"You want to know me? Know all about me?" Edgar wheeled his horse, obviously agitated, but didn't bolt like she expected.

Behind her, she heard Seb mount up and gallop off. She didn't blame him; she could face her husband's ire.

"You want to know that my own mother abandoned me to a Chicago orphanage when I was four years old? That she promised she'd come back but she never did? Is that what you want to know?"

Her heart ached for him. Both for the little boy he'd been, all alone, and for the man whose closely held pain now clenched his jaw.

"Edgar—" She stepped toward him, but he wasn't finished.

"Or maybe that the director claimed to love me but put me on that orphan train anyway, when all I wanted was stay with her? She promised that I would find a family, but no one wanted me! Is that what you want to know?"

Her breath caught in her chest. "Of course I wouldn't have wanted those things for you—"

"Well, now you know."

The finality in his voice as he wheeled his horse, this time bolting away, shook her to her core.

He was gone.

And now she knew.

But she'd hurt him, too, with her insistent pushing.

She couldn't keep Emma safe. She couldn't talk to her own husband. Her failures were mounting higher and higher.

Edgar rode in the opposite direction of the herd. He couldn't face his brothers right now. He couldn't face anyone.

He was raw, rage filled, hot.

He rode into a brushy woods and ran off his horse, going knee deep in the little meandering creek they'd been following for three days.

Tossing his hat, he cupped his hands and scooped up handfuls of cool water, splashing his face.

The icy water did nothing to quench the burn inside him.

A twig snapped and he jerked around, water arcing from his hands.

Seb.

"You okay? You flew out of there pretty quick."

He nodded. Then shook his head.

Turned his back on his younger brother and ran both hands down his face.

"Should I have checked on Fran first?" Seb asked.

He squeezed, but the pounding in his head didn't dissipate.

"You yell at her?" His younger brother was looking for trouble, nosing in where he didn't belong.

"Could you go away?" he responded. "I need—"

He needed to take it back. All of it. But couldn't.

He splashed both hands violently through the water, getting wet and cold up to his armpits.

"Did it help? Yelling at her?" Seb pushed.

"No!" he burst out, hanging his head and sliding the fingers of both hands back along his scalp.

All that did was make him think of her, too. The tender way she'd cut his hair. She was driving him insane.

"No, it didn't help."

Seeing her tears had torn something open inside of him, releasing a flow of hot emotion that broke him.

Reopening an old wound like his that had scarred over didn't help, it just created more scar tissue, more memories he didn't need.

Unless the wound needed to be lanced.

He shook his head, confusion and that old pain warring with regret that he'd spoken to Fran like he had. She shouldn't have been prying into his past, but that didn't mean she deserved to be yelled at.

He needed a clear head. The cattle. He had to think of the cattle first, and Emma's safety.

"You could always...oh, I don't know. Apologize," Seb said.

Before Edgar could turn and read his brother the riot act, he heard hoofbeats heading into the distance. He looked over his shoulder to see Seb's retreating back.

He was alone.

He hadn't felt this alone since Jonas had fit him into his family. He'd been accepted immediately, been made a part of the group. Was expected to pull his weight and was taken care of in ways he hadn't known since he'd come to the orphanage at a young age.

Now, with his brother's disapproval stinging and himself worn raw from the confrontation with Fran, he felt like that four-year-old boy again.

And it hurt.

* * *

She'd ruined it all.

Thankfully, Emma claimed not to have heard the altercation with Edgar. She remained quiet and withdrawn as they got closer and closer to their destination.

What could they expect when they arrived?

Edgar hadn't said what he planned to do with them until they reached Calvin, but he wouldn't just leave them unprotected if men were following them, would he?

She hadn't known him long, but she couldn't imagine he would.

She trusted him to keep Emma safe. Had since the beginning.

He'd proved his mettle when he'd rescued Emma during the rainstorm on the range.

He was a man who took seriously the care of his own. His loyalty to his father proved as much.

What did she have to do for him to see her as a real wife?

Where was God in all of this?

She'd watched Edgar circle the herd for a good part of the past hour, taking minutes to speak to each horseman. Making plans?

She saw him exchange words with Ricky, both men wearing fierce expressions. Things were obviously tense between them.

He never looked back at the wagon.

Her stomach hurt. Worse than when she realized Tim didn't love her.

Nearly as bad as when she'd realized Daniel wasn't coming for her and Emma.

When Edgar got them settled, she would be very much on her own. Unless she could change things.

But that wasn't the worst of it. She hated that Edgar was hurt. Hated that he kept it so well hidden. Had his brothers even known that his pain ran so deeply, that he still felt it?

She would apologize if she could, but if Edgar remained at a distance from her, what chance did she have? She didn't know how to ride a horse—not really—and chase him down.

The sun had long passed its zenith, and her belly was warning her it was suppertime when Matty turned back from the herd and approached the wagon on his horse.

"Ladies," he greeted them.

"Hello, Matty," Fran replied.

Emma stirred in the back of the wagon.

He sidled his horse up to the wagon, matched its pace with that of the horses Fran drove.

"Is Edgar all right?" Fran asked, because she couldn't contain the question.

Matty winked beneath his Stetson. "I have faith he'll come around, don't you worry. He hasn't always been such a crotchety grandpapa, you know."

His words comforted her, a little. Edgar had his family. And his family was obviously important to him.

"Ed's worked up a plan to get y'all in town to the train station. Interested in hearing it?"

She was interested in knowing why her husband didn't come and tell her the plan himself. Was he still that furious with her? Or avoiding her because her questions had cut too close to the true source of his pain?

"Of course," she said.

Matty tossed a bundle and she caught it by rote. Juggling the reins, she revealed a pair of…men's trousers and a cowboy's woolen shirt?

She looked at the cowboy askance. "What's this?"

"Ed says it's time for your second riding lesson. He wants ya to put that on."

She held up the trousers between two fingers. "I can't wear this. It's not appropriate."

"Maybe not in a big city, but my ma's been seen wearing trousers a time or two workin' on certain chores on the ranch."

How peculiar. Heat rose in her face just thinking of it.

"And I'm going to…ride? Dressed as a cowboy?" She was having trouble understanding this plan of her husband's.

"Exactly." He tossed his cowboy hat to Emma, beneath the canvas cover of the wagon. "Ed wants you to tuck your hair up in that hat as best you can. Wants you to try to pass for a cowboy."

"But…won't anybody looking at me know that I'm not an accomplished rider?"

He shrugged. "The horse is a pretty well-trained cutter. All you gotta do is hold on, and he'll do the work for you. 'Sides…Ed thinks someone looking for two women won't be paying too much attention to a green-horn cowboy."

"So they'll only find one woman in the wagon. Emma."

That didn't comfort her at all.

But Matty was grinning. Widely.

And someone else was approaching from the herd. Not Edgar, much to her disappointment. A closer look revealed Seb.

"Nope. Someone lookin' at the wagon's gonna see *two* women."

She exchanged a wide-eyed look with Emma. "Seb?" she gurgled, barely able to get the word out.

Matty chuckled. "Yep. He ain't too happy with Ed's idea. But it's just until we get the cattle into the holding pens at the rail station. After that, the boys will be free to escort you ladies to the hotel and keep an eye on ya. Just in case."

Well. This plan was either ingenious...or insane. She didn't know which.

"Shouldn't Emma ride out, and I'll keep driving the wagon?"

He shook his head. "It'd work if she could ride at all, but two men riding double might raise questions and merit a second look. Seb's a good shot, and the rest of us'll be keeping an eye on the wagon anyway."

Fran didn't argue that she had *very* little more experience than Emma. She'd left Tennessee and vowed to do whatever she had to do to keep her sister safe.

And if this was it, she would do it. No matter how foolish she looked or felt.

And she did look foolish, she concluded a quarter hour later as she descended from the wagon dressed like a cowboy. They'd given her Seb's boots and left him to go barefoot. Even with a sock rolled and stuffed into the toe of each boot, she felt clunky and awkward in the men's footwear. Maybe it would be better on horseback.

Her neck was exposed beneath the cowboy hat.

And she thought that probably anybody who took a look at her would be able to tell she was a woman. Wouldn't they?

She'd passed her dress out of the back of the wagon while Emma had helped her put on the cowboy garb. Now Seb appeared from behind his horse, where he'd donned the dress over his own trousers.

Lanky as he was, his shoulders still stretched the

fabric of the dress. She sincerely hoped he didn't tear it, or she'd have nothing left to wear at all.

He didn't look happy, stomping in bare feet back to the wagon.

Matty looked like he was barely suppressing his laughter behind lips clamped together until they were white.

"Well, Fran here might pass for a cowboy, but you sure don't make much of a girl. You'd better stay in the back of the wagon."

"Then who's going to drive?"

"Emma," the cowboy said with a nod at Fran's sister.

Fran began to protest. "She hasn't driven a wagon before—"

"Ed said you might argue and that I should remind you something about coddling."

She opened her mouth to argue—the man wouldn't even face her but he was going to get onto her for trying to protect Emma.

Emma broke in. Quietly, with a beseeching look at Fran. "I can do it. If something happens, Seb will be right there in the wagon. Right?"

Matty winked at the younger girl, a brotherly admiration apparent on his face. "Exactly right. None of us are gonna let anything happen to you."

"Are you sure?" Fran asked.

Emma's lips pinched with determination.

Fran gave in with little grace—because she didn't seem to have much of a choice.

Had Edgar somehow known that having a chore to do would put a little starch back into Emma, when Fran hadn't been able to help her sister do it herself?

Matty boosted her onto the horse's back and she

clung to the knob on the front of the saddle, but the animal didn't move. Not even a quiver.

The cowboy grinned at her. "I'll be right beside ya until we get to the herd, then I'll give ya some instructions. Mostly just stay out of the way of the cattle. If they start getting out of control, one of the other boys'll come to your aid."

She managed to get the horse moving in a placid walk. Praying that she didn't look too awkward.

Praying that all this preparation was for nothing.

But knowing there was a chance it wasn't.

Edgar had promised himself he would stay away from Fran.

But he found his horse gravitating toward her around the herd regardless.

He had never imagined that a woman wearing trousers would look so good. Her slender hips and the definition the trousers gave to her legs… He had to wrestle his wayward thoughts into submission several times, like chasing one of the stray steers back to the herd.

What was it about her that kept drawing him, even over the discomfort that she now knew about his past?

Matty had only ridden by and given a short report, but Edgar wasn't surprised that Fran hadn't complained about his zany plan. She hadn't complained yet, no matter what he'd asked, no matter how hard it was on her.

Right now she didn't look comfortable in the saddle, but at least she hadn't fallen off.

They were coming up to the outskirts of Tuck's Station when a dozen head decided to wander away from the main herd, right in front of her.

Her cow pony started skirting them, just like it was supposed to. The burst of speed turned into a trot.

And she started bouncing in the saddle.

He moved in to help, rounding the steers and pushing them back toward the herd. He pulled up next to her. "You doing okay?"

She reined in the pony, clutching the saddle horn with her other hand. White-faced, she attempted a smile at him. "Mostly trying not to fall off."

Somehow he found himself wanting to smile back at her. Even now. "Emma okay?"

"Yes, I think so. She was when I rode out anyway."

He nodded.

"Edgar, I really am sorry—about before. About pushing into your past."

He went hot and then cold. Surprised that she'd brought it up. He steeled his features. Squinted into the sun pretending to watch the herd. "I don't like to talk about it. But I shouldn't have yelled at you."

He could practically hear his ma blasting his ears for not apologizing the right way. "I'm sorry," he choked out.

He chanced a look at her. Her clear, assessing gaze had him shifting in his saddle, and the animal beneath him scooted to one side, probably wondering what burr Edgar had got under his caboose.

His little wife did tend to get under his skin.

"Let's just leave it be, all right?"

She nodded, but he still felt as though her eyes saw too much.

Was this what a real marriage was like? Someone else knowing the dark parts about you? It was uncomfortable....

But also...

Now that she knew, now that the secret was out there, there was a relief in not being forced to hide it anymore.

They rode quietly together over the next hill, and the town of Tuck's Station came into view, nestled in the valley. Close enough almost to touch.

Finally.

"Stay close," he said as he idly scanned their surroundings. Arriving from this direction afforded him a nice view, something he'd been counting on.

No one in sight, except those that looked to be working around town. The town wasn't any bigger than Bear Creek, and the goings-on looked to be normal. Someone loading a wagon near the livery; a couple of people were passing on the boardwalk. The saloon was quiet, but it wasn't late enough in the day yet for it to be busy.

The holding pens at the train station were empty, which was a surprise. He'd expected to see some activity there. It might be nothing, or it might be something. The agent in Bear Creek had said the train was running, and he had to get the cattle to Cheyenne.

"Do you…expect trouble?" Fran glanced over her shoulder toward the wagon.

He'd told Seb to keep it close to the herd, even if it meant his brother and Emma would be eating trail dust. So far everything had gone according to his plan.

"Don't know. John tried to track the men following us earlier today and it seemed like they just disappeared. So we want to be prepared for anything."

He saw her swallow, her neck slender beneath the hat and disappearing into the neckline of one of Seb's second-choice shirts.

Then he had to swallow hard and avert his eyes, and those wayward thoughts.

Someone might be following them. Or in front of them. Right. Focus on possible danger. Not his enchanting little wife.

"We're going to push the cattle right into the holding pens over there at the rail station." He pointed to the fenced area to one side of town. "Should be able to just send the cattle in with no issues."

The pens were out in the open. No cover, except for the train station. Nowhere for men to hide if they were after Emma.

"By the time the cattle are penned, the cowboys will circle around to flank the wagon and we'll have enough men to watch out for Emma—and you—until I can get things settled with the ticket agent."

This time when she looked at him, her eyes were moist.

"What?" he asked. A little gruffly, because he wasn't sure what had her upset now.

She shook her head slightly. "Just…thank you. For getting us this far."

Her gratitude had him shifting uncomfortably again. What had he done, exactly, other than save Emma from the rushing water? Put Fran to work, that was what. And she was thanking him. It rubbed him wrong, somehow.

His horse neighed, telling him exactly what it thought of Edgar's discomfort.

"All right, old boy," he said to it, settling in his saddle.

He nodded to Fran. "Let's get them in. Stay close to me."

And she did.

When he told her left, she went left. The longer the afternoon wore on, the more comfortable she got in the saddle. It helped that the pony was experienced and not green-broke. By the time they'd driven the last few head into the pens, she was reading his cues without him having to instruct her. And her beaming smile buoyed him into almost forgetting about their trouble.

Until he got to see the ticket agent.

He'd sent Fran to the wagon with the cowboys after sending his brothers a hard look that said they'd better look after the girls.

And now in front of the ticket agent, he got an answer he did not want to hear.

"What do you mean, the train's not running today?"

The man reminded Edgar so much of the agent back in Bear Creek with his mannerisms and thinly veiled disdain that Edgar had to wonder if they were long-lost cousins.

"Trains can't get through from the east," the man said, jerking one finger back toward Bear Creek. "On account of the broken tracks."

That made sense.

"So until the next train comes in from the west—" now he jerked his finger the opposite direction "—there's no train to take your animals to the next station. Sorry."

He didn't sound all that sorry. His words sounded rote, like he'd said them several hundred times in the past few days.

This wasn't good. Edgar had a day and a half left to get the cattle on to Cheyenne, like his pa had promised the buyer. If he had to drive the cattle like they had been doing, it would take all of that time and maybe more. There was no room for error or bad weather.

"When does the next train arrive?" he asked, barely reining in his patience with the man before him.

"Scheduled for tomorrow. That's if it's on time, and there may not be room for all your animals."

"What do you mean?"

"Farmers around here booked their animals on the next stock cars. I don't know how many cars will be on the train, but those who've paid first get first right to load their animals."

Edgar gritted his teeth. "So even if I wait till tomorrow, you can't guarantee I can ship my cattle on?"

"That's right."

Edgar turned away from the ticket window, slapping his Stetson against his thigh.

This was a delay he could ill afford. His pa had given his word about those cattle and left it to Edgar to get the job done. It wasn't Edgar's fault that the tracks had broken, and it wasn't his fault that they'd been delayed by the weather.

But none of that mattered. He'd made a promise to his pa that he would follow through on the deal, so he had to.

He moved off the platform to the boardwalk that lined the town's one main street. A glance over at the holding pens and a nod from Matty indicated that things were calm there. Could he trust Ricky not to get into trouble?

A glance in the other direction didn't reveal anything suspicious. Just folks going about their business.

He sighed.

Looked like they were going to be staying the night. He might as well give the town marshal a heads-up about Fran and Emma. If Fran had been telling the truth and the men after them really did have nefarious intentions, they'd stay far away from the law. He could also try wiring his pa's buyer in case there was a delay with the railroad.

And he remembered the state of the girls' dresses. He had a little spending money left from the previous summer that he'd tucked into his pocket when he'd left the homestead. Up until now, he'd been thinking the cash would help get the girls settled in Calvin, but now he had another thought.

A sudden hankering to see Fran in a pretty dress.

Chapter Twelve

"Are you sure you won't come down to supper?" Fran asked Emma.

They'd spent the late afternoon sequestered in the hotel room Edgar and his brothers had escorted them to. After a lovely hot bath in which she'd scrubbed away days of trail dust, Fran began to feel human again.

And then the dresses had arrived. Store-bought and prettier than anything Fran had had since she was a young girl, a deep green for her and a paler green for Emma. Had he meant them to be an apology? She didn't know.

They'd arrived via the front desk clerk, along with a note from Edgar requesting they join him for dinner.

Before he'd settled them at the hotel, Edgar had asked them not to leave the room. But she'd been able to ask the clerk for paper and an envelope and had asked the man to return in an hour for the missive she composed.

She probably shouldn't have taken the liberty. But she couldn't forget Edgar's obvious pain when he'd spoken of his mother's abandonment and the director of the Chicago orphanage. So she'd written to the institution on his behalf and asked if the woman was still there, and if so, to send details on what had happened back to Edgar in Bear Creek.

It was a long shot. No doubt the orphanage had changed directors or maybe the woman wouldn't even remember Edgar with all the children she must be helping. But Fran felt she had to try.

She doubted he would appreciate her interference. Knew he would likely hate that she'd done it.

But she would be in Calvin by then, too far away for him to complain to.

She prayed that he would get an answer that would give him some peace. That by knowing with a man's wisdom what he perhaps hadn't seen as a child, he could settle his mind over it.

If he wouldn't let her in, at least she could do this for him.

Now a light tap on the door shook her from her musings.

She cracked the door to find Edgar there, wearing his same cowboy garb, but with his hair and beard damp and his cheeks ruddy, as thought he'd just scrubbed up for supper.

His eyes took her in from the hem of her skirt to the top of her now-shining hair.

"You look…real good in that."

She flushed hot and reached up to touch the back of her hair. It had had to be a simple bun, because she'd lost some of her pins between all their outdoor adventures and had no way to acquire more.

But his appraisal made her feel she didn't look simple at all.

"Thank you," she murmured.

He looked to the room behind her. "Emma ready?"

"She doesn't feel up to going down for supper."

His eyes narrowed. "Is she sick? Didn't she like the dress?"

"I think she's just frightened. Still."

"Seb said she did great with the wagon." His statement seemed more like an argument than a question.

"Well, we're in town now."

She saw a muscle in his jaw tick. She could hear him silently accusing her of coddling her sister. "Tell her to get out here."

"No."

His eyes widened at her refusal.

She lowered her voice, glancing over her shoulder. Emma stood at the window, peeking out from behind the curtain, apparently ignoring them or unable to hear their low voices.

"I've seen how well your high-handedness works with Ricky. You were fighting again this afternoon—"

He inhaled sharply and his eyes darkened. His frown deepened.

She tried cajoling. "Can't you ask one of the cowboys to stay and watch over Emma? Please?"

He looked like he was biting down on his back teeth again. "Fine."

"Fine," she repeated.

The moment hung tense between them. She thought perhaps he might want to kiss her again. But that was silly, wasn't it? Why would fighting make him want to do that?

He stomped down the hall and spoke to the tall cowboy standing at the end. She thought his name was John, but she hadn't learned all the cowboys' names yet.

The other man nodded, and Edgar returned to her. He tilted his chin down and raised his eyebrows, silently asking if she was satisfied.

She was. She took his arm, saying a quick goodbye to her sister over her shoulder.

Emma didn't reply.

Fran bit her lip as she followed him down the hall and past the cowboy, down the stairs to the hotel lobby.

She'd intended to stay compliant, try to convince him to give her a chance. And look how quickly she'd gone back to her quarrelsome self.

But she didn't want to push Emma, not when her sister had seemed slightly stronger after the adventure driving the wagon.

She blinked away thoughts of Emma. Fran should enjoy tonight. It might be her last decent meal in a while.

They descended the staircase and found the hotel restaurant crowded.

"The clerk said all these folks have been delayed by the train," Edgar murmured. "He promised they could seat us, though."

But when they were ushered to a table shared with two other folks, he went pale.

Edgar lost his appetite when the waiter seated him and Fran.

Right up next to RuthAnn Hurst and her daughter, Melody. Edgar knew them from Bear Creek. RuthAnn had thrown Melody at him over and over again a couple years back. The mama hadn't accepted that he wasn't interested in her daughter.

What great companions to have for supper. Sure to make him look even more a fool in front of Fran.

"Good evening," Fran murmured as she settled into the seat.

He could barely take his eyes off her. Her dark hair shone clean and beautiful under the lamplight. And that green dress...looked even better on her than he'd imagined when he'd seen it in the store window.

Mrs. Hurst's eyes widened when she caught sight of Edgar.

"Evening, Mrs. Hurst. Melody," he greeted. He could at least start the evening politely.

"Mr. White." RuthAnn's greeting was devoid of warmth, and her lips pinched white.

But Melody smiled at him. "Hi, Edgar."

A tall man joined the two ladies at the table meant for six. He balanced a toddler on his knee. The kid hadn't had his first birthday yet, judging by the lack of hair and drooly fingers-in-mouth smile.

"My husband, Beau," Melody introduced. "And Beau Jr."

Edgar nodded to the man. Well, good for Melody.

"And my wife, Fran."

He didn't even stumble over the word.

RuthAnn's eyes widened, and her lips seemed to pinch even more. Melody's eyes brightened with curiosity.

Luckily, the waiter interrupted them before RuthAnn could comment.

Fran ordered a potpie and a side of okra. Then she added on dessert. He found himself grinning. He could admire a woman who wasn't afraid to eat. At the White family dinners, the boisterous group often meant a person had to fend for themselves. Something told him Fran would fit right in with his family.

He cut that thought off before it could take him somewhere he didn't want to go.

On his other side, Melody listened to the waiter recite the daily specials.

"I guess I'll have the meat loaf...."

"Are you sure, Mellie?" her mother interrupted. "I've ordered it before and their portion is enormous. More than any one girl needs."

The older woman looked down the side of her nose at Fran, as if she was appalled by his wife ordering dessert.

Fran smiled at him, either ignoring or unaware of the slight. "After three days of trail fare, I'm hungry for a real meal." Ignoring it.

"You've been on the cattle drive *with* the men?" RuthAnn's incredulous gasp didn't seem to affect Fran at all.

He grinned at his wife.

Melody looked at her husband tentatively, but the man was distracted by the wiggling baby now reaching for his mustache.

"All right. I'll have the chicken, then," Melody told the waiter.

Her mother nodded approvingly.

The waiter left and RuthAnn turned on him. Or rather, on Fran.

"How long have you been married to this...cowboy?" she asked, voice falsely saccharine.

"Only a few days," Fran replied, exuding friendliness.

He tried to catch her eye, give her some kind of warning, but she'd turned toward the older woman and didn't see. He didn't know what would be worse—for Fran to admit their plans for the marriage or for word to get out more than it already had about his marriage.

"My Melody here had her cap set for him a couple of years ago."

"Mama!" Melody gasped, looking to her husband. The man seemed only mildly interested in the conversation, still wrestling the toddler on his lap.

Edgar hoped for the husband and the kid's sakes that their food arrived quickly. And that the kid was hungry.

"Until he told her off in front of the whole church. Said he wasn't interested in marrying anybody at all."

"Mama," Melody gasped, her face reddening. "Edgar, I'm sorry." She looked between him, her mama and her husband. Then to Fran. "It didn't happen like that at all."

Fran had her eyes on him. And she seemed to be brimming with mirth, barely holding back laughter.

"As I remember, it was you who had your cap set for me on Melody's behalf," Edgar drawled.

The older woman began to sputter.

"Seems like Melody's done pretty good for herself, though," he went on with a nod to the husband, who seemed content to watch all the drama. Smart man.

"Thank you, Edgar," Melody said. "Beau and I live in Boise and we're very happy. We're up for a visit with mama and were trying to get home on the train."

But RuthAnn wasn't done. She turned all the way to face Fran. "I hope you know what you've gotten yourself into, dear."

Fran's tiny smile was a warning to *him.* "Oh, I know all about Edgar's aversion to women."

"He's an uncouth, rough—" RuthAnn motioned to his head and he assumed his beard "—well, cowboy."

Fran looked at him, letting her eyes linger on his face a little longer than was polite.

Color crept into his cheeks at her intimate perusal.

He remembered vividly the times he'd tried to put her off with his ill manners, things that would've made his ma take him by the ear.

For a split second, he wished he'd tried harder, showed her that the trail boss wasn't all there was to him.

But she only grinned at him. "I'm aware of his faults."

Her look and the smile she extended to the rest of the table conveyed without words that his positive attributes were enough to counter such faults.

It gave him pause. Did she...genuinely like him, even though he *was* uncouth and unkempt, a cowboy down to the bone?

Was she out of her mind?

Their food arrived, piping hot, and RuthAnn was distracted by ordering her daughter around as Melody tried to settle her son enough to feed him.

"You all right?" he asked Fran in a low voice when the others were focused on the young boy.

"Of course." She smiled at him, dazzling him once again. The play of lamplight on her features just enhanced the beauty that was there.

He was hard-pressed to remember why he wanted her to stay in Calvin.

He needed to focus on the job, and then worry about what to do with Fran.

He'd wired his pa's buyer earlier in the day and the man hadn't been sympathetic to Edgar's plight with the train. He'd said if the cattle weren't there on time, the deal was void.

Not good.

And what was Edgar going to do about his brother? He should probably check on the boys, and on Ricky.

But he couldn't muster the energy to leave, not when she kept shining at him like that.

"Melody, not like that," RuthAnn snapped at her daughter as the younger woman struggled with her son, now on her lap.

And got rewarded with a smear of brown gravy across her cheek.

Edgar wasn't much good at reading women, but he knew enough to see that Melody was near tears. Probably more from her ma's fussing and embarrassing her than from dealing with her son.

"Here," he said.

He picked up the tot and plopped him on his own knee.

Beau Jr. looked up at him in amazement, eyes wide and focused on Edgar's face.

"Hullo, little man. You want to give your ma a break? I don't think she's gotten to eat one bite of her food," he said.

He gave the boy a piece of bread from his plate, and the kid squeezed it tightly and started to gnaw on it, mostly drooling all over Edgar's pant leg.

Edgar kept one hand on the youngster, who was wiggly but not any more so than his nieces and nephews or brothers and sister, come to think of it. He ate with his other paw, just like he'd done dozens of times before at Sunday lunch.

Melody and her husband looked on in amazement.

But it was Fran's admiring gaze that he felt acutely as he finished off his plate. Appetite restored.

In the lobby, RuthAnn disappeared up the stairs but Melody and her husband and baby remained.

"I'm sorry about Mother," she said.

Edgar shrugged it off.

She touched Fran's forearm. "I hope you didn't take offense. Everyone around Bear Creek knows the White family, and Edgar is known for his responsibility now that his two older brothers married. He's a fine catch."

Fran's cheeks pinked. "Oh... Thank you."

"Listen," Beau said. "This was the first time in the month we've been down here that Beau Jr. has been calm."

"It's true," Melody said. "I think being around Mother puts him on edge."

Edgar wisely kept his trap shut about that.

"Would it be too much to ask—" Beau started, and then cut himself off.

"Y'all want to take a walk around the town? Let me and Fran watch the kid for a half hour or so?" Edgar asked.

The relief on the man's face was almost comical. "Would you mind terribly?"

"Not at all," Fran said, reaching out for the toddler. He came into her arms easily, reaching for one loose curl that had slipped out of her hairdo and rested on her neck.

Edgar wanted to do the same thing.

He ushered her outside of the noisy lobby.

The evening air cooled her flushed cheeks as they brought little Beau Jr. outside and found a quiet spot at the end of the boardwalk between the hotel and another building.

The little tot seemed enamored with crawling up and down the step. Repeatedly.

"He's getting dirty," she pointed out.

"They didn't tell us to keep him clean," her husband pointed out. "Only to watch him. Besides, little boys need to get dirty every once in a while."

She smiled as he sat on the top step, long legs reaching all the way to the ground. He supported the boy with one large palm as Beau Jr. pulled up, using Edgar's pant leg for support.

"You're good with him," she said.

"Lots of practice." He grinned back at her over his shoulder.

The sight of him sent a thrill of pure joy through her. Imagining him with a child of his own, of their own, sent a pang of longing so close to pain throbbing right through her heart.

"Have you never wanted…children of your own?"

He didn't answer.

She thought perhaps she'd offended him until she saw him staring at a man lounging against the outside of a building across the street, partly hidden by a support post.

"You know that guy?" Edgar asked, voice low.

"No. Why?"

He stood, bringing Beau Jr. and tucking the boy against his side easily, as if he did it every day.

He took her hand and for a moment her heart soared.

Until he said, "He's been watching us since we stepped out of the hotel."

A shiver went through her. Could he be one of Underhill's men?

"He might be trying to figure out where the kid came from. Are you a good little distraction? Are you?"

Edgar's high-pitched baby talk eased her a little. He wouldn't let anything happen to the child. She knew that, knew him.

She could trust him to take care of her.

"What should we do?"

"Nothing. He ain't making any moves. I'd better check with the boys. Where'd your parents get to?" He switched midstream to talking to the little boy again, though his eyes strayed over the tot's head across the street.

"Do you want me to walk down this way a bit—"

He caught her arm before she'd moved an inch. "I want you to stay right where you are."

She was caught in the intensity of his eyes until a feminine voice rang out, "There you are. Beau Jr., were you a good boy?"

Edgar turned to release the toddler to his much more relaxed parents, manufacturing a smile.

He was protecting her. Not only Emma, but her, as well.

There *was* something between them. She knew there was.

Should she tell him about Underhill's accusations? She didn't know if they would hold water this far from Memphis, but she didn't want anything to come between them, not if there was a chance of making this relationship real....

Melody and her husband had barely turned away when Seb came running up the dirt-packed street, dust flying being him. He was red faced, as though he'd been running flat-out.

Edgar stiffened beside her, his arm coming almost naturally in front of her. Protecting her again. "Trouble?"

"Ricky," Seb gasped.

Edgar ushered Fran to the room she was sharing with Emma with barely a peck on the cheek and a squeeze of his hand—not the good-night he'd been hoping for.

He left the girls under John's watchful eye and followed Seb down to the marshal's office, where his brother was in a holding cell with two other men.

Ricky bore the marks of a fistfight, a purpling bruise on his jaw and a scraped cheek.

"What do you think you were doing?" Edgar demanded, stomping right up to the bars.

Ricky got to his wobbly feet. He reeked of alcohol and was decidedly tipsy. Just what they needed.

Seb and Matty came behind Edgar but stayed in the jail doorway.

"Havin' a little fun," Ricky slurred.

"By starting a fight?"

"Didn't start it. Finished it, though." Ricky belched, sending a waft of nasty-smelling hot breath in Edgar's direction. Ricky laughed.

Two others in the cell with him snarled, though neither made a move. One of them clasped a slab of meat over one eye and the other looked completely soaked.

His brothers shuffled their feet, and Edgar looked back to see the marshal thumping his way into the jail, making the small outer room pretty packed.

"We don't take too kindly to rowdy cowboys damaging property," the older mustached man said.

"I understand." Edgar straightened his shoulders, trying to think how his pa would handle this mess. "My brother's sorry—"

"You don't speak for me! I'm right here!" Ricky rattled the bars, his sudden irrational anger bursting forth.

Heat flared in Edgar's cheeks. His temper sparked but he tamped it down, knowing that whatever happened tonight could get back to Bear Creek. Or maybe they'd need to do business in the future here in Tuck's Station. Couldn't his brother think of things like that before he did something stupid like this?

"Shut up," he told Ricky.

"Pa might've left you to run the cattle, but you ain't my pa, and you ain't in charge of me."

Edgar wondered if his brother meant to sound so

childish. It sounded like something a two-year-old would say.

A glance at Seb and Matty showed they were just as flabbergasted and embarrassed as Edgar was. Only Ricky seemed oblivious as he kept rambling on in the cell.

"There's going to have to be restitution," the marshal went on.

"How much?"

The number the man quoted had Seb whistling low. It would eat up pretty much all of the profits Edgar would have made from driving the extra cattle to sale.

"I can take care of myself—" Ricky went on, still slurring his words.

"Yes, and look where it got you," Edgar mumbled, his temper getting the better of his mouth.

Ricky rattled the bars close behind where Edgar stood. "What? What'd you say to me?"

He reached through the bars and took a swipe at Edgar. Of course, the alcohol slowed him down, and Edgar was easily able to duck backward and avoid the hit.

Matty moved in, getting between them to try to calm Ricky down.

"I'm gonna have to hold him overnight," the marshal said.

"He don't care," Ricky yelled, getting loud again.

Edgar's anger snapped. He shoved Matty aside and put his fist through the bars, grabbing Ricky's shirt. "I care what's right. I care about those girls. If one hair on their heads gets hurt because of your foolishness, I'll whip you so good…"

They both seemed to realize what he'd said at the same moment.

He cared about Fran. Not the cattle.

Ricky watched him with a smirk that made Edgar uncomfortable.

His heart pounded loudly in the sudden stillness.

The marshal pulled him away with a hand clapped on his shoulder before he really had time to process what he'd said so thoughtlessly. "What's this about girls in danger?"

An hour later, parked in the hallway outside the girls' room, back to the wall and Stetson over his face, the altercation with his brother replayed in Edgar's head.

How had things gotten so wrong-footed with Ricky? He didn't respect authority. The boy was twenty years old—plenty old enough to be responsible for himself. But he didn't have a grain of common sense in his head.

Ricky could ruin everything. The sale of Pa's cattle.

He'd already ruined Edgar's night with Fran.

He thought back to her face across the supper table. She'd defended him to RuthAnn Hurst. Maintained a lively conversation with the rest.

And when she smiled that intimate smile, just for him…

Even now, his heart started pounding.

Remembering his objections to being married was getting harder and harder.

He hadn't known Fran long. How could he trust someone who had only been a part of his world for a span of days?

She hadn't lied to him. Not once. Not even when she'd been clearly uncomfortable answering the questions he'd asked.

Back at the jail, the marshal had been concerned about the possibility of them being followed. If the men coming after Fran and Emma had had legitimate cause, there would've been some kind of notice to the local law. And there hadn't been.

It had settled something deep inside Edgar. It wasn't exactly a verification that Fran's story was true, but it was close.

Seb had shared that he'd asked around town, as unobtrusively as possible, and found out there'd been a couple of strangers in town the past few days. Not causing trouble, but snooping around.

But the marshal didn't have enough manpower to help them, especially once they moved the cattle out.

If anything happened, they were supposed to let the marshal know. Lot of good that did.

The man hadn't seemed particularly inclined to help them anyway, not after Ricky's bust up at one of the saloons.

What would Fran think? Before supper, she'd challenged him by saying his forceful way with Ricky wasn't working.

Tonight's revelation at the jail had been a shock. Had he been softening toward her all this time?

Was he actually beginning to trust her?

Maybe the next two days on the trail would clarify things for him.

He didn't have to solve everything tonight. He was torn up about Ricky, tired from sleeping on the ground and watching cattle at night.

At the end of the cattle drive, could he really give their marriage a true chance?

He didn't know.

But for the first time…he wanted to try.

Chapter Thirteen

Fran woke to a light tap at the door with a foreboding sense of panic building in her chest.

What had happened the night before? Edgar had never returned to let her know the resolution of Ricky's situation. Or if they'd discovered anything about the man watching them on the street.

It was still dark outside the hotel window.

Another light tap on the door had her out of the warm bed, her feet bare and the plank floor cool enough to jolt her fully awake.

Had Underhill's men found them?

"Fran?"

The surge of relief at hearing Edgar's voice through the wood panel actually brought tears to her eyes.

She blinked them away and cracked the door open.

In the soft lamplight in the hallway, he was a welcome sight, rumpled shirt and Stetson and all.

She tucked her hair, loose down her back, behind one ear and made sure she was hidden behind the door. She didn't have a wrapper after all.

"You girls ready to ride out?"

"What? You just woke me up, and Emma's still

sleeping..." She let her words trail off as she registered the corner of his mouth that had ticked upward. And then she played back his question in her mind. "No railroad?"

"No." Nothing more, just the simple answer.

"Ricky all right?" she asked.

Shadows in his eyes darkened.

She wanted to throw her arms around him. Comfort him. But in her state of dishabille, that would be terribly improper. Even though they were married. Someone could pass in the hall and see.

She settled for a wobbly smile. "I'll wake Emma."

The morning had passed in a blur of rounding up the cattle in the near dark and passing out of Tuck's Station.

They'd left town before the sun had come up. She suspected it was Edgar's way of protecting her and Emma from whoever might be following them.

But it made for a drowsy morning, especially with the bright spring sun glaring in her eyes.

She was glad to take a midmorning break.

Emma had been quieter than ever. She hadn't slept the night before. In their shared bed, Fran had felt her constant restlessness.

She was ready for this to be over. Would Underhill's obsession with Emma never end? What possessed a man to enter such a crazed state?

She waved to Edgar as she stepped down off the wagon. Emma went to take a private moment in some nearby brush, and Fran just walked a bit away from the wagon, stretching the kinks out of her still-sore muscles.

The grass in this area was taller than her knees and dotted with wildflowers. It smelled fresh and springy, and she felt hope for the first time in a long time.

He hadn't made any declarations. But didn't actions speak louder than words? This morning had given her a tiny kernel of hope.

Contemplative, she sat down among the prairie grass, letting the sun warm her shoulders.

Then she thought she'd like to feel it on her face, so she laid down and spread her arms, face turned up to the sky.

It stretched, limitless and blue, like the possibilities before her.

Could she and Emma be happy on a ranch? She thought so. Could Emma find peace? Without a constant shadow over them, Fran was hopeful.

She'd gotten used to the work of a cattle drive. And although the daily chores of a homestead were probably much different, working alongside the cowboys had given her the confidence that she could do what needed to be done.

How would Underhill make his move? He was sly, deceptive, controlling, dangerous. She couldn't trust that he'd given up.

But those worries seemed far away in the warm morning sunlight.

She closed her eyes for a moment and the sunlight shone pink against her closed eyes. Soft shadows— clouds from high above—flickered.

She smiled.

She could be happy here. She knew it.

A shadow fell over her face.

She opened her eyes, raising up on her elbows to face the man standing over her.

"What are you doing?" Edgar's voice revealed his curious confusion.

"Enjoying the day," she retorted, lying back down to

stare up at the puffy clouds against the blue sky. "You've been driving all of us so hard I thought I could take a few moments for myself."

He settled beside her in the grass, heads tucked together, only inches apart. "Tyrant that I am, I'm only giving you two more minutes," he said. He sat his Stetson on his chest.

He took a deep breath. She felt more than saw the motion, as his feet were pointed in the opposite direction of hers, and she couldn't really see his chest.

"How long has it been since you stopped to smell wildflowers?" she asked, genuinely curious. "You haven't stopped working since I met you."

"It's not always so bad," he murmured. "Things around the homestead slow down in the winter months. There's time for reading, games… But in spring there's planting, calves being born, steers to sell…"

They were silent for a moment before he went on. "And I guess my brothers are probably right—I've been working more and not taking time to slow down and have fun like I used to."

"Too afraid some eligible girl might catch your fancy?" she asked, only half teasing.

He snorted. "Didn't stop you," he said, reaching over to tweak her nose.

"Ha." She swatted at his hand, and he captured her fingers. Slowly, he interlaced their fingers, surrounding her hand with the warmth of his larger one. He kept her hand, their clasp resting lightly on his shoulder.

"Just didn't—don't want to let my pa down. With Maxwell gone to medical school and Oscar married, more work falls on him."

"But doesn't your eldest brother still live on the ranch?"

"Yeah, across the valley. But he's busy with his own family."

"And the other brothers? Seems like they're all of age…able to help, take on more responsibility…"

He turned his head, the soft grasses beneath him rustling.

She turned to meet his gaze straight on. From only inches away, the intensity of his blue eyes caught her breath.

"And what of Ricky?" she asked softly. "Maybe he could bear a little more of the load?"

"You're not going to let my excuses stand, are you?" he asked.

"Should I?"

That one corner of his mouth kicked up. "You're intent on turning every cranny of my life inside out, aren't you? The only one who challenges me."

"Only what needs it," she murmured.

He moved toward her and gently kissed her forehead, a brush of his beard against her skin.

She waited for him to apologize, or say the kiss had been a mistake, but none of that came. Was he beginning to soften toward her?

He pushed to his feet and extended a hand to her. She accepted his help to stand and brushed at the few pieces of grass that clung to her skirt.

"I'm not going to get a frog in my supper, am I?" he teased, making her giggle.

She knew they needed to push forward; he'd told her earlier that it was imperative to get the cattle to Cheyenne on time or the buyer would back out of the deal.

But he graced her with a long, level look, showing her some deep emotion in his gaze, before he released her hand and turned to mount up. He waited for her to get into the wagon before he rode off.

Something was changing between them. She could feel it.

If they could get things settled, would she really get the fresh start she wanted? Would Edgar accept her as his wife—for keeps?

That question distracted her for the rest of the afternoon.

Edgar might have gone a little crazy. It was the only explanation for the thoughts swirling through his head all day.

Ricky was hungover and useless. Angry and distant. But thoughts of Fran kept Edgar from being able to maintain an appropriate level of anger toward his wayward brother.

When he'd left Fran after finding her daydreaming in the prairie grass, he'd imagined her sprawled in the spring grasses back at his pa's homestead. With him beside her.

They'd stopped briefly for lunch. All she'd done was hand him a cold biscuit and a thick slice of ham, but when he'd ridden out to spell one of the other cowboys he thought about what it would be like to see her rumpled and with her hair unbound over the breakfast table.

And that distracted him. Matty had to whistle at him, and Edgar realized he'd allowed a whole troupe of steers to escape past him. He spent the next several minutes rounding them back into the main herd and lecturing himself on keeping his mind on task.

Which worked until he started thinking about seeing

her around the supper campfire. Maybe…maybe they could sneak away and he could steal a kiss….

He was on the opposite side of the herd from the chuck wagon when a group of riders thundered over a bluff and into view.

Fear sliced through him, sharp and painful in its intensity. He *must* be falling for her if a threat against her had this powerful an effect on him. The fear was followed by a deep sense of unease.

A sharp whistle to his brother and a wave at the horizon sent Matty—and his brace of pistols—back to the wagon. They'd planned for this. Seb and John also rode toward the wagon as Edgar made his way around the herd.

Although the approaching men didn't seem to be in any hurry—they came on at a steady walk.

Edgar didn't like the numbers. By his count, there were sixteen of them, and twelve cowboys in his group.

Except his cowboys were busy keeping the herd in line.

Without at least a few riders constantly circling, the herd would scatter. If they wandered too far, it could take hours or even days to round them up again.

And he didn't have that kind of time, not with the buyer's deadline looming.

Which meant he couldn't spare many of their twelve to keep guard over the girls, should they need it.

It wouldn't be a fair fight, if lead started flying.

He'd given Fran a pistol to hide in the front of the wagon, but dearly hoped she wouldn't need it to protect her sister.

By the time Edgar thundered up to them, the wagon had rolled to a stop and Fran and Emma stood huddled between his brother and the wagon's scanty protection. The riders neared.

Edgar jumped off his horse, leaving it standing untied behind the wagon. If he or the girls needed to take off, having it unencumbered would be important.

Both girls were whiter than the wagon's canvas cover when he stepped up between them. Fran relaxed infinitesimally as she registered his presence.

"This the Underhill you been worrying about?"

She nodded, mouth pinched tight. "In the middle, on the black horse. I don't know the other men."

The horse was a beautiful animal. Well cared for, with good lines. Obviously expensive. Fran had said this Underhill had money, and riding that animal, it was obvious.

The men around him...not so much. They had the look of cowpokes, unless a body looked closer. Their clothes were in good condition—not worn like the other cowboys he'd been riding with these past few days. Their saddles were tooled and fancy.

They looked like hired guns.

And that he didn't like at all. If the man's purpose was legitimate, why all the firepower? The last thing Edgar wanted to do was put his brothers, or Fran and Emma, in harm's way.

Matty was out in front of the wagon and spoke over his shoulder. "Saw something shiny reflecting from the man on the big bay. Might be a lawman."

He almost didn't hear Fran's soft gasp as Seb said, "Pretty sure the one on the gray dappled is the same man we saw back at Tuck's Station, too."

Edgar let his palm rest on Fran's lower back. "I'm not going to let anything happen to you. Or Emma."

She whispered something under her breath, but he

couldn't make out the words as the riders reined in with a rush of hoofbeats and creaking leather. Had she been praying?

Underhill reined in and smiled evilly.

Chapter Fourteen

Fran couldn't help shivering as Mr. Underhill's cold glare flicked over her and rested on Emma.

"You've brought me on a merry chase, girls."

The man on a huge brown horse slid down. Matty had been right. There was a silver star-shaped badge on his chest. "These them, Mr. Underhill?"

"Yes. That is Fran and Emma Morris."

"What's your business with my wife?" Edgar asked. Steady at her side, a mountain of a man she could count on.

If only she didn't know that Mr. Underhill would do anything in his considerable power to have what he wanted.

Underhill's eyes flashed briefly in surprise. Maybe he hadn't expected her to have married a cowboy.

"These ladies have traveled far from their home in Memphis. I've come to take them back."

Edgar crossed his muscled arms over his chest. "I've heard you're the reason my wife and her sister left Tennessee. Fran, Emma, you want to go back?"

She shook her head quickly, and saw that Emma did the same on Edgar's other side.

Mr. Underhill took a long look around, taking in the cattle now moving on up the hillside, the wagon, the number of men standing around.

"You've got a big herd there. On your way to sell them, I believe?"

Why had he changed the subject? Fran knew his shrewd gaze would miss nothing, but she didn't understand the change in topic.

Edgar nodded slowly.

"It would be a shame to not have enough cowboys to get your cattle where they're going on time."

"You threatening me and mine?" Edgar asked, voice level.

Emma whimpered a little on his other side. He rested a kind hand on her shoulder. Fran could still see her sister shaking.

Fran couldn't help noticing that his other hand rested at his hip, just above the revolver in his belt. Why had she left the gun he'd given her in the wagon?

"Of course not," he said, voice just as calm as Edgar's. Even a little cold.

"Good. Because if you were, I'd want you to know that you might have a few more guns than we do, but that doesn't mean you'd all get away unscathed."

Underhill bared his teeth in a semblance of a smile. "I must confess to being a little surprised Miss Morris has found herself such a…passionate champion."

That made two of them. She hadn't wanted to think about what would happen if Edgar had to stand up for her against Underhill, but now that it was unfolding, she worried for her husband. She knew what Underhill was capable of.

And she'd fallen for the rough-edged cowboy. She loved him.

The realization hit her hard, as if she'd been struck.

It didn't seem possible. She'd only known him for a few days and for most of that time she'd been afraid for her life, on the run, overly emotional.

And he'd been a rock through all of it, steady and unyielding. Someone she could count on for the rest of her life.

She wished she'd seen it sooner. What if she never got the chance to tell him?

What if something happened to him because of her? She couldn't even countenance it.

She must've made some noise of distress, because Edgar looked down on her with a puzzled gaze.

She shook her head minutely, fear and love and distress all entwined inside her.

"I can see you're a man of some intelligence," Underhill said, bringing Edgar's attention back to him.

Edgar grunted.

"So let's talk about just whom you are protecting."

Fran's stomach dipped. He couldn't accuse her...not all the way out here, in Wyoming.

"This is a federal marshal." Underhill motioned to the man with the badge. "He has accompanied me all this way in an attempt to get back something that was taken from me."

Fran knew exactly what it was. Emma.

"No doubt Miss Morris has told you that she and her sister escaped Memphis, running from capture."

Edgar nodded. She watched his eyes scan the men before them, planning, thinking. But he was also listening.

"Did Miss Morris also tell you that she stole a valuable family heirloom from me?"

She flinched. It was the only sign she made that she'd been expecting the accusation, but it was enough.

At her side, Edgar went completely still. She couldn't be sure he was even breathing.

"I didn't steal anything," she said quietly. The words carried over the space between the men and the horses.

But they didn't faze the man beside her.

"She snuck into my home and took a valuable French vase worth at least five hundred dollars."

"I didn't," she argued.

"Then she and her sister ran, attempting to evade the authorities. If the vase wasn't so priceless, I never would've sought them this far, at this expense."

"Where is the vase?" she cried. "Where is the money? I have neither."

She turned to Edgar. Matty and Seb and the other cowboy watched, too. "Why would I have gone on the orphan train if I had five hundred dollars?"

"To escape," said Underhill.

Edgar's unblinking eyes stayed on her face, but she couldn't read him, couldn't tell if he believed her.

With what she knew about his lack of trust in women in general, she didn't know what he was thinking.

"I have proof." Underhill's voice rang with satisfaction. As if he knew he'd won.

No! This couldn't be happening. It was wrong, all wrong. The man was pure evil.

"Where is the proof? It's a lie!" she cried.

"Back in Tennessee. Its very existence is why I was able to persuade this federal marshal to accompany me here to fetch the two of you."

"He's lying." She breathed the words, entreating Edgar with her gaze to believe her. "Please…"

The man with the tin star didn't bat an eyelash. "It

will be up to a judge to decide. I'm to take you into custody now, miss."

And no doubt by the length of time that would take, Underhill would've already had his way with Emma.

"Please," she said again to Edgar. "Don't let him take Emma," she begged.

She couldn't allow Emma to be hurt. She'd come so far, done everything in her power to prevent it. Married a cowboy, traveled all this way under slightly more than primitive conditions, given her heart…

"You said Fran was the one who stole from you," Edgar said, turning away from her to face Underhill. "She and I are married. There's a legal document at the courthouse back in Bear Creek that says so. And that means *Emma* is given into my custody."

Fran's knees threatened to give way, so strong was her relief.

He barely glanced at her. The coldness in his eyes… The warmth she'd seen, what they'd shared earlier in the meadow was gone.

Her heart was breaking.

"You said Fran's the one who stole from you. Then Emma doesn't have anything to do with it. Emma stays with me." With the firmness in his voice, there was no arguing with Edgar.

Some of the men's horses shifted. The marshal looked back at Underhill.

Matty and Seb put their hands on their guns.

"And Fran's my responsibility. I won't turn her over to a gun-toting posse. She ain't that dangerous." His voice was devoid of any humor. "I'll deliver her to the sheriff's office in Cheyenne."

Underhill looked furious.

But he wasn't the one who spoke. It was the federal

marshal. "How do we know you won't run with her? She's a fugitive."

"Well, you could take my word for it. Or you—just you, Mister Marshal—can ride along with our outfit to Cheyenne. In the meantime, we've got a job to do."

His words were dismissive, but Underhill didn't appear to want to let it go that easy.

He marched over to the federal marshal and they conferred in low tones. It looked like he wasn't getting the answer he wanted, as his face reddened and he gesticulated angrily.

Edgar remained a cold stone mountain at her side.

"I didn't do what he said—"

"I don't care," her husband interrupted, voice dead and quiet. "It doesn't matter to me at all." *You don't matter to me at all* was the unspoken meaning behind his words.

Mr. Underhill swung up into his saddle. "I will see you in Cheyenne," he said, his voice a cold promise.

But Fran couldn't even feel the fear she knew she should. Her heart was breaking into a thousand tiny pieces.

Edgar didn't believe her.

After all of this, after she'd told him the truth the entire time they'd been together, his heart was too hard.

Underhill and his cronies thundered over the hillside, scattering part of the cattle. Edgar didn't like the way he'd taken one long hard look at Emma before he'd galloped off.

The marshal stayed behind.

"Edgar?" Seb asked quietly.

He shook his head. He couldn't talk to anyone, not right now. "You stay with the wagon." He leveled his pointer finger at Seb. Seb, who'd gotten him involved in this mess in the first place. Sort of.

"I don't want either of the girls alone for one second. Understand?"

Seb nodded gravely.

Edgar turned to his horse. He told himself he felt nothing. That he was completely numb.

But it didn't help. Pain and betrayal seared through him.

Fran had lied.

Straight to his face. The whole time she'd been with him.

He didn't know about the stolen goods. The way Fran had gone pale and her lack of surprise at Underhill's accusation, plus the fact that she'd kept something so huge from him, was incriminating enough.

If she was innocent, why hadn't she told him from the start?

She tried to talk to him as he moved toward his horse, but he had no capacity for talk right now—not without losing his temper.

How had she fooled him so completely? He, who had been determined to be unaffected by her wiles?

He felt sick, completely sick.

A stone-faced Matty sidled up to him as he made his way back to the herd. "Doubt we've seen the last of Underhill."

Edgar rolled his shoulders beneath his shirt, but the tension in him remained. Maybe it was ingrained so deeply he'd never get rid of it now.

"He seemed too slick. What he said—"

"I don't want to talk about it," Edgar snapped.

He was too raw. He felt as if he was five years old

again, and had just realized that his ma wasn't coming back to get him like she'd said. Disappointed and hurt…

…because he loved her.

What a fine time to realize it. At the same time that his faith in her had been shattered.

Well, emotion didn't have any place on a cattle drive. He had a job to do.

"We've got a job to do," he reminded his brother and himself. "Get the cattle to Cheyenne. That's it."

"Then what?" Matty asked.

"I don't know." He really didn't.

They made camp late, after nightfall. Fran didn't know if Edgar pushed so hard for the sake of his papa's cattle sale, or because he wanted to reach Cheyenne to get rid of her.

She had a guess as to which it was.

He'd stayed away from the wagon the entire rest of the afternoon, although Seb had stayed beside them the whole time. The federal marshal had ridden several paces behind or beside them.

She didn't know what to think about that man. Either Underhill had enough sway back in Memphis to convince the lawman to ride along and apprehend her, or he'd paid off the man. Whatever the case, it didn't bode well for her when they got her in front of a judge. If he could manufacture evidence enough or pay witnesses, she could be convicted of a crime she didn't do.

But at least Emma would come out of this unharmed.

Edgar's refusal to listen, to consider her side of things, hurt. But she knew he'd been in a hurry to get the cattle moving again after facing off with Underhill and his associates.

She held one tiny sliver of hope that he'd be considering things over the afternoon and would at least allow her to explain once they stopped for the evening.

Maybe that made her foolish, but she couldn't give up.

What they'd shared earlier in the day, lying together under the spring sun and simply *being,* was real. It wasn't the passion they'd shared in the stolen kisses— although that was there, too, underneath. It was the *relationship,* the friendship, the togetherness.

That was what she didn't want to lose.

And if she could convince him of it, that was what he needed, too.

Seb had taken over the reins as it got darker, and when Edgar finally called a halt, he guided the wagon into a shallow wash. The grasses were so tall in this meadow that with the wagon hidden in the depression, only the very top of the canvas was visible unless one was so close they were nearly on top of it.

"Edgar says not to use a cook fire tonight," Seb told her in a low voice.

"But what about the cowboys?"

"It'll be hardtack and more cold biscuits." He didn't look thrilled about the prospect, but he winked, obviously trying to reassure her. "We'll be in Cheyenne before you know it and we'll sort all this out. And get a hot meal!"

He hopped out of the wagon and met the marshal several feet away, guiding the other man several more feet as he chatted with him. They were too far for her to hear what was said.

Fran didn't feel good about the man being in their camp, but it wasn't as if she had a choice. At least Edgar hadn't sent her on with Underhill and his men.

A large form approached through the darkness and her heart leaped with simultaneous fear and hope.

"It's me."

Matty.

Her heart thumped once in disappointment. "Everyone okay out there?"

"The cowboys are a little on edge."

"And Edgar?"

He simply shook his head, a frown overtaking his expression.

"I need to talk to him," she said.

He shook his head again. "He's out making the rounds, talking to the others. We'll have a watch on you girls all night."

Between the men she knew would be keeping watch over the cattle, and now this… She guessed none of the cowboys would be sleeping tonight. Guilt surged, but her protectiveness over Emma won out.

"Could you…take me out to him?"

"He wants you girls to stay put."

She'd asked, but couldn't really imagine having such a conversation in front of his brother and her sister anyway.

"Then…is there any chance… Could you ask him to come to me?" She hated that her brother-in-law saw the tears she was fighting to keep at bay. Hated that she had to resort to nearly begging because of her stubborn husband.

"I'll try." Matty gave her a sympathetic smile. "How's Emma?" he asked, with a glance at the canvas.

"Scared," Fran answered honestly. Emma couldn't stop shaking, no matter how much Fran reassured her. She was scared for Fran, panicking at the thought of Underhill taking her away.

Fran hated that the fear had returned to her eyes, wished that there was a way to comfort her sister, but she knew there wouldn't be until this all had ended.

And the way things were going, Fran couldn't see a way to a good resolution for all of them.

Emma's safety was the most important thing.

"Ed said to remind her about the lesson from yesterday morning. He said he'd left y'all a present earlier."

She nodded, reading between the lines to his true meaning. The shooting lesson and the pistol that Edgar had left them before Underhill's appearance. She was a little surprised Edgar hadn't taken it back, but she was glad of the extra protection. She didn't know if Emma could shoot a man, but she thought she could, if her sister's life depended on it.

Matty took his leave, promising to relay her request that Edgar come talk to her.

But he never came.

Chapter Fifteen

"You're being an idiot."

Edgar didn't react to Ricky's statement. He stayed in his squat, bent over his horse's hoof. The animal had picked up a stone in the last few minutes of the day's drive and Edgar needed to remove it and let the horse rest for a while.

"She's up in the wagon, crying. Wants to talk to you," Matty added.

Edgar shifted, edging his shadow out of the weak moonlight. He was working mostly by touch, but he'd asked for no fires, so he was doing the best he could.

He ignored his brother's mention of Fran crying.

"Edgar—"

"I heard you," he burst out, head against the horse's flank. "Aren't you supposed to spell John about now?"

Grass crunched, as though his brother was pacing a circle, but Edgar didn't turn to look. He'd gotten enough accusatory looks from both Ricky and Seb all afternoon. He didn't need one more.

"Edgar—" Ricky started.

"If I was going to take advice, it wouldn't be from you!" he burst out. He couldn't take the both of them ganging up on him.

"You think you know everything!" Ricky countered. "No one else can ever be right—"

"Because that's the way it is!"

Ricky threw a punch.

Edgar caught it in his palm, Ricky's fist smacking against his flesh. His brother's eyes were a little wild, about how Edgar felt right now.

"Right ain't always right," Ricky muttered after a long, hard stare passed between them.

"This ain't solving anything!" Matty exclaimed from behind them.

"What's to solve?" Edgar asked. He turned away, kept his head low, so his brothers wouldn't see the emotion welling up in him. "She lied to me."

"You sure about that? Underhill could be the one lying."

"With a federal marshal along for the ride?"

It seemed preposterous. And if it was an unfounded accusation, why wouldn't she have told him sooner?

Even if she hadn't outright lied, at the very least, she'd omitted some very important information.

He couldn't trust her.

And he obviously couldn't trust himself. She'd grown on him with her noncomplaining attitude, her protectiveness of her sister…but maybe it was all an act. Or maybe she really was willing to do anything to save Emma.

"You talk some sense into him yet?"

The third voice—Seb's—had him on his feet almost instantly.

"What're you doing out here? You're supposed to be with the wagon," Edgar barked.

Both Seb and Ricky looked at him, faces serious,

and he turned away, taking off his hat with one hand and shoving his other hand into his hair.

It just reminded him of Fran, how she'd washed and cut it.

"We know you care about her," Seb said. Low and soft, like Edgar was some flighty filly to be brought around by gentle speech. "Kinda hard not to notice."

"I don't want to," he growled.

"You can't just let them take her away," his youngest brother pushed.

"She says Underhill wants Emma. If that's true, then he doesn't have any reason to push for her to be incarcerated." Unless she really had stolen from him.

"You're gonna make that gamble? What if he gets so mad about being thwarted that he tries to punish her?"

"I don't know!" he thundered, spinning to face his brothers. "I don't know anything anymore. She's got me all mixed up and turned around!"

He threw up his hands and his Stetson went flying into the night.

"We started out four days ago with a job to do. We've still got to get the cattle to Pa's buyer. *That's* what I want to focus on."

Cattle were easy, even if it was going to be a challenge to get them to the buyer on time.

Cattle didn't tie him up in knots, didn't turn everything from black-and-white to gray.

Or rainbow colored, like looking at the sun behind closed eyes.

"Will you please go back to the wagon?"

Seb considered him for a long moment. Finally, the younger man crossed his arms across his chest. "No."

"What?"

"I'm not going. If you want to make sure Fran and Emma are protected, you go."

He turned to Matty, but found no help there. Ricky was trying to hide a faint smile behind one hand but not succeeding.

"I guess you're not going, either," he said, disgusted with their maneuvering.

"I'll just get one of the other hands to do it," he threatened.

Seb shrugged. "If you want to be that big of a coward. She's just one woman. Nothing to be scared of."

"A woman who wants to talk to him," Ricky threw in. "That can make for a dangerous creature indeed."

Edgar wasn't laughing. Neither was Ricky.

He wasn't up to seeing Fran. He was afraid she would be able to convince him of her innocence and convolute his thinking.

But he couldn't leave Emma unprotected, either. He'd made a promise.

Fran clutched the pistol in the folds of her dress, sitting awake in the dark.

Seb hadn't come back, and neither had Ricky.

Beside her, beneath the canvas wagon cover, Emma was wide-awake, too. Fran couldn't see her, but she could hear her sister's near-panicked breathing.

"How come one of them isn't back yet?"

But what Fran heard was her sister's fear. Fran reached out a hand in the darkness and Emma clasped it painfully.

"Edgar promised to take care of you," Fran said. "And I trust him."

Because she still did, even if he let Underhill take Fran. He'd given his word.

"Well, I don't!"

The vehemence in Emma's voice surprised Fran. "What?"

"When you married him, he promised to take care of *you*. If he lets that Mr. Underhill and that marshal take you, he's breaking a promise."

The sound of Emma's soft sobs prompted Fran to tug her closer and put her arms around her younger sister.

"Oh, Emma. God's going to work all this out." She had to believe it. Otherwise what had all her effort been for? "He must've put Edgar right in our path, and must've surrounded us with all these cowboys for something, don't you think?"

Emma quieted. "I don't know."

"Well, I do."

And thinking like that made Fran realize something else, too. What if God had put her in Edgar's path for a purpose? To open his heart from those wounds of his past?

She held Emma until the girl quieted, and then left the weapon with her sister.

She had to talk to Edgar, now, tonight, even if it meant saying her piece in front of his brother.

Hopping onto the wagon seat, she hissed, "Ricky! Seb! Matty!"

There was silence, but she had an awareness that she wasn't alone. There was someone out there. Why didn't they answer?

"Ricky!" she called again, this time a little louder.

She stepped out of the wagon into the waist-high grasses, intent on finding whoever was out here and making them take her to see Edgar.

"I know you're there! Matty!"

Grasses rustled, and for a moment she was frozen with fear. What if she'd gotten it wrong and it was one of Underhill's men?

"It's me."

Edgar came out of the darkness, the moon's weak light falling on his broad shoulders and illuminating his Stetson, leaving his face in shadow.

"Oh. Good."

He looked ominous in the moonlight, tall and unapproachable. "What's the matter?"

She swallowed the lump of fear and emotion that seemed lodged in her throat. "I need to talk to you."

"You should get back in the wagon. Get some rest."

Unspoken, his message was that she could talk, but he wouldn't listen.

He took her elbow in a very impersonal way and turned her back toward the wagon, but she dug in her heels. They were only feet away, she didn't want Emma to overhear everything that was said.

"Do you really think I'll be able to sleep?" she asked.

He let go of her elbow and moved back a step. Distancing himself from her.

"There are others around, keeping a lookout over you and Emma." His voice was cold, distant.

As if he'd already cut himself off from all emotion concerning her.

Tears burned the back of her throat.

"Not because of that," she said, and had to clear her throat to try to dislodge the tears.

"You said, more than once, that I've turned your life upside down. Did you never stop to think that maybe God put me on that train in Wyoming for just that reason? It wasn't a coincidence that we met and married—"

"No, it was a mistake." He'd gone tense, muscles taut. Closed off to her.

"No, it wasn't," she breathed, tears now blurring her vision.

"It should never have happened. I should've found some other way to fix things back in Bear Creek."

She shook her head, held on to her middle with both arms. She took a shaky breath, and she knew he heard it because he shifted his feet as if he was uncomfortable.

She wished she could see his face so she could better tell if he was just pushing her away or if he really had completely shut off his emotions.

"I never lied to you." She said the words as softly and levelly as she could. "Underhill is the one lying about me."

He didn't answer, staying distant in the dark.

"You can say what you want, but I know what really happened," she said. "I got too close, didn't I? You've kept yourself isolated out here on the ranch. You claim to want independence, but I think you've really been hiding all these years."

He flinched as if she'd struck him.

She went on, "You were so hurt by what happened in your childhood that you didn't want to let anyone come close again, so you made excuses. You claimed not to trust women, claimed you never wanted to marry... All because you were afraid of falling in love."

"What—"

She interrupted him this time, pushing on his chest with the force of her emotion.

"You're afraid of letting me in—and that's a fool thing to be, because I'm here and I'm..."

She stopped.

She'd almost blurted, "I'm in love with you."

But she couldn't give that to him, couldn't declare her love when he was standing stone still, silent, determined not to let her in.

"I won't hurt you," she said instead.

And she waited.

He assessed her in silence, for a long time, and she began to hope…

But he only said, "I've got to spell John with the cattle. Seb will be here shortly. Tell Emma to keep that weapon close. I don't want any surprises."

And gave her a nudge toward the wagon.

She was blinded by tears as she fumbled her way into the covered space.

Emma was there, holding on to her. Comforting her. She should have been doing that for her younger sister instead.

She didn't have any hope left. Edgar had taken it all with his callousness, with his refusal to believe that she was more than her circumstances.

What now?

Emma would have her happy ending, but for Fran only darkness remained.

Edgar made his way back to his horse, chest hot like he had a spike of fire through his sternum.

There was a reason he'd wanted to be far away from Fran.

Seeing her tears, her face white in the moonlight, pleading…

It was enough to give a man permanent heartburn.

How could he trust a woman like her? He couldn't. Running away made her look guilty. The presence of the federal marshal compounded it.

If she was innocent, why all the hullabaloo?

He knew the story of how the insane man who'd become obsessed with Penny had attempted to get Penny's pa out of the way and tried to kidnap her as well, but what if this situation wasn't the same?

He didn't know anymore.

And he had a job to do.

He passed Seb on his way to the wagon to guard the girls. Edgar would spell John, and at least two of their guys could get an hour or so of rest.

Edgar wouldn't sleep anyway.

The cattle were edgy, restless when he took a slow circle around the herd. He ranged out farther but didn't come across any of Underhill's men.

Then a bunch of coyotes started yipping off in the distance and he thought that was probably what had the cattle spooked. It didn't take much.

He warned the other riders, and then spelled John. He ground tied his horse and walked a bit, swinging his arms to create some warmth in the cooling night air.

The girls would be all right.

He'd take Emma home to his ma and…then what? How would he explain that he had a wife but she was in custody of a federal marshal, awaiting trial?

His ma would not be happy.

And she would probably demand he go down to Tennessee and see what had happened with the trial.

He thrust a hand through his hair.

His own decency would demand he go after her. Even if he didn't want her in his life, he would have to finish it.

He'd promised to get her a start, hadn't he? He was man enough to provide at least that for her.

His horse nickered and he turned. In the dark, he could barely make out the form of his animal. He'd wandered farther than he'd thought, just like his thoughts.

He had one job to do. One.

Get the cattle to Cheyenne. He could worry about his wife and all the trouble following her after that point. Whether that meant going to Tennessee or staying here with Emma for now, he didn't know.

He couldn't think about the things she'd accused him of—using his pa's ranch as a place to hide.

It rankled.

Mostly because his brothers had said the same thing.

He wasn't a coward.

Was he?

Between all the emotion of the day and knowing Underhill was somewhere close by, Fran couldn't sleep.

Judging by Emma's rapid breathing, she wasn't sleeping, either.

"It feels like we're too exposed in this wagon," Fran whispered.

"I know."

Fran sat up. "If we aren't sleeping anyway, maybe we should just be out with the cowboys."

Rustling came from Emma's side of the wagon bed and she popped up. "Can we?"

They scrambled to find their shoes in the dark. And Fran had an idea.

"Do we still have Seb's trousers and shirt?" she asked.

There was a long pause before Emma responded. "I think so. Why?"

"You should put them on. If the men are looking for you, it could make a difference to what they see in the dark."

Emma didn't argue with her, which told Fran the depth of her fear. It was a struggle getting her dress off and the trousers on in the dark confines of the wagon bed.

Fran helped her pin her hair as closely to her head as she could and then they were ready.

Fran stuck her head out of the canvas first. "Seb? Ricky?" Somehow, she knew Edgar would've left.

No answer.

Had they fallen asleep? Or ridden farther out?

Or worse, had they detected a threat?

Sudden fear, real and physical, lodged in her throat.

"Emma!" She barely breathed the name, and was relieved to the point of tears when her sister appeared at her elbow.

They clambered out of the wagon as silently as they could. Two dark forms, larger than men, moved in the grass nearby. The horses, unhitched from the wagon and ground tied.

"Let's ride out," she whispered to Emma.

"But—"

"It'll be quicker."

"But there aren't any saddles. And the horses are huge."

She was right on both counts, but the increasing urgency Fran felt had her tugging her sister toward the animals.

There was a rustling behind them, close to the wagon. Fran's heart pounded in her ears, drowning out their footsteps, making her strain to hear.

If it was one of Edgar's brothers or one of the cowboys, why hadn't they called out? Surely they would know she and Emma were frightened and seek to reassure them.

The only answer was that it wasn't one of Edgar's men. It had to be one of Underhill's.

Fran pulled Emma to the nearest horse. She reached out to touch the animal's shoulder and it neighed softly. She didn't dare whisper a greeting to the horse.

It took one step away from Fran.

Edgar had told her the animal could sense fear—no doubt it was picking up the chills that were running through her that very moment.

But they didn't have time for her to comfort the animal.

Fran made a cradle out of her hands to boost Emma onto the animal's back.

"Fran!" Emma squeaked.

"Shh!" she hissed.

The trousers made it easy for Emma to straddle the animal's wide back, but Fran knew well how awkward it felt.

She curled her sister's hands around the horse's mane, barely able to reach.

"Hold on tight," she breathed.

"They ain't here," a man's voice said quietly.

Fran scrambled to where the horse was tied. Her hands shook so badly that she couldn't get a good grip on the leather ties. And in the darkness, she couldn't see what she was doing.

"Please, God." She whispered the fervent prayer, unable to find words but hopeful that He understood her urgency, her fear for Emma.

If Underhill took her, Fran could lose Emma forever.

The ties loosened, and Fran flipped the leather reins over the horse's back.

"Fran!" Emma cried softly.

"They've got to be here somewhere." That was another growly male voice, not one Fran recognized.

The grass rustled, getting closer. She was out of time to spirit Emma away.

"You've got to go," she told her sister.

"Not without you."

She attempted to reach to the horse's back, but her

foot caught in her skirt and there was no way she could pull herself up on the large animal without help or a stepping block.

"Emma, go!"

She slapped the horse's rump at the same moment that a yellow square of lamplight shone on them, lighting Fran's form and the horse's backside.

Blessedly, Emma remained in shadow as the horse thundered away into the night. Fran prayed it ran fast and right to Edgar.

"Hey!" an unknown male voice called out.

She lifted her skirts and ran. The long grasses clung to her.

She could hear the loud huffs of someone, several someones, following her.

There was nowhere to hide. In the open prairie, there were no trees or bushes.

She was disoriented, trying to remember in which direction the cattle were located.

She dared not call out. What if Underhill's men had done something to Edgar and the cowboys? If she made too much noise, it would be a beacon for the men behind her to find her.

Her breaths came in gasps. She tried to stifle them, trying with all her might to be silent as she ran through the night.

"Get her!" came a shout from behind—closer than before?

Could she just lie down in the grass? What would keep the men from finding her?

She kept running, desperate.

Where were Edgar's cowboys? Surely she should have run right into them by now.

Lungs burning, mind spinning, she cried out when someone grabbed her arm and twisted it brutally.

"Gotcha now, girl," said an angry, huffing voice.

She struggled, jerking and kicking and spitting. Trying everything she could to get away.

She connected with something—the man's shin, maybe?—and his hold loosened. She ripped her arm away and tried to run again, but smacked into a hard body. A second man.

She screamed as loudly as she could.

Until a dirty hand clapped over her mouth. "No one close enough to hear ya, missy," said a smooth, cold voice.

She struggled again, but it was no use. One of them cruelly yanked her arm behind her back, sending a spike of pain up through her shoulder and making her cry out, the sound muffled behind the hand blocking her breathing.

"She ain't going nowhere," the man holding her grunted. "What about the other one?"

"She wasn't at the wagon. Abe thought he saw a boy rushing away on a horse. Hard to see in the dark."

"Let's go see if Abe caught up to the kid, then."

Fran struggled frantically as they dragged her back toward the wagon.

Thoughts screaming, she couldn't find air and the edges of her vision began to blacken.

Emma. Did Emma get away?

Chapter Sixteen

The sky was slate gray when Edgar startled awake.

In the swirling haze between sleep and consciousness, he'd remembered the wedding vows he'd spoken to Fran days before. He'd promised to honor her and comfort her.

And to love her.

He wasn't a man to break a promise.

The shock of the realization—what he'd promised all those days before—held him immobile, leaning back against the large, flat rock he'd found in the night.

He hadn't meant to fall asleep, not with the threat of Underhill's men hanging around.

Now, trying to shake the sleep from his noggin, his promise from their quick wedding service stuck in his mind, stuck in his craw.

He'd said he would love her.

And he did.

He loved her.

No matter that she might be a fugitive from the law or might've omitted something important the whole time he'd known her. None of that kept his emotions in check.

None of it kept his heart safe.

He already loved her.

She'd challenged him to be more than his past.

And he'd pushed her away.

From the start, she'd done more than he'd asked of her, even when what he was asking—like driving a team all day—was difficult for her.

She'd done everything she could to protect her sisters.

And wouldn't he have done the same? He'd pitched that snake out into the night to keep it from even having a chance to bite Seb.

Would she be able to forgive him for not listening to her the night before, when she'd come to him?

He would imagine so.

Because unlike him, when bad things happened to her, like her parents' death or her brother's abandonment, she hadn't shut down. Somehow she'd kept her heart open for a big lug like him.

He was astounded by what she'd given him, even if she hadn't said the words.

He had to go to her.

He pushed himself off the ground, heading for his horse a few feet away. He'd left the animal saddled in case there was trouble in the night.

He was a little surprised that things had been quiet. He'd half expected Underhill to attempt something— either against the cattle or with the girls.

And then he registered the silence.

It was almost eerie in its totality.

No cowboys whistling. Not even a cricket chirping or a whippoorwill calling. The cattle were still, as if they were poised on the edge of…

Shots fired broke the early morning stillness and startled him.

His horse nickered and bobbed its head, but didn't bolt.

Unlike the cattle.

They scattered.

He heard several surprised shouts from the other cowboys, but didn't have time to dwell on it.

Several steers headed right for him and he jumped into the saddle, quickly guiding his horse to join them.

They jostled him until he was sure his leg was bruised. He gripped the horse with his thighs, fighting to stay on. Then he gained his seat and his horse got a burst of speed. He got in front of them far enough to look behind.

The cattle had gone in all directions, and he caught glimpses of the other cowboys riding along, trying to guide them into one cohesive group. Without much luck.

The largest group of cattle was headed to the east. Without anyone out front to try to turn them.

His stomach dropped, and fear coalesced in his veins.

Those cattle were headed straight for the wagon, where Fran and Emma were.

He hesitated.

Among the cattle like he was, he couldn't turn his horse too sharply. If a steer plowed into the side of his animal, they'd both go down and be trampled.

He urged his horse in that direction as best he could, fighting through the cattle.

It was like riding through molasses. Like trying to swim across a raging river.

Nearly impossible.

He started praying that the girls had been awake, had heard the thundering hooves and had somehow known to get on one of the draft horses. If they could stay on the horse long enough for it to outrun the cattle, they might have a chance....

But then he remembered they were city girls. What if they'd thought the noise was a thunderstorm? After the last disaster, would they even stick their heads out of the canvas wagon cover to see?

Fran was smart. He had to remember that, to think positively.

They were going to survive this.

He kept pushing his horse, fighting through the cattle, but he could tell it was a losing battle.

Then he caught sight of Ricky doing the same from the opposite direction. Ricky was a little closer.

But the first of the cattle were also closing in on the wagon.

Edgar couldn't see any movement around the wagon. Where were the girls?

The horses weren't where they had ground tied them the night before.

Had the girls managed to escape somehow?

Or had the animals panicked and managed to tear their ties from the ground, only saving themselves?

Fear and desperation drove him to push his horse too hard. The animal stumbled, and Edgar desperately tried to right the both of them.

To no avail.

He cried out as his horse went down, surrounded by the horde of racing beasts.

"The big one went down."

The man with the binoculars spoke, his voice slightly muffled.

With her hands tied in front of her and sitting on the

horse behind one of Underhill's men, Fran could only see some of the cattle racing around.

At the man's words, everything went perfectly still and silent.

The big one?

Edgar?

She could see the other men's mouths moving, knew the stampede must still be unfolding in the slight valley below them.

She couldn't hear any of it.

Edgar had fallen? In the midst of the stampede?

Could he survive that?

She didn't know, and the fear and desperation choked her. She closed her eyes, praying for Edgar, praying for Emma—the men, including the federal marshal, hadn't found her in the dark, and Fran could only hope she'd reached one of the cowboys or was far, far away.

Edgar couldn't be gone. She hadn't had a chance to tell him what she should've told him the night before. That she loved him.

She'd chickened out because he'd distanced himself from her and because he'd been right—she should have told him about Underhill's accusation from the start.

If she had, would they have gotten to this point? Would Edgar still be hurt—or worse? Emma lost and alone?

She didn't know.

The horse shifted beneath her and she struggled to keep her balance with her hands bound.

"Let's get her back to the boss," one of the men said.

She ducked, hoping that her unbound hair obscured her face enough for them to think she was Emma. The longer they went without chasing after her sister, the safer Emma would be.

* * *

Edgar shoved to his feet, trying to shake off the jarring sensation of falling.

The horse had stumbled, and they'd both gone down, but blessedly, the animal seemed to be okay.

It struggled to its feet, eyes rolling and white around the edges, head raised in fear.

"Easy, boy," he said, loud enough to be heard over the thundering hooves.

A steer brushed by, close enough to knock into Edgar's shoulder. He staggered.

Kept his feet by sheer force of will.

He had to get to Fran.

The horse seemed to know the danger they were in—if they didn't get up, they could be killed.

Edgar waited as the animal pushed to its feet and then threw his leg over its back.

They were moving again, Edgar feeling that he'd be battered and bruised tomorrow morning.

It didn't matter.

He had to get to Fran.

He pushed his horse, edging toward the wagon.

He could see cattle crashing over where the wagon had been.

Heart in his throat, he wondered if they'd survived. They had to. He had unfinished business with Fran.

Ricky got close enough to take a look and shouted back to him, waving his hat.

That was either good or bad.

Edgar quit fighting the herd and spurred his horse.

He passed one of the rangy beasts. Another.

He kept going, even though his eyes blurred with emotion, and sweat poured into them and stung.

He kept pushing, because he had no choice.

An eternity passed, watching the backs of the steers, until he edged out in front. Looking to the side, Ricky had done the same.

There were two ways to stop a stampede. Wait for the cattle to tire themselves out, or get out in front and lead them in a circle.

Edgar and Ricky signaled each other and started turning the herd back to the south. It took time.

Time they didn't have.

But the other choice was to let the cattle run and possibly hurt themselves, possibly damage homes or other people who might be out on the prairie.

Soon Matty, John and Chester joined them, pushing the cattle into a tighter and tighter circle, until they didn't have anywhere else to go and had to stop in a tight bunch.

Edgar took off his hat, waving it in front of his face to cool the sweat from his brow. Ricky untied a handkerchief from around his neck and mopped his face.

"You all right?" Ricky asked. "Thought you were a goner. Nasty spill you took."

"You fell?" Matty asked.

Edgar rolled his shoulders. "I'll be sore in the morning. What about the girls?"

Ricky shrugged, mouth tight. "Wagon was smashed to bits by the time I got there."

Heart thundering, Edgar wheeled his horse. He trusted the other cowboys to take care of the cattle. He had to see for himself what had happened to the girls.

Ricky and Matty trailed him.

"What of Seb?" Edgar called over his shoulder.

"Dunno. He was on last watch with the girls. Didn't see him with the cattle, either."

Edgar had hopped off his horse even before they'd

reached the wagon. Ricky was right—the wagon was crushed. One side had been completely obliterated; the other was in large pieces. Remains of food were mixed with grass and mud.

There was no sign of the girls.

Heart in his throat, Edgar turned over the largest piece of the wagon—part of the bottom panel. He was afraid of what he would find beneath, but only found hoofprints and smashed grass. No blood.

"They're not here," he said. "They're not here." Repeating the words sent a wave of relief spiraling through him. Sharp and painful and joyful enough to cover his eyes with the sheen of tears.

Fran was still alive. Somewhere.

"You all right? You got pale all of a sudden," Matty observed.

"Yeah." He turned in a circle, scanning the horizon. "Any sign of the draft horses?"

Ricky took a turn looking around. "I haven't seen 'em since last night when they were tied by the wagon. What're you thinking?"

"The girls have got to be somewhere," he said. "Either they got on the horses and escaped—"

"Or Underhill and his men have got them."

Edgar went to his horse, grabbed his rifle. "You thinking the stampede was meant to be a diversion?"

"Could be." Matty shoved back his hat.

Ricky had been quiet and serious since they'd gotten back to the wagon.

The morning sun was bright and warm on his shoulders. Edgar's mind spun, trying to determine the best course of action.

He was a planner, someone who looked at every angle before he acted.

But if Underhill had the girls, he didn't have time to plan. If the man had caused the stampede to delay Edgar from following him, he could already have a lead on them.

And where was Seb?

Where were the horses? If they tracked down the horses, would they find the girls?

In the midst of his mental scrambling, a shrill whistle brought his head up.

There was Seb, leading one of the draft horses by its reins. Riding double with another hand.

Except as they got closer, he saw that the second person had long dark hair cascading down her back and was clinging to his brother, obviously not comfortable on the horse.

His heart began to race and he found himself running toward his brother.

Only to be disappointed.

Seb's passenger was Emma.

Then he saw the dark stain on the side of Seb's face and jaw, running down onto the shoulder of his shirt. Blood.

Edgar's heart pounded. Seb had been hurt.

"They've got her!" Emma cried out before Seb had brought the horse completely alongside the three men.

"Who's got her?" he asked, knowing before she even said what he knew was coming.

"Underhill's men. They came in the night—"

"What happened?" he asked his brother, helping Emma off the horse.

"They got the jump on me. That marshal hit me over the head," Seb said. He was obviously upset, jaw tight with emotion. "I'm sorry."

Edgar squeezed his brother's knee briefly. "I'm due

my share of blame. I fell asleep. We've all been exhausted from pushing these cattle. We've been on edge the past two nights. It's not your fault."

Seb shook his head, jaw still tight.

"Are you all right?" Edgar asked. He held Seb's gaze until his brother nodded tightly.

Edgar knew his brother would get over it eventually—especially when they got Fran back.

"Start at the beginning," Edgar said to Emma. "What happened last night?"

The girl was shaking. He took her hands and had her sit down on the grass before she fell down.

He squeezed her hands gently. "Can you tell me? We need to know what we're riding into."

"Fran and I were scared in the wagon. We...we couldn't tell if any of you cowboys were close by...."

Seb grunted and shifted, his horse shifting with him.

Emma sniffed. "And Fran got this idea to ride out to you. She said since we couldn't sleep anyway, we could be awake with the cowboys!"

Edgar found the corner of his mouth turning up, even with the fear and desperation filling him. That sounded like Fran.

"We still had the trousers and shirt, so she made me put them on, just in case...."

He squeezed her shoulder when she started to break down.

"And we sneaked out, got to the horses...and there was noise behind us and voices...not you..."

She could barely get words out now, sobbing into her hands.

"Calm down," he said, rubbing her back. "We're going to get her back."

"She got me up on the horse and slapped it. I can't ride! I was so scared—"

"That's about when I came to," Seb said tightly. "Somehow I hung on to the horse, didn't go down. Then her horse must've run past me. The rush of air about knocked me out of the saddle. I took off after it, not knowing who it was."

"I couldn't make it stop. It just kept running."

"But you did a good job of staying on," Seb told her.

She just shook her head, dissolving into sobs.

"I lost them in the dark, had to wait until it lightened up a little to follow the tracks. The horse was tucked up next to the creek, winded and worn-out. And she was still clinging to him like a burr on a dog's butt."

"Good job." He hugged Emma again from the side, the same way he would've hugged Breanna if it had been her.

"But…but they've got Fran," Emma gasped. "You've got to get her back—"

"We will."

He had no other option. Fran belonged to him.

And she would expect him to comfort Emma. "But she wanted you safe. That was important to her. And it's important to me."

She quieted, staring into his eyes. He did everything he could to return her gaze levelly. He'd promised her sister his protection from the beginning. He wouldn't shirk that duty now.

"I want you to stay with her," he told Seb. "Until you get back to Tuck's Station, ride as fast as you can. Bring the town marshal and any men you can round up to help us. And settle Emma with the preacher."

"What about the cattle?"

Yes, what about them? They'd come this far, pushing

the men past their endurance, endangering his wife…
all so he could make the buyer's deadline.

"There's a box canyon about a quarter mile west of
here. I remember passing it on a drive with Pa several
years ago. Have John and Chester drive them into it,
then come after us."

He went to his horse and mounted up. "We're going
after her."

He looked to Ricky. "I need you. Everything else
between us can wait. Are you with me?"

By the time Matty and Ricky rounded up the other
cowboys, Edgar realized they had a major problem.

The cattle had scattered in all directions before
they'd gotten them under control, and the hoofprints of
that many stampeding cattle had obliterated any tracks
from Underhill's men.

Smart.

It forced them to waste time ranging out to find the
real tracks.

Edgar worried for Fran. What would Underhill do
when he realized he'd captured her instead of Emma?

They were running out of time. He knew it.

A single shot brought his head up. Ricky. On a bluff
within sighting distance. Must be about a quarter of a
mile away.

He must've found the tracks they were all looking
for.

Edgar kicked his horse into a gallop, noting that the
other cowboys were making for Ricky's location, too.

Before he'd gone half the distance to his brother,
a lone rider coming from the wrong direction caught
his gaze.

Edgar's hand went to his rifle by instinct, and he went to meet the man.

He got close enough to see that the man rode like a city boy. The horse wasn't any kind of decent. Seller probably took him for a ride. He was pale, not like he'd been surprised, but like he was sick.

And his dark hair and features were familiar.

"Hallooo!" Edgar hailed the man.

The man reined in the horse—badly—and his hand went to his waist. Armed.

"I'm looking for a pair of young women," the dark-haired man called out. "My sisters."

His familiar features suddenly made a lot more sense. "You Daniel?"

The man's shoulders relaxed the slightest bit. "You seem to know who I am," the man said. "Might I have the pleasure…"

Edgar took off his hat. Took stock of himself. Hair, tangled and matted from his hat and the wild ride that morning. Beard, too long. Clothes, trail dusted and well worn.

He didn't look like much.

"I'm Edgar White. Riding with my brothers and some other cowboys. I'm Fran's husband."

The brother looked surprised. "I understood she and Emma only came West several days ago. How did you come to marry her? Have you taken advantage of my sister?"

Edgar supposed he deserved that suspicion, but he had a little of his own. "I understood you abandoned the both of them. What do you care that she's in trouble now?"

Daniel's face took on the look of a thundercloud. "Is that what she told you?"

Edgar shrugged. "In as many words." Although Fran had been more worried about what had happened to her brother than anything else.

Daniel suddenly coughed. And couldn't stop. He hacked and hacked, nearly unseating himself from the horse. If the horse hadn't been so old and uninterested, it might've taken offense, but as it was, it stood still, grazing on some of the grasses in front of its feet.

Finally, the cough stopped. Daniel took a white kerchief from one pocket and dabbed at his mouth.

The violent cough had brought some color to his cheeks, but he still looked peaked.

"I've been ill."

Edgar could believe it, judging by the other man's pallor. "All right now?"

Daniel nodded, still looking as if he could vomit or fall from the horse. "Where are my sisters?"

"Emma is with one of my brothers. Riding back toward Tuck's Station."

The other man didn't look particularly happy that she wasn't right there. "And Fran?"

"It's complicated."

The suspicion returned to Daniel's face. "What do you mean?"

Edgar's horse shifted beneath him, reminding him of the urgency of the situation. "Ride along, and I'll explain," he told Daniel.

By the time they reached the other cowboys, Daniel had been filled in and seemed angry at both Underhill and Edgar.

Edgar didn't blame the man.

"What's going on?" Edgar asked as they joined the other cowboys.

John, the best tracker among them, stood over a spot

on the ground. "Looks like several of them convened here and stood for a while. Maybe right after those shots scared the herd into a stampede."

"Can you tell which direction they went?" Edgar asked. His horse was fairly dancing beneath him, reading Edgar's anticipation of the chase.

"Yes, that way," John pointed.

"What's the plan?" Ricky asked.

The other cowboys looked to Edgar for direction, and even Daniel seemed ready to defer to him. Seemed like the city boy didn't really know how things were out there in the West.

"I don't have a plan," Edgar admitted. "I just have to get her back."

Underhill had not been happy to see her.

Fran sat silently among the tall grasses, hands bound before her, head down. She pretended the prairie could hide her, would keep her safe until Edgar came. She knew he would, if he was alive.

She listened to everything.

Underhill's men had left the overlook shortly after their exclamation that Edgar had gone down amongst the stampede.

Surely he'd survived. Surely God wouldn't have let him die like that.

Not without giving her time to tell him she loved him.

She needed to keep her head, and figure a way to escape Underhill and his men.

Her only comfort was that they hadn't found Emma.

"She can't have gone far," Underhill argued now. "She was with them up until nightfall, right?"

The federal marshal nodded, shifted the cigar he was chewing to the opposite side of his lips.

He was in on it. That had been a surprise to Fran as the sun had come up. Underhill must've paid him off. Or maybe he wasn't even a real lawman, she didn't know.

But knowing that he'd been collaborating with Underhill and apparently had assaulted Seb just made Fran angry.

And made her escape more urgent.

"Somebody got away on a horse, just before we grabbed *her*," one of the other men reminded them all.

Underhill glared at her, but Fran simply turned her head on her bent knees and stared out at the horizon.

"You think the cowboys are still hiding her?" asked another of the men. "We've got more guns than them. Let's go back and get her."

Underhill shook his head. "We can get away with taking one girl back to Tennessee for trial. If we murder several men...someone will notice."

"What if they come after her?" another of the men asked, motioning to Fran.

If Edgar was alive, and did come after her, he wouldn't bring Emma, would he? He'd promised to protect Emma, and that would be bringing her right into the hornets' nest of danger.

Would he even care enough to come after her?

She didn't know.

And that was why she was doing her best to get herself out of this situation.

She'd worked at the knots behind her hands. Her skin felt chapped and raw beneath the rough ropes, but she had managed to loosen the bonds somewhat.

One problem was that she had to make sure Underhill or his men didn't notice.

She'd also been unobtrusively attempting to gauge their surroundings. They'd convened near a wooded area. She thought if she could somehow get away from the men, she might have a chance in that direction. The trees were close together and it wouldn't be easy for horses to move through them, meaning the men would be forced to chase her on foot.

But she wasn't sure she was faster than them, especially hampered as she was by a skirt.

Other than the wooded area, there was open prairie all around, which meant the men would be able to run her down on horseback.

Unless she was able to get on one of the horses.

If she somehow broke away, could she get onto the horse? There was one smaller pony, but it was on the other side of the men, far away.

Perhaps if she could make some kind of diversion.

Why, oh, why, had she left the pistol back in the wagon?

"We've got to do something soon," the man dressed as a federal marshal said. "Daylight's burning."

That meant her window for making an escape could be closing. She needed to make her move.

But what move?

There was a loud crack. A gunshot.

The men turned as one to face the noise—turning away from Fran.

She hadn't been able to get her hands untied, but she pushed to her feet anyway and ran on wobbly legs toward the pony.

One of the men shouted.

She didn't stop.

She reached for the saddle knob and got her hands on it.

The horse whickered and stepped away, maybe afraid of her skirt fluttering in the wind.

"Easy, boy," she said, even as the shouts behind her probably spooked the animal more.

She managed to get her foot into the stirrup and pulled against the knob.

Her leg swung over the saddle, and she squeezed the way Edgar had shown her. The animal jumped forward, but a larger horse and rider got right in front of Fran.

Her horse pulled up, rearing.

She shrieked and bobbled, tried to stay balanced, grasped the saddle as best she could with her hands bound, but she couldn't stay seated.

She hit the ground hard on her shoulder.

Rough hands grabbed her as the pony's hooves hit the ground only inches from her face.

She scrambled, arm screaming with pain, trying to get up, get away.

It was no use. The men were upon her, fighting against her.

A loud whip cracked.

Everyone stilled. Including her.

Terrified, breathing hard and in pain, she looked up.

Underhill stood close, a long leather whip in hand. His eyes were a little wild.

"You're the reason for all this," he hissed. "You've brought me on this chase and kept Emma from me—"

"C'mon, Mr. Underhill, sir," one of the men said, attempting to calm him.

The whip snapped again and the man recoiled, putting a hand to his cheek. His hand came away bloody.

There were murmurs from the other men.

It was clear Underhill had lost his mind, if he was attacking his own men.

He was dangerous and insane.

If the men were afraid, maybe she could convince them to help her escape.

"He's crazy," she said. Her voice wobbled, showing her fear, but she pressed on. "He's violent—"

"Quiet!" Underhill screamed, this time at her. The whip cracked again, a warning.

"Will you let him hit me—"

The whip cracked again and she rolled away, instinct bringing her arms to cover her head.

She cried out as the strike connected across her back.

Chapter Seventeen

Racing across the plain, his brothers, Daniel and the other cowboys following, Edgar knew real fear.

Fran was in danger. He could sense it.

This was all his fault. He should've kept her closer in the night, should've set more of a watch on the wagon.

But he'd been so worried about the cattle, and angry that she hadn't told him everything.

He'd been so awful to her.

If they found her, he would do everything he could to make it right for her. He'd beg for forgiveness if he had to.

His heart thundered in time with the horse's hooves.

Where were they?

He scanned the horizon. His eyes flew to each shadow and swell in the prairie. John had been in the lead at first, tracking the men's horses, until Edgar could make out the tracks, the indents, the broken grasses.

They weren't trying to hide.

Which scared him even more.

He prayed Seb and Emma were well on their way back to Tuck's Station. He should've sent both the girls back the day before after Underhill had shown up. Instead, he'd wagered their safety against an insane man.

And lost.

He caught sight of the horses first, seeing a commotion as several moved and one reared up.

He strained his eyes. Was that Fran who had fallen in a heap of skirt and dark hair?

There was a sharp crack. A gunshot? No.

A whip. He recognized the sound from branding, as some of the other cowboys preferred it as a way of guiding the cows where they needed to be.

He saw movement, just Underhill's men standing around. Fran on the ground.

He heard shouting over the ringing in his ears and then saw the whip fly through the air again, saw Fran roll on the ground, cover her head, flinch.

Blood bloomed across the back of her dress.

He was close now—he urged his horse forward, knocking one of the men aside.

The whip arced through the air again, but this time he threw himself off the horse and on top of a prone Fran.

The whip struck him instead, a sharp sting of pain across his back from one side to the other.

The pain was intense, a burn through his skin and down into his muscles.

How had Fran borne it?

He started shaking, realizing just what he'd put her through, all because of his stubbornness. How would she ever forgive him?

Through a haze of white noise, he realized some of the cowboys had engaged with Underhill's men. He heard sounds of fists meeting flesh and struggling.

He looked up to see several of Underhill's men ride

off. Cowards. What else did Underhill expect when he'd likely paid them to be there?

Edgar trusted his boys to take care of what needed taking care of.

Fran needed him.

She pushed against him. He moved his shoulders slightly, giving her room but keeping her pinned. "Stay down," he murmured. "You okay? Of course you're not okay." He could feel her shaking.

Underhill's voice rang out loudly. "She's cost me everything!"

"Let me up!" Fran insisted.

The red-faced man had exchanged his whip for a gun, and waved it wildly, spewing vitriol.

"Sorry," Edgar told her, keeping her tucked beneath him. He was sure her back was paining her. "If he starts shooting, I don't want you to catch a bullet."

He'd rather it be him, if it came to that.

He'd rather it be no one.

"Where's Emma?"

"Not here. With Seb." He twisted his head, trying to see between the shuffling cowboys' legs and milling, restless horses.

The scuffle had turned dangerous.

The federal marshal was trying to talk Underhill down. At this point, Edgar didn't know if he was on Underhill's side or regretting what he'd gotten himself into.

Underhill was having none of it. He pointed the pistol in Fran's—and consequently, Edgar's—direction.

Where was Ricky? Matty? He didn't want any of his men getting shot.

They were on the periphery, apparently thinking the same thing he was.

"Edgar, please." Fran twisted beneath him, maybe trying to see. "I can't breathe!"

He could see the federal marshal attempting to get Underhill's gun away from him.

And as they both scrabbled for the weapon, a lone rider trotted up to the group. Fran's brother. Had he been behind them this whole time, and just now arrived?

With the sorry excuse for a horse he had, Edgar wouldn't be too surprised.

Problem was, he didn't have great control over his animal and the horse aimed for the scuffling men.

The horse walked right into the two of them and the gun went off.

Beneath him, Fran jumped.

"It's all right," he murmured into her hair. Even though he didn't know if it was or wasn't.

Had Daniel been hit?

Ricky and the other cowboys were just about done sorting it out. Two of Underhill's men lay groaning on the ground.

Ricky reached up for the horse's reins and Daniel tumbled off. He rose to his feet, dusting himself off. Not hurt.

One less thing for Edgar to have to apologize for.

When Ricky moved the horse, the federal marshal was on his knees, and Underhill was flat on his back on the ground, a red stain blooming on his chest.

Ricky looked back at him, still holding the horse, and shook his head.

Underhill was gone.

Edgar pushed up off the ground, careful of Fran and her injuries. He had to clamp down on his back teeth as, helping her to her feet, he again spotted the red stain on the back of her dress. He tried not to let her see the violent scene behind where they stood, but she was too quick for him and edged around to see Underhill.

She gasped and looked away, squeezing her eyes closed.

Some protector he'd been.

He smoothed her tumbledown hair away from her shoulders. Underhill's strike had hit Fran completely across her middle back and up across her shoulders.

"Oh, darlin'," he crooned.

Her shoulders bowed, and a fine tremor went through her. Relief? Fear? He couldn't imagine the mess of emotions she must have been facing at that moment.

She looked up at him, then quickly away. "What about you? You're hurt, aren't you?"

"I'm a rangy cowboy who can survive a snakebite. What do you think?" he tried to tease, but she trembled again.

"Fran..." He touched her elbow lightly, conscious of how she must be hurting. He wanted to tell her how much he loved her. She looked up at him, but the words stuck in his throat. How could he ever apologize enough for not believing her, not trusting her when she'd needed him?

Her eyes clung to his face but then darted away. She went perfectly still.

"Daniel?" she asked, quiet and disbelieving. Then she cried out, "Daniel!"

Her brother pushed past Edgar and took her in his arms. "Frannie!"

"Ow!" Her exclamation was muffled by her brother's shoulder.

"Watch it," Edgar growled. "She's hurt."

Daniel shot him a scathing glare over his shoulder.

Fran pushed away. "What are you doing here? How did you find us?"

Daniel smoothed the hair from her temple. "You didn't make it easy, that's for sure."

Watching her greet her brother squeezed Edgar's stomach tight as a fist. She was shining with joy, even after everything she'd just been through.

Daniel turned Fran and started leading her away.

Edgar reached out for her, but then stopped.

Now that Daniel was there, Fran didn't need him any longer.

She didn't have to stay married to him. They'd been married under duress and she'd been forced into it by the judge. He knew that could be grounds for annulment under Wyoming law. Would her brother push her to annul their marriage?

Ricky came up beside him. "You want us to go after the others riding with Underhill's outfit?"

Edgar shook his head. "I don't think they're coming back, and the rest of us have had enough adventure for one day."

Ricky nodded.

Stood there silent at Edgar's shoulder as they watched Daniel make over Fran.

"You gonna just let her walk away?" Ricky asked finally.

He should have. He didn't deserve her. And if she abandoned him, it would be completely his fault. He hadn't proved himself to her—all he'd proved was that he didn't keep his promises.

She'd be in the right to walk away from him.

But...

"Not if I can help it," he told his brother.

Fran's relief knew no bounds. Emma was safe. Daniel was there, although he was thinner than she remembered and pale, as if he'd been sick.

And Underhill was dead, thanks to the federal marshal.

But what brought tears to her eyes was Edgar, safe and whole. He had survived the stampede.

She glanced at him over Daniel's shoulder, only to find him and Ricky standing side by side, a powerful pair of cowboys. Edgar's eyes were locked on her.

She was conscious of her ragged, dirt-covered appearance—she'd been rolling on the ground to escape after all, and her hair had long before fallen out of its pins.

She shouldn't care so much. She knew what he thought about her, that she couldn't be trusted.

In the face of everything that had happened, her determination to tell him that she loved him wavered.

She could tell him—later.

"We need to get Emma and get back to a town with a train station," Daniel was saying.

All of a sudden, Edgar was there at her brother's elbow, near enough for her to smell horse and man. "Fran's got to be exhausted. She needs to get to town to rest."

"She can rest after we get home to Tennessee," Daniel argued.

"She's my wife, my responsibility—"

"I can sleep in the wagon," she said, to keep the argument from escalating further.

Edgar looked chagrined. "The wagon didn't make it through the stampede."

A ripple of latent fear shook her. If the cattle had destroyed the wagon, big and bulky as it was, they could have easily killed Edgar when he'd fallen.

Then she thought of something else. "Your ma's recipe cards!"

It was a combination of her relief, bottled-up fear and distress that made her eyes fill with tears.

She tried to turn away.

Both men behind her gasped.

Edgar took her shoulders. Gently. "You need to wash up, and then we'll get you to town to see a doctor."

He meant her back. The stinging was constant, so she'd forgotten about it momentarily.

"I'll send Ricky back to fetch Emma—"

"How long will that take?" Daniel asked belligerently.

There must have been something between the two men. Fran rarely heard her mild-mannered brother angry, but he seemed really perturbed at Edgar.

She shook her head. "I don't want Emma to see—"

She met Edgar's gaze and one corner of his mouth turned up, a bit ruefully.

"Coddling," she whispered. Still tearful. "Can you… Could you—"

He didn't make her ask. "Let me see if I've got some clean cloth in my saddlebag."

He escorted her to a nearby creek—after extensive reassurance from her to Daniel—where the scrub trees shaded them from the bright morning sun and gave them a little privacy.

He'd found a washrag and now rinsed it in the creek. The water was icy against her upper back as he dabbed carefully at the cut.

His hands were shaking. Badly. And he was silent.

Was he still that angry with her for not telling the whole truth about what had transpired with Underhill?

She couldn't stop crying.

Partly, she was relieved that they were all okay, but partly she was afraid he would send her away with Daniel.

It was similar to what had happened two days before, during the rainstorm. The storm had come, and her emotions had overflowed like rushing water. Unstoppable.

Fran's silent tears unmanned him.

He had let her down. He was desperately afraid that she would leave—and he knew he deserved it if she did.

He bandaged her cut as best he could.

"We'll see the doctor in Cheyenne," he said.

She turned on him. "You'd better let me see to your back."

He stood dumbfounded for a moment.

"Didn't he get you with the whip, as well?" she prompted.

He nodded, jaw tight as he remembered all over again what that monster had done to her.

He knelt on the bank, shrugging out of his shirt.

Her hands were cool against his skin, but not as cool as the cloth she'd dipped in the creek. He jumped.

"Sorry," she murmured. "Will we make it to Cheyenne tonight?"

"Early this afternoon. Maybe even by lunchtime."

"With the cows?"

Ah, the cattle. He'd realized too late what was really important.

"I'll let Ricky and the boys worry about the cattle. I don't want your back getting infected out here on the trail."

"But what about your papa?"

He turned his head to the side but couldn't get a good look at her face.

Jonas would've known what was important well before Edgar had realized it. He imagined his pa would be pretty sore at him for letting Fran get into trouble like she had.

"He'll understand if the deal falls through. We can look for another buyer."

It wasn't worth jeopardizing Fran's health. Infection could be deadly.

She hesitated, one hand resting on his shoulder. "Are you sure?"

He was. He just hoped it wasn't too late.

Knock, knock.

Still shaken from the events of the morning, Fran opened the hotel room door and a shaft of late-afternoon sunlight fell across the floor.

Emma.

Her sister vaulted toward her, knocking the door in, and Fran opened her arms in time to catch the younger girl in a firm embrace. Emma clutched her shoulders, avoiding the injuries on Fran's back that Daniel must have warned her about.

A shadow moved outside the hotel door, and for a moment, Fran's heart tripped, thinking it was Edgar.

But when he passed through the doorway, she saw it was Daniel instead, carrying a brown-wrapped package.

And she couldn't be disappointed that her brother was there, could she?

She pulled them both into the hotel room, laughing a bit tearfully.

"I can't believe you're here," she told her brother.

He set the package on the bed. "I almost wasn't."

His words stopped her. He was serious, deadly serious. Her brother, older by a decade, tended toward solemnity anyway, but the gravity of his words stopped her.

She and Emma sat on the bed while he told them just

how ill he'd been with tuberculosis and how he'd come to track them down. Hearing his story, she went from skepticism, to disbelief, to horror and then to thankfulness that God had spared her brother's life. He'd come close to dying, but she hadn't lost him.

Finally, Daniel shrugged out of her hug. "We'll get this situation with the cowboy taken care of and get back to Tennessee."

Fran shook her head. "Do you mean my marriage?"

He nodded. "You'll want to annul it, won't you?"

"No!"

Emma wrapped her arms around her knees. "He sent you that package." She nodded to the item sitting on the bed. Fran had forgotten about it until Emma's reminder.

When she twisted and reached for it, Emma let out a gasp.

Chagrined, Fran realized her sister must've seen the blood on the back of her dress.

"I'm all right," she reassured her sister. "It's only a cut—the doctor said it wasn't too deep. As long as I keep it clean it should heal in a week or two. And Edgar saved me from the second blow."

"He's the reason you were hurt in the first place," Daniel muttered.

She shot her brother a look before she ripped the paper to reveal a pretty lavender dress—clearly store-bought and of fine quality.

"I would say Underhill and his obsession was the real reason," she returned as she shook out the dress and stood up from the bed. She held it to her torso, fingering the lace-edged sleeve.

It was high quality, expensive. Edgar had sent it to her.

But why hadn't he come himself?

"You really want to stay married to a cowboy like that?" Daniel asked. "Do you know what life is like out here in the wilds? You'll have to work. Much harder than if you marry a businessman or some such."

"I'm *married* to Edgar."

"He hasn't been the most sensitive of men," Emma reminded her.

Fran didn't downplay their concern, but they didn't know him like she did. "His mother abandoned him to an orphanage when he was very small," she told them. She hoped he wouldn't mind her sharing his story, but she would need to make them understand if she was going to have any hope of remaining in the marriage. "That one event has shaped much of his thinking about women."

She shared what she felt she could without betraying Edgar's privacy too much.

Daniel still looked skeptical, but Emma seemed to understand that Fran couldn't just walk away.

"I'm in love with him," she finally whispered. "Scars and all."

Daniel just shook his head. "I'll give you a week. If he hasn't convinced me that he returns your feelings, I'll insist on an annulment."

One week.

It was longer than she and Edgar had known each other. But she didn't need more time to be sure of her heart.

She just needed a plan to convince a stubborn cowboy that she was right.

"What do you mean, he's gone?"

Seb's pronouncement that Ricky had disappeared set Edgar's teeth on edge.

Edgar had forced himself to leave the hotel and go out to meet the herd and his brothers as the sun was setting, only to find his youngest brother as the lead rider. After eating trail dust and drawing the overnight watches, Seb had managed as trail boss for the last patch into town.

"There's been a burr under his saddle for a long time," Seb said.

But he'd ridden out with Edgar to save Fran. Hadn't that meant anything?

How could Ricky have just *left?* Abandoned the family?

It hurt.

And it quelled the plans that had been spinning in Edgar's mind all afternoon. What to do about Fran?

"What am I supposed to do?" Edgar asked the mostly rhetorical question of the bovines as he scratched the back of his suddenly aching neck.

He stared at the cattle, willing a different answer to show itself to him.

Now that the cattle were in Cheyenne, it shouldn't have been too difficult to find another buyer, but it could take time—days—to see a deal through.

He'd been planning to hand over the duties to Ricky. His brother was of age, was business minded enough to handle the transaction.

And now he was gone.

Which left the duty to Edgar.

He'd promised his pa he would take care of it.

And he'd promised Fran he would take care of her.

"D'you think Fran will wait for me back at the homestead for a couple of days?" he asked Seb.

His brother shrugged. "Don't see why not. Unless that brother of hers talks her into movin' on."

That was a real worry. Daniel didn't seem to harbor much respect for Edgar, and he could well understand why not. Edgar was sore at himself for putting both girls in danger, and couldn't forgive himself for letting Fran get hurt.

Would she understand if he asked her not to make any decisions until after he got the cattle sold and got back to the homestead? He hadn't made the best of showings as a husband and would like her to see him in his familiar surroundings, where he might be able to impress her with his work.

"If I was you, the thing I'd regret most was not asking her," Seb said.

He slapped his brother on the back. "You are wise beyond your years."

Seb just grinned. "I know. Don't tell Ma."

Chapter Eighteen

Three days later, finally home, Edgar snuck behind the bunkhouse and eyed the main cabin. Waiting, hoping for a glimpse of Fran.

The early-morning light reflected off the kitchen window where his ma usually spent the morning washing up. He couldn't detect any movement there at all.

Another two weeks and Ma and Pa would be home. Would he have a wife to show off to them?

It had taken a couple days to work out the issues with the cattle buyer. They'd been blessed to find a new buyer when the other had backed out.

In the meantime, Fran had agreed to come home to Jonas's place, her brother and sister tagging along.

Edgar had arrived late the previous evening, and although he'd seen Fran briefly, he hadn't had a chance to really talk to her. She'd had some leftovers that she warmed on the stove for him and Seb and Matty.

While they'd been settling the cattle deal, it was obvious she'd charmed Davy in their absence. He was all smiles in the bunkhouse the night before, until Edgar had had to tell him about Ricky.

Now that Edgar was there, he was unaccountably nervous.

What if she really couldn't forgive him for letting Underhill take her, and for his momentary doubt of her trustworthiness?

If she walked away, he would deserve it.

And with her brother there, probably encouraging her to do so, what chance did he really have?

But he wasn't a kid anymore. When his ma had left him at that orphanage, he hadn't been able to do anything to stop her.

With Fran, he could try. He could proclaim his love, or at least let her know how he felt and let her make the decision from there.

He had to try.

He looked down at the piece of mirror and straight razor in his hand. Might as well give the best showing he could. Fran had cut his hair, but it was time—past time—that the beard went away.

He walked around the side of the bunkhouse to the wash bucket back behind. He assumed his brothers were working or in the barn, since he hadn't seen hide nor hair of them yet that morning. Better to shave in privacy.

He dunked his whole head in the bucket. The splash of cold water was bracing. He shook like a dog, droplets slinging through the air.

He worked up a lather with the shaving soap and spread it into his beard.

He took a deep breath and only hesitated briefly before he took the first swipe with the razor.

With every stroke, he thought of Fran. Of the way she'd cut his hair, her tender care for him when he'd been nothing but harsh to her.

Of her in the moonlight, begging him to let her in.

Of kissing her.

He ran his palm over one side of his freshly shaved face and wondered if she had been right when she'd accused him of hiding.

Did he let himself reach such an unkempt state to make sure no eligible girls got close? Was that the real reason he'd always kept distant?

Why had he let himself be so closed off?

Was it too late for him?

"There he is."

A voice snapped him from his thoughts. He tossed his towel over the side of the barrel and let the straight razor fall to the ground.

He turned to see Davy, Seb, Matty and Fran's brother waylaying him.

"Whoa!" Seb exclaimed.

"Who is that?" Matty teased. "Don't recognize ya, pardner."

He sent a stream of water from the top of the wash barrel splashing toward them. "Morning, boys," he said. What was going on?

"Dan here wants to talk to ya," Seb said.

He nodded, facing off with Fran's brother.

Although Dan was only slightly shorter, Edgar probably had sixty pounds of muscle on the man—Dan was slender and still looked like he could stand to gain some weight after his illness.

"You've regained a little color," Edgar commented.

"It's been a relief to be reunited with my sisters and to have the accusations against Fran resolved. I wired some business acquaintances back in Tennessee, and it seems the witnesses Underhill claimed could accuse her didn't exist. There is no case against her." But instead of looking relieved, Daniel looked very serious.

Edgar was glad they'd been reunited. Families should be together. That was why his responsibility for Ricky and his brother's desertion still weighed heavy on him. But while Ricky was of age, the girls had needed a protector.

"How's Emma?" he asked.

"Having nightmares nearly twice a night. She wouldn't tell me—the difference in our ages—but Fran has shared some of it." The other man looked weighed down by his sister's situation.

But he seemed to rouse himself from his internal musings. "Fran seems to have developed some affection for you," Daniel said, and Edgar's heart thumped wildly.

Did he still have a chance to win Fran?

"And he wants to know what your intentions are," Seb put in gleefully.

Davy stood looking on, arms crossed and silent.

"I…" Edgar hadn't even expressed his feelings to Fran yet. He didn't want to tell her brother he loved her first. "I care about her. I want to make things right for her."

"Do you really think you can? Do you even know what she's been through? What it's been like for her, a city-raised girl thrown onto the prairie with a bunch of cowboys?"

"Fran's tougher than you think" was his immediate response.

Daniel did not look pleased with the comment. His expression grew even more perturbed.

"I'd like to know where you were when the girls needed you," Edgar went on quickly. "Fran wrote to you more than once." He hated that he sounded so confrontational, but was not sure he appreciated someone who hadn't been there for Fran taking him to task.

"I don't have to explain myself to you," the other man said.

Edgar gave him a long look. He was Fran's husband. He didn't have to explain himself to her brother.

"I've had a bad bout of tuberculosis," Daniel finally said. "It came on quickly, and I suppose the truth is I almost died."

Seb stepped back from the other man.

Daniel smiled ruefully. "My doctors have assured me that I am no longer contagious." He looked back at Edgar. "As soon as I learned of our parents' deaths, I came looking for the girls. I found that they'd left the finishing school, been to the orphanage and sent West. The woman who ran the orphanage told me of their troubles with the unfortunate Mr. Underhill—"

"He got what he deserved," Seb interrupted.

Daniel shook his head. "I believe it's up to the courts to mete out punishment."

"He was trying to shoot her," Edgar put in.

Daniel shrugged, eyes hard. "We're getting off track here. I want to know whether you intend to do right by my sister or not."

Davy finally broke in. "I'd like to know that, too."

Edgar looked at all of them watching him expectantly. "Yes. I want her around…." It was such an understatement that he choked on it. "I…I love her."

Daniel didn't look totally appeased, but Seb's face had lit and Davy was smiling.

A wagon rolled up the drive, distracting all of them.

"Looks like the neighbor."

"Wonder what he wants."

It didn't take long to find out.

* * *

Fran had been so relieved to see Edgar the night before that she'd begun crying again, so she'd rushed inside with the excuse of warming some supper for the cowboys. But it was really to hide.

And this morning she was still hiding inside the Whites' warm kitchen with its overlong plank table. When she should've been outside locating her husband, she was slinking around indoors.

She was afraid he was going to send her away.

With Daniel there and available to take care of her and Emma, the stark fear for their survival was gone.

Especially with Underhill out of the picture. Although Emma still had some healing to do from the whole encounter.

No, Fran's fear had to do with loving the incorrigible cowboy and knowing there was a chance he couldn't return her love because she hadn't been upfront with him about Underhill's accusations.

The kitchen door opened and he was there, filling the frame with his height and wide shoulders.

"Morning." He took off his hat and hung it on a peg near the door.

When he turned back to the kitchen, she caught sight of his face and sucked in a surprised breath.

"You shaved," she said.

He nodded, red climbing his cheeks. Without the thick blond beard, she could see how easily his fair skin changed color.

He was even more striking without his beard. A sharp jaw and fine, full lips... Even his nose appeared handsomer.

He rubbed a hand across his jaw as if she was making him uncomfortable, and she realized she was staring.

"What're you doing?" he asked.

She turned, grateful for the excuse to delay, even for a moment. She needed to gather her thoughts. She was going to tell him that she loved him. She just needed to get her courage in line.

"I made Daniel bring us back to where the wagon had been that night," she admitted. "I was able to salvage some of your mother's recipe cards. I've been copying the recipes to new ones, so she will still be able to use them."

Most of the old cards were readable, though mud spattered and torn from the cattle's destructive hooves. The new cards were stacked neatly in the center of the table. It was a paltry offering, because Fran knew some of the cards held sentimental value for Edgar's mother. The project had really been to keep her hands busy while she'd waited for his arrival.

Remembering the mangled, decimated wagon cinched her chest tight. Half of it had been sheered completely away, splintered to dust.

"The men…" She took a breath. She'd cried so many tears in the past few days, purging her fear and desperation. She didn't want to relapse into a sobbing ball of emotion now. She wanted her husband to see her strong.

She started again. "Underhill's men had said you'd fallen in the stampede."

He nodded slowly, idly fingering one of the cards with her handwriting on it. She watched his broad fingers sweep across the tabletop.

Seeing him alive, hale and healthy and vital, clogged her throat with emotion.

He glanced up at her, seemed to see she was struggling. His hand closed over hers, and he squeezed. "I'm all right."

She fought off the urge to throw her arms around him. She didn't know where they stood.

"What about you?" he asked, hand still warm around hers. "Your back?"

"Sore," she admitted. "Probably about the same as yours."

His jaw tightened—it was so much easier to read his expressions without his face covered in the beard.

"This was awful nice of you." He motioned to the cards spread across the table.

"It was my fault they were on the wagon," she reminded him.

She'd meant the words to be somewhat of a jest, but he shook his head. "Underhill coming after you wasn't your fault. And his boys starting that stampede wasn't your fault, either."

Now tears truly did mist her eyes. He folded her to his chest as hope rose in her heart.

He held her close for a long moment.

"If that's true, then Ricky leaving wasn't your fault," she whispered.

At her words, he set her slightly back, his face dark and upset.

"Seb told us last night," she admitted.

His brow creased. "Pa left me in charge. I should've done something about it."

She touched his hand. "You did. Every day, he knew you loved him, knew he could come to you if he chose. But he chose to leave instead."

He hung his head, eyes squeezing shut.

The fact that he was showing her his emotion, not shutting her out, made her heart soar. Did this mean he wanted to be with her?

"Can we…can we talk?" she asked through a throat tight with hope.

He nodded slowly. "I think we should. Let's start with this."

He put an envelope on the tabletop between them and crossed his arms over his chest.

Curious, she picked up the missive. Spidery handwriting listed the return address as being in Chicago.

Chapter Nineteen

Edgar watched Fran's face go pale as she looked at the letter's return address.

He'd quickly recognized it from the orphanage where he'd been abandoned as a child. And he'd only had to read the first part of the letter to discover Fran had a hand in the letter's arrival.

And it was clear by her expression she recognized it, too.

"You want to tell me what that is?" he asked.

"A letter?" she said, as if she wasn't sure.

He raised one eyebrow at her. Let her squirm. After all, she'd been nosing into his personal business. Again.

She sighed heavily, as if expelling all the air out of her entire body.

"All right," she said. "I sent a letter to the orphanage in Chicago. I hoped it might give you some closure, that someone might know about your mother."

"When?"

"Back at Tuck's Station. Before you came and got me for supper." She spoke in a small voice, chin tucked down.

She was adorable.

He waited until she peeked up at him, then held out his hand, palm up.

"Let's have it."

She handed it to him, looking up at him from beneath thick lashes. "You're not...mad?"

"Dunno yet," he teased.

She shifted on her feet, raising up on her tiptoes to see as he ripped open the envelope.

He went to a bare spot on the long table and motioned her to come with him. "Sit with me?"

She didn't hesitate, and his heart bumped as she settled in at his elbow, her ear brushing his shoulder.

He unfolded the letter, his stomach dropping as he did so. Did he really want to know why his birth ma hadn't wanted him anymore? Why the director had put him on that train?

Wasn't the past better off just left where it was—in the past?

Fran bumped his upper arm with her shoulder. "You don't have to be afraid of whatever is in there," she said quietly. "You've built a life that suits you. You have a... family that loves you." She hesitated. "Whatever that letter says, you won't lose any of that."

She was right. She'd been right the whole time. Telling her about his mother and the director, just saying the words aloud, had somehow lessened his pain. It didn't hurt *more* to share his burden with someone else, it hurt *less*.

He cleared his throat. "'Dear Edgar and *Mrs. White*,'" he read.

He had to stop and glance at her askance.

Her cheeks had gone a little pink, and she didn't directly meet his eyes. He went back to the letter.

"I was so glad to receive your letter. Next week will be my last as director for the orphanage here, and so I might not have received it if it came at a later time. God's timing is always right!"

He had to stop. "She always used to say that," he remembered to Fran.

She placed her hand over his wrist and squeezed gently.

"Edgar, you have been in my heart many times over the years since I last saw you. Many prayers have been sent Heavenward on your behalf. I am so happy to know that you were adopted into a good family. Sending you West on the orphan train was the hardest thing I have ever done.

You see, I loved you as my own son. Perhaps I should not have let myself get so close to you, or negated your attachment to me in some way, but it couldn't be helped. You were such a bright, helpful boy. Often playing pranks, but not in a malicious way. You just wanted to make the other children laugh.

Though I loved you deeply, my calling and my duty was to the orphanage. What kind of life would you have had, being shackled to a single woman whose job was taking care of so many other children who have so many needs to be filled? I hoped—oh, how I hoped—that you would find a family with both mother and father who would see your joyful spirit and take you into their home and fill you with love until you were overflowing. I am brought to tears of joy to know that that seems to be the case.

I loved you so much that, although it broke my heart, I wanted what was best for you. I hope that with the understanding of a man, you can now see that."

He had reached the end of the first page and had to stop. The tightness in his chest made him temporarily unable to go on. Priscilla had loved him. Loved him enough to give him up, so he could have the better life she'd dreamed of for him.

Fran sniffed.

He cut his eyes to her. She dabbed at her eyes with part of one sleeve.

When she saw him looking at her, she gave a wobbly smile.

He dropped the letter on the table and swung one arm around her shoulders. Holding her close was like coming home all over again. Having her there beside him made reading the letter bearable. Not only that, but he never would've had the letter if it weren't for her.

She sniffled a little, and then wiggled away. "Finish it."

He shifted the first page away to see there was a second. Did he really need to know what had made his ma abandon him?

"I don't need to finish it. Knowing Priscilla loved me is enough."

She looked up at him, her eyes shining and a little exasperated. "C'mon. You'll never be settled unless you know."

He steeled himself and picked up the second page. Because she was right.

"As to your mother, the truth is that she was very sick when she brought you to the orphanage.

Over the years, I have seen many parents have to
leave their children in my care for a myriad of
reasons. Often, the parents are more sorrowful
than the children, who cannot really understand
what is happening.

Perhaps your mother claimed she would return as her own way to comfort you. Perhaps she
thought she would get better. I don't know what
prompted her to give you a promise she could not
be sure of fulfilling.

I was notified several months after your arrival
that she had passed away. You and I did have a
conversation about it, but how much does a child
of five really understand about death?

Know that your mother loved you, and did her
best for you when she could no longer take care
of you herself. I don't know why she was on her
own or what might've become of her family, but
her tears on the day she left you in my care told
me of her love for you.

With my retirement looming, I find that perhaps I might enjoy a trip to the Wild West. If you
would welcome me, I would love to visit the boy I
knew and discover the kind of man he has become.
Sincerely, Priscilla Henderson, Director."

Edgar stared down at the page for a long time, emotion clogging his throat.

His ma had been sick. Dying.

And that was why she'd left him.

Not because of anything he'd done.

It was both a comfort and a blow. His ma was gone.
But she'd loved him.

Fran was quiet beside him. Unusual for her.

He cleared his throat. The shimmer in her eyes wasn't unwelcome anymore.

"Are you...angry now?" she asked softly.

Was he? She'd nosed into his business without his permission. But she'd given him a gift no one else had been able to. "No. No, I'm not angry."

He turned to her, straddling the bench. His gut clenched. She'd been open to him since he'd come in. Now it was time to make his declarations.

She deserved the best of him. And that meant opening his heart. Even if it was the scariest thing he'd faced. What if, after everything that had happened, she found him wanting? The only thing more frightening was the thought of losing her.

He opened his mouth.

And the door burst open.

"Lunchtime yet?" Seb called out. Emma followed him in, though Daniel was nowhere to be seen.

"Do you want some help with the recipe cards?" Emma asked, coming to the table.

Seb banged around the kitchen.

They obviously weren't leaving, and he didn't intend to say what he needed to say with an audience.

"You want to take a walk?" he asked.

Fran followed Edgar from the house and past the barn. When she and Emma had been at the ranch overnight that first day, she'd been exhausted from travel and fear. Now that she'd had a couple of days to learn the lay of the land, she loved its unique charm.

The main cabin had obviously originally been built with only two or three rooms, and then been added on to multiple times. The barn was older, the bunkhouse newer to serve the growing family. Extending off the back of the barn was a large corral with several horses. Across the valley, she could see another cabin tucked in among some trees. A small creek cut across the land and sparkled in the late morning sunlight.

Edgar marched her past all of it. He seemed like a man with a goal, intent on reaching some destination.

She followed him, her heart light although she was unaccountably nervous. She'd been surprised that her letter had been answered so quickly, but Edgar's neighbor had been in a nearby town and picked it up for him. She'd been even more surprised that Edgar hadn't been angry, that he'd opened up to her.

It had increased her hope exponentially.

They passed the creek and climbed a gentle hill, moving through prairie grasses that reminded her of the moments they'd shared lying out in the field near the chuck wagon.

She slowed without really realizing it, swirling one hand through the tops of the soft grasses.

He turned back. "Am I walking too fast for you?"

"No. I'm just dawdling. Daydreaming."

He reached out one hand to her and she took it, his large, warm clasp welcome. He drew her to his side and she looked up at him—all the way up to his dear face.

"Don't send me away," she demanded, as softly and cajolingly as she could. "I…" And then she paused, unable to say she loved him without knowing how he truly felt. "I want to make our marriage work. We are a good fit for each other."

"You think so, hmm?" He asked the question in such a level voice, without inflection and with no expression on his face, that for one moment her stomach dipped low.

Then he hauled her into his arms and pressed his face into her hair, his breath hot on the crown of her head.

"I love you," he murmured.

She could feel him shaking. She wrapped her arms around his middle and hung on as tightly as she could.

"I didn't want to, not at the beginning," he said, ducking his head to brush a kiss on her cheek and speak into her ear. "You turned my life upside down and showed me that I needed to be shaken out of my safe rut."

He pulled back and framed her face with his hands. "Do you… Are you sure you can be happy in Bear Creek? On this ranch? With me?"

She saw the genuine fear behind the question, the remnants of that little boy who had watched and waited for his mother to come back for him every day.

It made her eyes mist a little.

"Yes. Because I love you, too."

He kissed her until they were both breathless, then held her tightly, his joy evident in his sudden loud, effervescent whoop.

She laughed.

"I was thinking we could build a little cabin of our own. Right about here. You get a pretty picture of the valley…." He whirled her around to see what he was talking about, without letting go of her.

"Your sister can stay on if she wants…."

She took in the surrounding view. The barn and main house in the distance, the arching blue sky and wildflowers all around.

"…raise horses, and of course the cattle, a cut of the family herd…"

And her husband, making plans.

She'd arrived in Bear Creek afraid, running for hers and Emma's lives.

And God had given her this man, and this new life.

It was much to be thankful for.

Epilogue

"Keep 'em closed. No peeking." Edgar cupped his hand over Fran's eyes, just in case.

She sighed. Then giggled.

"You know I saw the cabin yesterday," she reminded him.

"But the roof wasn't on yesterday," he parried right back.

Riding his big black with her just in front of him gave him the perfect opportunity to hold her close—so he did, as he guided the horse up the hill to their newly finished home.

Home.

He hadn't realized that the word could mean a person. He knew that now, no matter where he went, with Fran by his side, he'd be home.

After two weeks together, the emotion, the completeness, still brought that uncomfortable warmth to his chest. Only he was getting used to it now.

They crested the hill where he'd first shown her his dream spot for building a cabin of their own. Between his brothers working with him well into the night for several days, and a house-raising party the folks of Bear

Creek had held the previous weekend, Fran would have a home of her own. Today.

Just in time for his parents' homecoming later that afternoon.

He was looking forward to having Fran to himself. He thought Breanna would probably be happy to share her room with Emma for a bit, and Daniel planned to stay with the brothers in the bunkhouse.

Between the rush to finish their house and the heavy spring chores, he felt like he'd barely seen his wife since he'd come home from selling the cattle. But now that was all about to change. Even though the chores would continue—ranch life necessitated that—he would have time in the evenings with her.

His brothers had teased him mercilessly, but he'd also caught the tail end of a conversation that sounded like they were planning on letting him take it easy for several days, a sort of "working honeymoon."

The old Edgar might've insisted on taking on his share of the work, but with his new outlook on life and love, he would take their gift and be thankful.

He was unaccountably nervous about showing the finished place to Fran. As she'd said, she'd been up there every day, checking on the progress as the place was built.

But what if she didn't like it?

She hadn't said as much, but he imagined her parents' home and the finishing school she'd attended in Memphis had been well appointed, nice.

But this was all he had to offer her. It was snug, but small. He'd modeled it after Oscar's place, with hewn logs for the walls and glass windows where he could fit them.

It was a house that could survive many Wyoming winters, a place they could grow old in together.

Maybe with a passel of kids around them.

"All right." He drew up the horse a few yards away from the front door. "No peeking."

He slid off the horse and reached up for her.

She came into his arms, eyes still closed, totally trusting him. It was a gift he couldn't take for granted, not after what had happened—and what could've happened—with Underhill.

Her nose wrinkled adorably. "Did you light a fire?"

With her waist already in his hands, he took the opportunity to draw her to his chest, tucking her in close. "Had to test the new cookstove," he said against her temple. "Didn't want the place burning down around you the first time you make my supper."

She hummed, the soft noise vibrating through his chest. Then pushed against him. "I thought you were going to show me the house, not sneak me away up here to steal kisses."

He brushed one across her cheek. "Maybe it was both."

Then he let her go, gently spinning her with his hands at her waist to face the house. "All right, you can open your eyes now."

With her in front of him, he could only see the side of one cheek, but she gasped and then looked back at him, and her eyes were shining.

And all the long nights and backbreaking work were suddenly worth it.

"You planted flowers?" she asked, turning toward the house and taking several steps forward. He followed.

He'd thought the two scraggly bushes and overturned

mud that Seb had insisted on planting on either side of the doorway had been ridiculous, but maybe his brother had been right.

"Roses," he said. "Gift from Seb and a lady in town."

"And you've washed the windows," she murmured. "Emma."

She paused halfway to the building and craned her neck back. "The roof looks good. Nice and watertight."

He couldn't help that his chest puffed with pride.

"And you didn't let Daniel fall and break his neck, either."

And he deflated with a laugh. Fran definitely didn't allow his pride to get out of control. "It was a close call. Several times."

Her eyes danced at him.

He had been surprised that Fran's brother had wanted to help with their new place. The city slicker was as out of place as a peacock in a henhouse. But he'd promised to stay until the girls were settled. Who knew? Maybe the fresh Wyoming air would do him some good in getting back to full health.

"Can we go in?" Fran asked.

He ushered her to the front door.

She went still so quickly that he was half outside the threshold, eyes trying to adjust from being in the bright sunlight. He guessed she'd seen his wedding gift for her.

"What did you do?" She barely breathed the words.

"You wrote a letter on my behalf," he said. "I took it upon myself to do the same. Dan told me that his health had kept him from saving most of your parents' belongings when the mortgage defaulted, but I was able to get in touch with a nice lady who sent this on the train for me."

He'd left the cedar chest in the dead center of the living room, so it would be the first thing she saw when she came in.

She knelt in front of the long wooden box, hands shaking as she spread them on the worn, scarred top.

"I can't believe you did this."

She pushed open the lid and froze again. He thought he heard her sniffle so he moved up beside her.

She reached inside and held up a white, fancy-looking dress. "It's my grandma's wedding dress." She said the words almost reverently.

"Well, it's too late for you, but maybe Emma can wear it in a few years."

She sent a wobbly smile over her shoulder. "I was thinking the same thing."

Next, she untucked a stack of faded letters tied with a ribbon. "My papa sent them to my mama when they were courting."

And in the bottom was a family portrait. It was several years old, because she'd been a teenager in it, but it had all five members of her family together.

She set it down gently in the chest, then got to her feet and threw herself at him.

He caught her and her arms went around his neck.

"You're not upset?" he asked, because he still couldn't be sure about all feminine emotions.

She shook her head, the top of her hair brushing his still-shaved chin. "I'm so…happy. I can't believe— It's the best gift I've ever received."

She raised up on her tiptoes and kissed him.

Moments later, he held her face in one big paw. "That's exactly how I feel about you. You're the best gift God could have surprised me with."

* * * * *

Dear Reader,

Did you have fun getting to know the third White brother, Edgar, like I did? Matching up this rough-and-tumble cowboy was a wild ride, and I hope you enjoyed it, too. During my research, I learned a lot about how much work cattle drives really were for the wranglers and their animals, as well as what a "Cookie" really had to deal with driving the chuck wagon all day and cooking the afternoon away. I'm not the best cook, but I can't imagine making do over an open fire with cattle kicking up all that dust!

I would love to know what you thought of this book. You can reach me at lacyjwilliams@gmail.com or by sending a note to Lacy Williams, 340 S. Lemon Ave. #1639, Walnut, CA 91789. If you'd like to find out about all my latest releases in an occasional email blast, sign up at http://bit.ly/15lA19O.

Thanks for reading!

Lacy Williams

Questions for Discussion

1. Who did you relate to more in this story: the hero, the heroine or another character? Why?

2. What was your favorite moment in the story? Why?

3. Both Fran and Edgar suffered losses in their past that shaped the way they saw the future. Describe something that happened in your past and how it affected the way you view things.

4. How does Fran help Edgar grow and change during the story?

5. Fran tried to control the situation with her sister and the men chasing them. Did she succeed? How did her view of the situation change by the end of the story?

6. Edgar had a tumultuous relationship with his brother Ricky. Do you feel he handled the relationship well or poorly? What would you have done differently?

7. Do any of the characters in this story remind you of someone you know? Who, and why?

8. How do Edgar's brothers influence his thoughts and decisions?

9. Orphan trains resulted in both Edgar and Fran finding new families—although not in the same ways!

How do you think children riding the orphan trains felt as they traveled to unknown destinations to make a new start?

10. What was the theme of this story? What parts of the story really showed the theme?

11. Edgar never planned to marry, but God had something else in mind for him. Tell about a time when you had a plan but God changed it for you. What was the result?

12. What was your favorite scene in the book? Why?

13. When did Edgar's feelings for Fran begin to change? Why?

14. During the cattle drive, Fran was put in different situations she never imagined she would have to face. Do you think these situations made her stronger? Why or why not?

15. What was your first impression of Edgar? Did it change over the course of the story? Why or why not?

COMING NEXT MONTH FROM
Love Inspired® Historical

Available September 2, 2014

HIS MOST SUITABLE BRIDE
Charity House
by Renee Ryan
When Callie Mitchell is asked to help widower Reese Bennett find a prospective bride, she finds the idea of Reese marrying anyone but her simply unthinkable....

COWBOY TO THE RESCUE
Four Stones Ranch
by Louise M. Gouge
When a handsome cowboy rescues her father and takes them to his ranch, Southern belle Susanna Anders begins to fall for the exact opposite of all she'd thought she wanted.

THE GIFT OF A CHILD
by Laura Abbot
To help an abandoned child, Rose Kellogg and Seth Montgomery enter into a marriage of convenience. But can an agreement between friends lead to true love?

A HOME FOR HER HEART
Boardinghouse Betrothals
by Janet Lee Barton
Reporter John Talbot thinks he's found the story of his career. But when the truth he uncovers threatens to expose the father of the woman he's come to love, will he sacrifice his dreams for her happiness?

REQUEST YOUR FREE BOOKS!

2 FREE INSPIRATIONAL NOVELS
PLUS 2
FREE
MYSTERY GIFTS

Love Inspired.
HISTORICAL
INSPIRATIONAL HISTORICAL ROMANCE

"They're so cute," Brody said.

"Who can't like kittens?" Hannah scooped up another one and held it close, rubbing her nose over the tiny head.

"I meant your kids are cute."

Hannah looked up at him, the kitten still cuddled against her face, appearing surprisingly childlike. Her features were relaxed and she didn't seem as tense as when he'd met her the first time. Her smile dived into his heart. "Well, you're talking to the wrong person about them. I think my kids are adorable, even when they've got chocolate pudding smeared all over their mouths."

He felt a gentle contentment easing into his soul and he wanted to touch her again. To connect with her.

Chrissy patted the kitten and then pushed it away, lurching to her feet.

"Chrissy. Gentle," Hannah admonished her.

"The kitten is fine," Brody said, rescuing the kitten as Chrissy tottered a moment, trying to get her balance on the bunched-up blanket. "Here you go," he said to the mother cat, laying her baby beside her.

Hannah also put her kitten back. She took a moment to stroke Loco's head as if assuring her, then picked up her son and swung him into her arms. "Thanks for taking Corey out on the horse. I know I sounded…irrational, but my reaction was the result of a combination of factors. Ever since the twins were born, I've felt overly protective of them."

"I'm guessing much of that has to do with David's death."

"Partly. Losing David made me realize how fragile life is and, like I told your mother, it also made me feel more vulnerable."

"I wouldn't have done anything to hurt Corey." Brody felt he needed to assure her of that. "You can trust me."

Hannah looked over at him and then gave him a careful smile. "I know that."

Her quiet affirmation created an answering warmth and a faint hope.

Once again he held her gaze. Once again he wanted to touch her. To make a connection beyond the eye contact they seemed to be indulging in over the past few days.

Will Hannah Douglas find love again with handsome rancher and firefighter Brody Harcourt?
Find out in
HER MONTANA TWINS
by Carolyne Aarsen,
available September 2014 from Love Inspired® Books.

*Brave men and women work to protect
the U.S.-Canadian Border.
Read on for a preview of the first book in the new
NORTHERN BORDER PATROL series,
DANGER AT THE BORDER by Terri Reed.*

Biologist Dr. Tessa Cleary shielded her eyes against the late summer sun. She surveyed her surroundings and filled her lungs with the sweet scent of fresh mountain air. Tall conifers dominated the forest, but she detected many deciduous trees as well, which surrounded the sparkling shores of the reservoir lake.

A hidden paradise. One to be enjoyed by those willing to venture to the middle of the Pacific Northwest.

The lake should be filled with boats and swimmers, laughing children, fishing poles and water skis.

But all was still.

Silent.

The seemingly benign water filled with something toxic harming both the wildlife and humans.

Her office had received a distressing call yesterday that dead trout had washed ashore and recreational swimmers were presenting with respiratory distress after swimming in the lake.

As a field biologist for the U.S. Forestry Service Fish and Aquatics Unit, her job was to determine what exactly that "something" was as quickly as possible and stop it.

"Here she is!" a booming voice full of anticipation rang out.

A mixed group of civilians and uniformed personnel gathered on the wide, wooden porch of the ranger station.

All eyes were trained on her. All except one man's.

Tall, with dark hair, he stood in profile talking to the sheriff. Too many people blocked him from full view for her to see an agency logo on his forest-green uniform.

Tessa turned her attention to Ranger Harris. "Do you have any idea where the contamination is originating?"

He shook his head. "We haven't come across the source. At least not on our side of the lake. I'm not sure what's happening across the border." George ran a hand through his graying hair as his gaze strayed to the lake. "Whatever this is, it isn't coming from our side."

"Let's not go casting aspersions on our friends to the north until we know more. Okay, George?"

The deep baritone voice came from Tessa's right. She turned to find herself confronted by a set of midnight-blue eyes. Curiosity lurked in the deep depths of the attractive man towering over her.

Answering curiosity rose within her. Who was he? And why was he here?

For more, pick up DANGER AT THE BORDER.
Available September 2014
wherever Love Inspired books are sold.

LISEXP0814

Love Inspired HISTORICAL

His Most Suitable Bride

by

RENEE RYAN

No one in Denver knows how close Callie Mitchell once came to ruin. Dowdy dresses and severe hairstyles hide evidence of the pretty, trusting girl she used to be. Now her matchmaking employer wants Callie to find a wife for the one man who sees through her careful facade.

For his business's sake, Reese Bennett Jr. plans on making a sensible marriage. Preferably one without the unpredictable emotions that spring to life around Callie. Yet no matter how many candidates she presents to Reese, none compare with the vibrant, intelligent woman who is right under his nose—and quickly invading his heart.

**Offering an oasis of hope, faith and love
on the rugged Colorado frontier**

*Available September 2014
wherever Love Inspired books and ebooks are sold.*

Find us on Facebook at
www.Facebook.com/LoveInspiredBooks

LIH28278